KILGORE ANSWERED CHIUN WITH FILTHY PROFANITY.

"Failure after failure, that is the story of Harry Kilgore," Chiun chanted. "All who know of you also know you are prone to lose at every attempt."

Kilgore sneered. "Is that old man saying I'm a loser?"

"Yes, Harry Kilgore, The Magnificent Loser," Chiun taunted.

More filth spewed from Kilgore's mouth. He snapped off a shot. Chiun heard the *poot,* felt the pressure drop and slipped away as the blast came. Then he was right back where he was, unharmed and not even ruffled.

"You wanna be roadkill, old man?"

Chiun raised his hand, created an L shape with his finger and thumb and pressed it to his forehead.

CREATED BY WARREN MURPHY & RICHARD SAPIR

THE DESTROYER

MINDBLOWER

A GOLD EAGLE BOOK FROM

WORLDWIDE.®

TORONTO • NEW YORK • LONDON
AMSTERDAM • PARIS • SYDNEY • HAMBURG
STOCKHOLM • ATHENS • TOKYO • MILAN
MADRID • WARSAW • BUDAPEST • AUCKLAND

First edition January 2006

ISBN 0-373-63257-6

Special thanks and acknowledgment to Tim Somheil for his contribution to this work.

MINDBLOWER

And for the Glorious House of Sinanju,
at www.warrenmurphy.com

1

Professor Frederic Laft wasn't afraid of the dark. He'd walked across Goodrich Campus late at night a thousand times. Besides that, he was preoccupied by the news he had heard that afternoon. A former student, a bothersome young man, was apparently about to cause more trouble for him and others in the college of engineering.

The student in question was a disagreeable fool. Unpleasant, unkempt and unworthy—especially unworthy of the fame and fortune he grubbed for.

For years, Laft considered, the college of engineering had been striving to groom a star student, and a star student could only be produced by creating a certifiable engineering marvel. It had never happened until Harry Kilgore, a most unpleasant student, stumbled upon his innovation by accident; the man was too dense to have truly created the innovation. It was unthinkable to contemplate such a repellent human being emerging as the one and only star of the Goodrich college of engineering. To be required to make nice to that imbecile would be demeaning. Worse was the notion of watching Kilgore grow prosperous on the profits of his accidental discovery.

Laft had a way to make it not happen, and the strategy was sound. Another week and it would come to fruition, but then fate intervened. The little weasel somehow got wind of the plan. Today, the shoe had dropped when Professor Laft took delivery of a certified letter. It was in the pocket of his blazer now. Laft's patent application was being contested.

Professor Laft was taking the footsteps by feel as he turned around the rear of the Ferguson Halyard Gymnasium, where the grounds were seldom used except for overflow parking for popular sporting events. There were no lights, which didn't concern Laft. He knew every crack in the ancient sidewalk. At the end of the walk he turned around a maintenance shed onto the street-side walk and was just a half block from his own home on Professors' Row.

He wasn't thinking about home, but about his problem. He had in place the falsely dated notes and documents to prove he'd developed the idea for the patent long before Kilgore even arrived at the University of Oregon. It would be the word of a respected engineering professor with twenty-two years' tenure at Goodrich college of engineering against that of a slovenly, unpopular doctoral candidate.

"Yes, I suggested he pursue this line of research," Laft would explain. "The young man, quite frankly, was bereft of original ideas for a doctoral thesis. Perhaps it was unethical to attempt to help Mr. Kilgore, but he had worked so hard to overcome his shortcomings. I wanted him to at least have a chance of earning his degree. I suppose I learned a hard lesson myself."

Oh, that sounded good. Laft had wanted to avoid any public scrutiny at all, but it was inevitable now, and a little false evidence and a lot of sincerity would make the problem of Harry Kilgore go away.

"Hi, Prof."

Startled, Laft slowed his steps. There was a car parked behind the Halyard Gymnasium. It was so dark he could hardly tell it was a station wagon. There was a man busying himself with the car.

"Hello?" Laft asked, and he kept walking. The man was opening the rear hatch of the station wagon. He didn't seem really interested in Laft. His voice was familiar. Probably one of his students. The rear hatch creaked when the man lowered it, then the car suspension groaned as the man knelt inside the cargo space.

The man didn't seem threatening, and he was a stone's throw from Laft. Still, it was odd that the man was parked behind the gym in the dark.

"Do I know you?"

The man inside the station wagon was busy, but he called over his shoulder, "Sure ya do, Prof."

Laft struggled to place the voice. "Security doesn't like people to park in this lot except when there's a game."

"I'm only going to be here a minute."

Professor Laft was startled when the voice clicked. "Harry? Is that you?"

"Sure. Who'd you think it was?"

"What are you doing here?"

"Setting things right."

"Is that supposed to be some kind of a threat?"

"Not at all."

Laft wasn't going to turn and run. Kilgore was unpredictable, but he wasn't a physical man. He wouldn't attack Laft, surely. As long as he kept his distance, Laft wasn't going to be intimidated.

"You want to strike some sort of a deal, Harry?"

"Not at all."

"You can't win, Harry. Not when it's my word against yours."

"Yeah, I figured that out." Harry hardly seemed to be paying attention. He was fooling around with whatever was in the back of the station wagon.

"So, you do want to make a deal?" Laft demanded.

"No way."

"So what are you doing here, Harry, besides wasting my time?"

"I'm doing field testing, Prof." Harry Kilgore clambered out of the rear of the station wagon, and a single green light glowed on the machinery like a happy green eye.

Professor Laft was slow to understand. "You mean, that's a working model?"

"Well, I won't know that until I run the test," Harry Kilgore said with a smile in his voice. "Wish me luck."

Harry Kilgore raised his hand with some small controller clutched in it.

Professor Frederic Laft understood the purpose of the machinery in the cargo area of the station wagon. He realized that it was the largest of its type ever constructed, and he realized that he was in extreme danger.

"Don't, Harry!" Laft cried. He was ready to give up his claims to Harry's invention. He'd go public with his duplicity. If only Harry would refrain from deploying the engineering innovation.

Too late. The engineering innovation was already functioning with a rumble of sound. Then all was quiet again.

"I'd say that was a successful test," Harry Kilgore said with satisfaction. "Don't you think so, Professor?"

The remains of Professor Laft made no reply.

CAMPUS SECURITY FOUND him first. Soon Goodrich police swarmed the scene. The county medical examiner wasn't far behind.

"Is this a fraternity prank?" demanded the county medical examiner when he jumped out of his car.

"No joke," insisted the chief of Goodrich police.

"Better not be."

The closer he got, the less it looked like a joke and more like an actual human body.

"He splatted," the medical examiner pointed out. "I never heard of anybody actually splatting before."

"I heard of jumpers splatting," the police chief said. "If they jump from way high."

The difference was that Professor Laft wasn't on the ground, but on the wall. He had splatted against the wall, and he splatted so hard he was stuck there.

"He must have been hit by a car," the medical examiner said.

"I guess so, but his front's not damaged. If a car hit him that hard, wouldn't his front be all smashed up, too? His facial bones are intact. Even his rib cage is solid on the front."

How'd you know?"

"Poked him."

The medical examiner wasn't prepared to explain it. He wasn't even a medical doctor, just an elected county coroner. For the first time he realized how stupid it was to have the people of the county elect an insurance salesman to be county coroner.

Sure enough, Professor Laft's front looked undamaged. His eyes were wide open and hadn't burst, and his body contours seemed unaltered. It was his back that was crushed flat—crushed with such violence his body exploded out of his skin and clothes and splashed in all directions.

"So," the police chief asked, "what do you think?"

"I think I won't speculate until after an autopsy is performed. Let's get him off the wall."

The police chief nodded seriously and asked, "You bring your spatula?"

THE PATCH OF SAND was known as Unreliable Island. Sometimes it was five acres of bulging sand peppered with strands of grass, and other times it was nonexistent—the sandy floor ten feet underwater. The ocean geologists explained that it had something to do with an unusual intersection of concentrated currents that pushed up the silt, then washed it away, then pushed it up again. The scientists claimed that, with careful study of the opposing currents and the tide tables, they would be able to chart the growth of Unreliable Island, but it just wasn't worth all the effort. Unreliable was a curiosity and nothing more.

If there was a cycle to submersion and eruption no human could learn it, and the island always seemed to be submerged when it was really needed. The coral in the vicinity invariably snagged boats during the periods when Unreliable Island was beneath the waves. The local shark population made survival in the open water a short-term affair, so shipwreck victims never lasted long. Then Unreliable Island would build up from the shallow ocean shelf and expose the broken skeletal remains for the next passersby to discover.

The locals, on a pair of Bahamian islands that were seven miles to the northeast, claimed a malicious spirit had been trapped on the island for a hundred years.

They spoke of a wicked bride who mocked her new husband mercilessly throughout their honeymoon yachting adventure, until the young man could stand it no more and stranded her on Unreliable Island. The bride died when the island sank beneath her feet and the predators closed in. The girl's tormented ghost remained, her heart still full of wickedness, so that she would gash the hulls of boats when her island was submerged. The locals claimed the wicked bride was still hoping to sink the boat belonging to her groom, even though he would have died of old age years earlier.

If the legend was true, then the bride ghost was probably sulking today, because Unreliable Island was above the waves at its maximum height, which was just enough island to serve as camouflage for the souped-up, low-profile cutters belonging to the United States Drug Enforcement Administration. The DEA needed a way to fool the drug runners' over-the-horizon radar, and Unreliable Island, on this day, was just the ticket.

THE DRUG RUNNERS HAD ALWAYS assumed the DEA would be unwilling to use Unreliable Island as a tool, and until today they were right. The DEA was riddled with so much inefficiency and bureaucracy and generally unreliable components of its own infrastructure that it usually steered clear of staging operations with any potential for surprise or miscalculation. Invariably, those who were responsible for making risky decisions were the ones who suffered the consequences of failure.

The lower ranks of the DEA were peppered with former senior agents who had made one bad choice—or who were blamed for making the choice.

Today, some up-and-coming project leader was informed that Unreliable was most likely above the waves, based on the recent ocean behavior and weather. This assessment was accompanied by intelligence that said Unreliable would be the location of today's drug exchange.

Special Agent Chou made the quick decision to stage an operation. The DEA had boats close enough to get into position before the drug runners. The delivery was a big one. Special Agent Chou took the risk, knowing full well that failure put him on the path to demotion and that the failure of the mission might come as easily as arriving at the drug-transfer point and finding that Unreliable Island was not, in fact, above the waves.

So far, so good. Unreliable was above the surface of the ocean. Even better, it was at its maximum height, making it an ideal hiding place for the low-profile DEA cutters.

Agent Chou's heart leaped into his throat when he saw the pair of drug boats closing in Unreliable Island for the exchange. The Colombian go-fast boat zipped in from southern points unknown, moving at incredible speed. The second boat sped in from the north from a hidden harbor among the hundreds of Bahamian islands.

The boats came without hesitation, because their radar and their instincts told them they were safe. They knew there were no boats in the area, and they could certainly monitor air traffic in the vicinity, and their lines of sight informed them that Unreliable Island was the only interruption on the flat, empty Caribbean Sea.

The drop-off should be a big one. Intelligence received by the DEA described an all-or-nothing run. It was one of those huge shipments that occurred when the shippers were extraordinarily confident that they had a secure route and were willing to risk a small fortune. The drugs on this run were worth many millions— a three-month production inventory from one of the biggest cartels in Colombia.

Agent Chou watched the two boats weave among the subsurface coral and rendezvous in the shallow waters off Unreliable Island, where they knew they were hidden from radar.

The Colombian boat pilot shoved the motor into reverse to bring his craft to a quick, sure halt in the churning water alongside the Bahamians' boat. As his trusted men snapped on the grapples, the Colombian pilot hurried to the side of the boat and, without a word, crooked his finger at the pilot of the second boat.

Time was short for the DEA. The drug runners were very good at what they did. They had practiced the exchange of cargo many times and knew how to accomplish it quickly.

Agent Chou estimated it would take them all of 240

seconds to make the exchange, and he clicked the countdown timer on his watch at the moment the grapples were in place and the two boats became connected to each other.

THE BAHAMIAN PILOT held his index finger out to the Colombian. The Colombian presented a small aluminum device with an opening less than an inch in diameter. The Bahamian inserted his finger into the aluminum device.

It was an effective little piece of electronics that some of the most professional drug smugglers were employing. The portable fingerprint-reading device was equipped with a tiny, motor-driven guillotine inside.

Since the two men had never met, the Colombian had no way of knowing for certain if the Bahamian pilot was the correct man. Photo ID was worse than useless. Only biometric technology could be trusted when one was exchanging, on an anonymous basis, goods that could be measured to have street values of many millions of U.S. dollars.

Rubber grippers latched on to the finger with crushing power and the device scanned the finger. The pilot from Colombia looked at the pilot of the boat from the Bahamas, and the scanner made no noise whatsoever. The Colombian's eyes shifted. He apparently had not expected the operation to take this long.

The Colombian wasn't worried. He knew that the device took many readings at various levels of sensor intensity, as a way of insuring an accurate read. The

Colombian didn't bother to explain this to the Bahamian. The Bahamian sweated.

There had been a few false-negative readings in the past. When the device decided that the finger it was reading was not the finger it had been expecting, it reacted at once. The disk blades inside the device began spinning so rapidly that by the time the victim heard the whir, the blades would already be cutting through the flesh and into the bone. By the time the victim felt the pain, the digit would be half-severed. By the time he tried to shake the device off, it would have fallen off by itself, with the victim's finger still locked inside.

The advantages of the system were manifold. Drug pirates were extremely reluctant to target the forward-thinking drug runners who utilized such methods. Brutal criminals with no fear of putting themselves within close proximity of the ruthless cartels were too afraid to put their fingers in the shiny silver box. Piracy attempts on cartels who used the device had dropped to almost nil.

In addition to the suffering of having one's finger amputated, the victim would almost surely lose his life, too, later if not immediately.

The amputated finger could not be removed from the device. Unless the pirates managed to attack and subdue the cartel shippers at once, they couldn't get the device back. Even if they did, it was well known that the device contained a satellite phone that communicated the digital image of the finger of the would-be pirate. The fingerprint would soon enough be identified, and the cartel would place all its resources behind finding and exterminating the would-be pirate.

The man in the Bahamian boat was no pirate, and yet he didn't trust the little aluminum device. As the seconds ticked away, he became certain the device was malfunctioning, about to decide on a false reading and sever his finger. Soon after that, the men from Colombia would wipe out him and his boys.

The device clicked. The Bahamian almost jumped out of his sandals. The Colombian chuckled as the device slipped off; the click was the sound of the rubber grips releasing.

The Colombian didn't need to say a word to his crew, who began at once to remove plastic-wrapped bales of merchandise from beneath the fake floor of the go-fast boat. A portable ramp was placed against the rail, latched into position, and the bales began riding up the ramp quickly, propelled by the eager Colombians.

The Bahamian crew hustled to intercept the bales that came flying over the rail, and stowed them in their own safe compartment. The transfer moved ahead as planned, which meant it should be off-loaded from the Colombian boat to the Bahamian boat in just minutes.

Agent Chou observed the sudden haste to transfer the shipment and he knew the time had come. He nodded to his own cutter crew and made the wide hand gesture that was the silent signal to the second DEA cutter to begin the interception.

Now was the opportune moment, when the cargo was half on one craft and half on the other, while the boats were grappled and the crews were engaged in rushed activities. Striking at them now made them most vulnerable. The fact that the cargo was partially delivered would create the highest degree of uncertainty.

Agent Chou didn't have much time to move in, and since his aircraft support could not be staged nearby, they could not be there in time to lend support. They needed to be called in now if they would be of any help at all.

"Bird One," he said into the radio. "Come in, Bird One."

He got no response. And this ticked him off. The radio equipment was spotty, and he couldn't understand why the DEA couldn't get some decent damned communications equipment.

"Bird," he said finally, "we are moving in now. You go ahead and join us when it's convenient."

He gave a second hand gesture, handed the radio off to another agent and grabbed the windshield frame as the boat came to life with a muffled roar. The DEA cutter tore out from behind Unreliable Island, and the second cutter came out on the other side. Both spun and flashed across the surface of the water toward the pair of grappled drug boats.

Agent Chou saw the reaction already on the drug boats. Just for a moment, the drug runners froze and stared across the water. He loved it when he took them by complete surprise, especially the real professionals.

THE COLOMBIAN BOAT PILOT hit the red panel switch of the emergency disconnect on the grappling brackets. He stepped behind the boat controls and gave it gas. He spun the boat in a hairpin turn and away from the attackers, palming the wheel to weave between the dangerous fangs of the coral that waited just under the surface of the sea.

The Bahamians had reacted too slowly to the ambush and couldn't get enough speed going. One of the DEA boats swerved across their bow. The Bahamians were forced to veer sharply, slowing themselves considerably and creating a perfect broadside target for the DEA gunner with the grenade launcher. He fired the launcher, and the OC pepper-spray round plopped onto a seat inside the Bahamian boat, then belched acrid smoke. The Bahamians wretched at the rails until the gas was too much for them, then they flipped over the sides into the blessed relief of the water. The boat stalled. The Bahamians were caught.

Fools and amateurs, thought the Colombian boat pilot as he took in the entire unfolding catastrophe in a backward glance.

"Set up to fire," he ordered.

His crew waited, like the professionals they were, until the second DEA cutter came within range, then they sprayed machine-gun fire into the air.

The DEA cutter was especially outfitted for chasing drug smugglers, and it was actually gaining on the expensive, customized go-fast cartel craft.

"More fire," he snapped to his men. "I want them shitting their pants."

His men obeyed without question, emptying their weapons at the pursuing DEA cutter but getting nowhere for it. The rounds that made contact with the boat were bouncing off the bulletproof windshield and the armored hull.

The Colombian swore quietly. The DEA craft didn't even need to catch up to the Colombians, but only had to keep the Colombians in sight long enough for their aircraft to close in with its standard arsenal of machine guns and sniper rifles. A helicopter could lay waste to the Colombian boat without even getting within range of the Colombian weapons.

"Here comes their air support," announced one of his men emotionlessly.

The Colombians were fearless. They had been in tight fixes before and they usually got out of them. But the boat pilot had no idea how they were going to escape this time.

The pilot heard an exclamation from one of his men. "The Americans have something new up their sleeves."

The pilot looked back. The DEA boat was fifty yards to the rear and pacing them, but the helicopter wasn't coming to join it. It was dangling a piece of equipment such as he had never seen before. The thing hung a few feet below the helicopter on heavy chains and seemed to weigh the aircraft down. It was round and silver, and fluted at one end. The Colombian pilot had no idea what it was, but he knew it couldn't be good.

He adjusted the controls slightly, hoping to pull a little more speed out of the boat, but there was no speed left for it to give.

"What is the chopper doing?" he shouted.

"It is staying near the island," one of his man said.

"The Americans have control of the Bahamian boat already," he replied. "What are they doing?"

He didn't get an answer until he heard the crack of thunder. It was curious sound on a bright, sunny Caribbean morning. The thunder came from the island. When the Colombian captain turned to look, he was just in time to see the remains of the American's cutter flying to pieces. Most of it was already below the surface.

"What happened?" he shouted. "Did they explode?"

"The chopper bombed them," one of his excited men said.

"You are seeing things!"

"Look!"

The pilot looked back and witnessed the second DEA cutter slowing. The agents on board were agitated. They cut speed as the helicopter sped toward them, slowed and hovered over the cutter. The special agent on board the vessel was waving his arms at the helicopter and yelling.

The cylindrical device hanging below the aircraft had some sort of a hornlike aperture at the bottom. The Colombian had never seen anything like it.

Nothing came out of the aperture, but there was a boom of thunder, right on top of the DEA cutter. There was no light, no smoke, no spark of fire, but the cutter collapsed and plunged into the ocean. The waving special agent seemed to get squeezed hard and he spurted his insides out in all directions. The cutter and the DEA agents were transformed into floating debris.

A cheer rose from the Colombian boat. "It's on our side!" shouted one of the men.

The captain wasn't so sure about that. His fears were confirmed when the helicopter came after his boat.

"Shoot! Aim for the pilot!"

The helicopter tilted and jerked as if the man at the stick were on his first solo flight, but the pilot managed to get a couple hundred feet of altitude as he come over the Colombian boat. The Colombians were firing straight up into the belly of the strange, dangling weapon, only to see the rounds bounce off the metal. The Colombian captain twisted the wheel, but the weapon was working already.

One moment there was nothing but Caribbean wind, and the next there was a tremendous pressure from high above. Too much air in not enough space. The air couldn't stay compacted like that and it surged out of the compression core. The boat was raked with monstrous wind that bowled over the gunners, swept some over the side and flung others into the seats and the hull plates. The pilot felt his body pushed into the wheel of the boat as if he had a ton of concrete on his back. The steering wheel collapsed. He couldn't breathe. His ribs popped in quick succession. The force of the air vanished, and he collapsed on the deck on his back.

Whatever the weapon was, it had been less intense than the strike that squashed the DEA boat. The Colombians' boat was still afloat.

But all his men were dead, their bodies snapped and broken. A minute later, the Colombian pilot was dead, as well.

The helicopter unfurled a grappling hook on a steel chain. It slammed into the deck of the Colombian go-fast boat, and the barb hooked on a seat pedestal. The helicopter towed the boat high onto the sands of Unreliable Island and released the chain.

Another chain snagged the empty Bahamian boat and dragged it to land, then the chains holding the weapon were winched high into the belly. The chopper came in for a landing. Billowing clouds of sand swirled around it, and the pilot seemed to lose sight of the land until he touched down with a crunch.

The pilot sat inside waiting for the sand to settle, then he stepped out with his shirt collar pulled up over his nose and mouth. He stepped back and examined the helicopter's collapsed skids, his scraggly, long hair flapping in the breeze.

Then he went to the Colombian boat, and looked inside.

"Yech!"

He clambered in, gingerly moved the bloody remains of a Colombian from the deck hatch and began tossing out bundles of shrink-wrapped cocaine. When he had them all he climbed out and made several trips to the helicopter, where he stowed the bales in the rear.

The Bahamian boat contained no bodies, but as he was hoisting out cocaine bundles, the man stopped.

On the opposite side of the boat was a wet blood trail and a disturbance in the sand. Somebody with an open wound had crawled out of the sea onto Unreliable Island—and it had happened after the helicopter deposited its smooth snowfall of sand.

Somebody had survived in the water and come ashore to escape the predators. The man followed the tracks in the sand to a bloody mound of sand. Whoever they were, they were hiding from him.

He finished loading the cocaine from the Bahamian boat into his helicopter, then started her up. The sand swirled. The aircraft rose, fell, then rose again. It hovered unsteadily in the air, and the weapon was lowered into position on its rattling chains.

The weapon made a tiny poof of sound, and the surface of Unreliable Island became a maelstrom of shrieking wind and sand. When it died down seconds later, there was a Bahamian lying in the sand where his hiding place had been. The Bahamian's skin had been a rich, dark coffee color, but now it was vibrant pink. The sand had scoured his flesh.

He got to his feet, stumbled and clawed at the sand. He looked up, but he was blind—the sand had scoured his eyes until they burst and the vitreous jelly streaked his cheeks. Still, the Bahamian heard the helicopter, and he shouted at it.

The weapon *pooted,* the thunder cracked right on top of the land, and Unreliable Island became a blinding sandblast that took the Bahamian's flesh off. The body flopped in the frantic sandstorm. The boats disintegrated. Another thunder crack scoured the sandbar below the water level. When the maelstrom ended and the waters rushed in, Unreliable Island was again below the surface of the Caribbean Sea.

2

His name was Remo, but one day soon he would come to be famous in urban legend as the Sunglasses Man, gallant savior of coeds in distress.

He didn't know he was about to become legendary. He didn't *want* to be legendary. He just wanted to pick up some of the trash on this stretch of shoreline so he could go back to his summer vacation.

"You'd think the cops would do a better job watching the beach," he complained. "I guess I can't blame them. This isn't even inside the city limits, is it? And there are miles of beach and not enough cops. I'm sure they get all kinds of crap from people who are always saying stuff like, 'You'd think the cops would do a better job watching the beach.' You know?"

The clerk said nothing, but he rolled his eyes up, then down, then this way and that way. Remo Williams used his fingertips to adjust the clerk's spine slightly. The clerk inhaled for the first time in more than a minute.

"You sound like a St. Bernard woofing," Remo said.

"Couldn't breathe," the clerk said.

"I know. I'm the one who made you not breathe, re-member? And I can do it again."

The clerk got to his feet and tried to run, but Remo's Fingertips of Power were now firmly pinched on his elbow. The clerk froze again, but at least his lungs re-mained functional this time.

They were standing in the cool sands near Myrtle Beach, South Carolina. Summer came early here from Remo's perspective—he most often made his home in the northeastern United States.

"Last few weeks I've been camping out at Piney Point," he told the clerk. "It's nice. Do you know the place?"

The clerk's eyes rolled back and forth. His whites were very white in the only light, which came from a chill, pale moon and the pinpricks of frozen stars.

"Secluded, quiet, right on the beach. I catch my own dinner a lot, so it's convenient. I've had a rough couple of months and I was kicking back, relaxing."

The clerk tried to make his body work, but all he managed was a grunt.

"If you mess your britches in the middle of my story, I'm gonna be really mad at you. Madder than I am al-ready. Where was I? Oh yeah. Relaxing. Kicking back. When all of a sudden, my father tells me there's a prob-lem at Myrtle Beach and I have to go take care of it. When my father says I have to do something, I do it. No arguing and no complaining, not ever. I'm a con-siderate son. So here I am, doing what the old guy tells me to do. Which leads me to you.

The clerk felt the Ring Finger of Doom switch a knob of his vertebrae at the base of his neck, then his body seemed to sag. He could move again—but only his mouth.

"Answer the question," commanded Remo, Supreme Wielder of Deadly Digits.

"I swear I don't know what you're even talking about."

"Problems. On the beach. Kids complaining. Kids not having a good time."

"I don't know!"

"Kids being mean to other kids? Making the other kids go home? See, my father's one of the merchants on this beach. He's got a booth a quarter mile south of here, and all of a sudden, traffic's way down. Why?"

"How should I know?"

Remo Williams pinched the ball of the clerk's thumb—just a little pinch, but the pain was as big as the great black Atlantic Ocean.

"Oh, shut up." Remo pushed the clerk over. The clerk inhaled between screams and got a mouthful of sand, which led to a choking fit. Remo tried on a pair of sunglasses from the clerk's beach stand to kill time.

It was pitch-black outside. Why would anybody buy sunglasses at night? The screaming and coughing were now barks of agony.

Remo lifted the clerk to his feet. "Finished?"

"Don't do that pinchy thing again, please, God."

"I promise you I *will* do that again. *Unless.*"

"What? *What?*"

"Answer the question. What's the problem on Myrtle Beach? Why's traffic on the decline? Why are the kids going home?"

The kid was almost hyperventilating. "Because girls are being, kind of, taken advantage of?"

"You know, I heard a rumor it was something like that. Tell me about it."

"Daters. The drinks are being spiked with Daters. They're drugs that make the girls get all, you know, willing."

"Willing? Find the right girl and all it takes is a few beers. Explain further."

The clerk was in a flop sweat, but he was helpless. "It knocks them out. You can do anything you want to 'em. They don't even remember it the next day."

Remo nodded seriously. "So, you make them unconscious?"

"Almost."

"Zombies, sort of?"

"Yeah," the clerk said.

"Then you have your way?"

"They don't even remember it the next day. It's like it never happened, man. You know, no harm, no foul?"

"Hi, girls," Remo said as a flock of scrawny girls in bikinis staggered past the Cool Shades Sunglasses stand. Like all the beach stands catering to vacationing teenagers, it stayed open for business until past midnight. The beach merchants understood that the best impulse sales came during an evening of drinking.

The girls came to the stand and giggled for the entire fifteen minutes it took them to pick out their sunglasses. Remo guessed the little females were too young even for a driver's license. A statuesque redhead, who might have been in her twenties, declared proudly, "I'm the chaperone. I'm the one who rented the hotel room."

"Impressive," Remo said.

"Wanna see it?"

"No, thanks."

"Oh, come on," the girls chorused. After all, Remo didn't look old enough to be their father.

He was, though, so he played the perfect professional sunglasses monger. He pointed out different brands of sunglasses propped on the displays, which were mounted on a plastic booth in the sand. The plastic was bright yellow, but it washed out to a gray in the darkness of night. The sunglasses stand had no lights except a penlight with a dying battery, which the clerk had flicked on only to count change. The dark didn't stop the girls from trying on sunglasses and posing in front of the plastic mirrors.

"What's with your friend?" asked a dark-haired waif in a black bikini. She exhaled grain alcohol and fruit punch.

"Too much to drink," Remo said. The clerk was frozen in his plastic chair, eyes wide, breathing shallowly.

"Is there any such thing?" squealed the dark-haired girl. The others laughed uproariously.

Remo wasn't interested in this crowd. He loved

attractive women, but high-schoolers were below his threshold. Even the tall redhead was young for his tastes—not to mention that he was repulsed by the sour-stomach smell of heavy drinking.

He took their cash and was alarmed when the girls proudly donned their new sunglasses to continue their midnight trek to the hotel. They drifted blindly toward the ocean, but the water lapping at their feet tipped them off and they swerved away from death by drowning with peals of intoxicated hilarity.

"They're easy targets," Remo remarked to the clerk when they were alone again. "Which makes me wonder why you need to spike their drinks with anything."

"What'll you do to me now?" the clerk asked.

"Tell me how you operate." Remo pressed both sides of the hidden panel in the kick plate at the bottom of the booth, and the stash drawer popped open. He tore a plastic freezer bag and examined the tea bags.

The sunglasses clerk explained, "Three grades of Dater. Twenty-five dollar, forty dollar and fifty dollar. You buy what you think you need. The fifty-dollar bags are the strongest. We take Visa and MasterCard, but not American Express."

"I see."

"Why don't you take some free samples?" the kid asked hopefully. "In fact, take them all."

"How would you work this into their drinks?" Remo asked. "Hey, look, you guys put little instruction tags right on the tea bag string. Pretty ingenious."

"Thanks. My idea."

"A fifty-dollar bag will do what? Say I hooked up with the tall girl with the tiger swimsuit and I slipped it into her cocktail."

"She'd be in outer space. You'd score for sure."

"Yeah? What about the little skinny one in the black suit? What'd it do to her?"

The clerk looked uneasy.

"Just might put her a coma," Remo answered his own question.

"We put warning labels on the tea bags!"

"You're lucky you haven't killed anybody so far."

The clerk looked extremely uneasy.

"At least," Remo added, "not that I knew about. I'd say you've put this whole scam together pretty well."

"Thanks, dude."

"On the other hand, my own daughter is just about victimization age."

"Oh."

"Yeah," Remo said. "Come on."

THE PLASTIC COOL SHADES Sunglasses booth was dragged down the middle of Myrtle Beach with the sunglasses clerk draped over it. The sunglasses on the rickety display stands wobbled precariously. It made an interesting sight in the middle of the night if you happened to see it—and somebody from the Shifting Sands Beach Lodge just happened to see it.

"Hey, it's the Sunglasses Man!"

It was his customers. The gaggle of girlies had their own fourth-floor lanai, and the whole flock was crowded out onto it. The scrawny brunette had her head through the bars and was about to projectile hurl, but everybody else was thrilled to see him.

"Come on up and have a good time!" It was the tall redhead, doing her best Statue of Liberty pose with a bottle of clear liquid that showed a tiny picture of a bat.

Remo was alarmed again—they were still wearing their sunglasses. He gave them a wave and kept walking, hoping his disinterest would send them back inside.

"Come on, Sunglasses Man!" the redhead shouted.

"Yeah, come on!" chorused the others.

Remo marched on. How'd he get in this pickle?

"Maybe this'll change your mind!" she shouted. "Look!"

Remo was only human. He *had* to look. The redhead was now twirling her tiger-striped bikini top on one finger above her head, and she was dancing. "Woo-hoo!"

The others refused to be left out. More bikini tops began twirling. Remo kept walking.

"Hey, Sunglasses Man, catch!"

The redhead flung her bikini top out to him. She flung just a little too far. She was just a little too tall. The iron rail on the old hotel balcony was just a little too low.

"Oh, bother." Remo mumbled to the clerk. "Wait here."

THE REDHEAD WAS FALLING. She wasn't so drunk she couldn't figure out that she was two seconds away from death. She screeched. She heard the rum bottle shatter, and in another moment she would shatter, too.

Then she was okay, nestled in the iron-strong arms of the Sunglasses Man. He was standing next to the pool, and it took her a moment to realize that he'd actually caught her.

He effortlessly pivoted both of them under the fluttering bikini top. It draped over her big toe.

"Oh, God," she moaned. "You saved me."

"I shouldn't have." He placed her on her feet in a glass-free spot.

"No, don't ever let me go!" She clung to his neck.

"Sorry, sweetheart."

The girls upstairs were cheering, except for the nauseous waif. "Go inside and sleep it off!" Remo ordered.

"Come on," pleaded the redhead. "Let's do it again."

"I'm out of here."

"I want you."

"Whatever." Remo slipped out of the lasso of her arms and hightailed it back to the beach. The redhead tried to chase him, but her feet tangled in her bikini top and she collapsed on the pool deck, skinning her most sensitive front parts.

"Come back, Sunglasses Man!" she sobbed. "I love you!"

Remo was already gone. The sunglasses on their

stands were swinging wildly, although, oddly, not one of them fell off. The clerk was swinging, too, and his limp head banged against the plastic with every step Remo took.

"I don't get why anybody would buy Daters anyway," Remo remarked. "How much easier could it be to score around here?"

REMO WASN'T GIVING himself enough credit. The truth was that women were highly attracted to him. It wasn't just teen party princesses on vacation, either, but all kinds of women.

Remo was the world's Reigning Master of Sinanju. The training he had endured gave him the ability to find the vulnerable nerve endings in the human body and exploit them in unusual ways. These were the skills he employed to get the cooperation of the clerk at the sunglasses stand.

Remo had complete control over his ability to find nerve endings. The business of attracting women was not so well under his control. It was a phenomenon that seemed to defy his understanding. Even for a man who controlled his body's heart rate, his circulation and his breathing like no other human being except Master Chiun, his mentor, he still couldn't quite get a handle on the process that made him superattractive to women. He could make it go away, if he really thought about it. But he wasn't sure *how* he made it go away and what a pain it was thinking about it all the time.

There was much, much more to being a Master of Sinanju, which at its surface could be called a martial art. Like other martial arts, Sinanju gave its practitioners a number of unique fighting skills. In fact, Sinanju was the first martial art, the original martial art. Over many centuries, bits and pieces of Sinanju knowledge were stolen by others and these fragments became the basis of all other martial arts. Karate and kung fu, the techniques of the ninja, the lost battle skills of a hundred vanished Buddhist monasteries were based on Sinanju knowledge. It followed then that all next-generation fighting schools, such as judo, could trace their development back to a sliver of light gleaned from the Sun Source of all martial arts: Sinanju.

What the other arts never understood was that Sinanju relied on so much more than just blocks, kicks and strikes. Sinanju was founded on expanding the human body and expanding the senses, and this relied, first and foremost, on breathing skills.

It was funny, Remo thought. Every living person knew how to breathe, right? But to start down the road to becoming one of the most skilled humans of all time, what you really needed to do was learn to breathe *fully*.

Remo's Sinanju-expanded senses enabled him to perform feats that seemed impossible. Seeing in near total darkness. Hear the beat of a heart, track the dilation of a pupil from ten paces, break rocks by tapping them with his knuckles. Sinanju improved his sense of balance—it even improved his ability to balance things other than himself, like a bunch of sunglasses on a rickety plastic stand being dragged down the beach.

The ancient tradition of Sinanju had sprung up in a little fishing village in what was now North Korea. The fishing was never good on that stretch of shore, so the Sinanju men worked as assassins, roaming the world to offer their services to king and emperor, plying their trade without weapons, taking their fee in gold. They became known as the world's preeminent assassins, and their fees were substantial.

The gold was sent back to the village of Sinanju, where the people eventually stopped giving their all to the occupation of fishing.

Remo, as Sinanju Master, usually went after bigger fry than greedy beach vendors, but tonight he wasn't on the company clock. This was a public service.

The clerk's hotel was just ahead, and it was a noticeable upgrade in cleanliness and room rates. The really expensive lower-level suites had balconies that opened onto the beach, and a quiet group of men was sitting around a table with a cooler of iced beer close at hand. They were on their feet long before Remo reached them.

"Sorry to spoil the chillin'," Remo announced.

"Who the fuck are you?"

"Found this on the beach." Remo brought the sunglasses booth to a stop and nudged the clerk, who flopped off the stand and slammed into the beach sand, motionless. "Says you guys are his associates."

"Who do you think you're messing with?" demanded the powerful-looking young man with cut chest muscles and bulging biceps. "Where's the cash?"

Remo looked from one guy to the next. "I can't help notice you're all wearing the same ring. Please don't tell me you're a fraternity?"

"Yeah. Who are you to care?"

"Does this little business with the drug dealing have the approval of the Greek council?"

"I don't know what you're talking about, but you sure got a big mouth."

"And you got fake chest muscles. I heard that guys were getting breast implants but I never met anybody who actually did it."

The belligerent college kid went wildly on the defensive. "What? What are you talking about? They're not fake. I work my chest three times a week. I'll kill you, asshole."

The sliding glass door slid open and an irritated male voice said, "What's the problem?"

"Get out here, Reg, we got a dilemma," said the guy with the breast implants.

Remo, whose hearing was far better than the hearing of anyone he knew, heard someone else inside the suite. A slurring female was in the hotel suite with Reg, and she wasn't there by choice.

"Oh, no," Remo said. "This just stopped being fun, gentleman."

"You got that right," the guy with the water-balloon pectorals snapped.

"Hi, Reg," Remo said to the alert, disheveled young man who came out of the hotel room in jeans shorts, pulling on a T-shirt. "You're just in time for the brainectomy."

"Who's getting a brainectomy?" Reg demanded, trying to get up to speed.

"You. Your friend with the fake boobs. All of you."

"I don't think so." Reg closed in on Remo Williams, as did all the frat brothers. It was seven against one.

The frat brothers didn't stand a chance.

3

The four old computer mainframes were nestled in the basement of a private hospital in New York, but they looked old enough to be in the Smithsonian.

However, it was just the cases that were yellowed and dingy. The guts were mostly new. Mark Howard had personally rebuilt the mainframes himself, piece by piece. New CPUs went in. New hard drives. Almost every connection and cable had been replaced in recent years. Phone lines were upgraded and then upgraded again. The mainframes, known as the Folcroft Four, were now many times more powerful than they were when Mark had arrived. The drives stored and mirrored many terabytes of data. The processors crunched more calculations per second than most global shared-processing networks. He couldn't even measure the capabilities of all its subsystems.

Part of the problem was the way in which the computers were rebuilt. One at a time, and in secret, the extraordinarily powerful components were purchased and brought to the hospital in Rye, New York. Individually,

Mark Howard would install them into the mainframes as best he could. Sometimes his biggest challenge was making the new component interface with technology that was ancient by the standards of the Digital Age.

But such was the nature of the facility in Rye that there could be no hint to the outside world that it was taking possession of computer power on such a immense scale. It was far more data-processing muscle than any hospital needed. Nuclear accelerators used mainframes on a scale like this. So did global weather analysis systems and the Pentagon and—well, that was about it.

Finally, Mark Howard had succeeded in reengineering all the vital components of the Folcroft Four. They were still using the old outer housings, but, like a tricked-out '67 Camaro, most of the working components were several generations removed from the originals.

Mark didn't think of it like an automobile, though. After all, high-performance automobile parts were easy to come by, and there were people all over the world with expertise in putting nonstandard parts on cars. The work on the Folcroft Four was more like removing the guts of a Douglas DC-3 and replacing them with space shuttle engines and controls. And doing it one piece at a time.

Without ever grounding the DC-3.

In fact, a lot of those components came from the aerospace industry. The latest upgrade was a chip set built for the European Space Agency and intended to power computers that monitored atmospheric conditions around launch sites and provided real-time analysis of possible weather-related anomalies. It took readings from thousands of sensors and converted them to an accurate, real-time map of the launch-site microclimate. They said it could monitor a breeze so light it wouldn't ruffle the flower petals in the garden beds. It factored in climate conditions around the globe, predicted their impact and learned from its mistakes.

Mark Howard wasn't sure it would help the European Space Agency reverse its mission failures, but the technology would help him crunch data. He had hacked into the systems of the chip producer and simply doubled the purchase order, then diverted the extra chip set on a cross-country series of shipping deliveries through several commercial carriers, the United States post office and a couple of private couriers. He doctored the delivery system on the last leg of the trip to send the chip set finally to a private rented box in New York City, but if those delivery records were ever audited, it would look like a wrong delivery caused by a paperwork snafu.

The chip set sat in an anonymous rented box under intense video monitoring. Finally, Mark Howard had gone and picked it up.

He'd gone through that kind of security process with each and every important piece of equipment—and the process was never-ending. He couldn't afford to let these computers be anything less than state-of-the-art.

He reconnected the network of fibers that tied the unit to its three siblings, and linked it to the racks of peripheral units. Then he powered up the unit. The old lights glowed to life. The flat-panel maintenance monitor recorded the start-up routines, the first-run diagnostics, the initialization application that analyzed the structure of the processor and reprogrammed it to operate in tandem with the other CPUs. Seconds later, the mainframe was operational again, and Folcroft had taken a giant leap forward in electronic thinking power.

Mark Howard smiled and shivered. The equipment room was like a meat locker, and a liquid cooling system sucked even more heat directly off the equipment so Howard could overclock the chips. He'd added twenty-two percent to the rated performance of the new chip set. The ESA wasn't going to get anywhere near as much performance from its components.

But then, the work of the ESA wasn't nearly as important as the work of Mark Howard, and the agency he worked for. That agency was secret and it used this private hospital, Folcroft Sanitarium, in Rye, New York, as cover for its operations.

To the public, Folcroft was under the direction of Harold W. Smith. Smith had administered the sanitarium for years, and he was renowned for his efficiency.

In truth, Smith was the first and only director of the U.S. federal agency known as CURE. CURE's staff was tiny. For years, Smith managed the agency alone. Mark Howard was added to the administrative team several years ago by the one man in the federal government who had knowledge of the existence of CURE— the President of the United States.

Adding Mark to the staff had been an ill-informed and impulsive step, in Smith's initial opinion, and yet Mark turned out to be a useful addition. He brought youth and vigor, intelligence and exceptional knowledge-gathering skills. He even had the technical skills to upgrade the computer systems that served as CURE's intelligence accumulation conduit.

Mark watched the small lights and displays tell him that all systems were go, and felt relief more than satisfaction. The maintenance monitor displayed the acceptance of an incoming call on the secure private lines. The call originated from a beach hotel in South Carolina.

Mark wanted to hear what that was all about. He secured the equipment room and rushed upstairs to the offices of CURE.

REMO WILLIAMS DIDN'T HAVE to dial phone numbers anymore. All he had to do was ask operator assistance to connect him to the phone for a certain fictional person or business. Somehow, this was supposed to ring the phone back at the office. He didn't understand how it worked, but it did seem to work—when he did his part right.

"What city, please?" asked the operator.

"Orlando. That's in Florida."

"Yes. What listing?"

Remo thought about that.

"Sir?"

"I'm trying to remember."

"You don't know who you're calling, sir?"

"It's an amusement park, I remember that much."

"There are several in Orlando, sir."

"Really?" He was being sarcastic. "Korean something."

"No listing," the operator announced.

"Yeah. It's there. Korean Oasis. No, that's not it. Korean Paradise?"

"No listing for any amusement park starting with the word 'Korean,'sir."

"Korean Conservatory? Korean Arboretum?"

"Sir, I searched under the word Korean. There's no such establishment as an amusement park with the word Korean."

"Korean Hothouse? Any of these sound right to you?"

"Sir, as I said, I did check for the word Korean."

"Check for Korean Hothouse."

"No listing. Please place your call again when you have the correct name of the listing."

"Did you try Arboretum?"

The woman sighed and typed. "No listing."

"What's like an Arboretum?" Remo asked. "A place where they plant stuff. A botanarium? A plantorium?"

"A garden, sir?"

Remo snapped his finger. "Gardens! Korean Gardens!"

"I've tried Korean already, sir."

"Try Korean Gardens."

"No listing. Excuse me, sir, there is a listing. Korean Gardens Enjoyment Center. Now, where did that come from?"

"'Arboretum'—guess I was trying too hard," Remo said. "Can you connect me to Korean Gardens?"

"Yes, sir." There was a click, then the line started to ring.

"I was trying too hard," Remo explained to the woman on the bed. She didn't even see him standing there.

A moment later he heard a familiar voice.

"Korean Gardens Enjoyment Center Security," she announced.

"Hi, sweetheart."

"Yes?"

"It's me."

"Me who?"

"Remo. Williams. Tall, dark and dead. Big wrists, smooth moves. You know."

"I'm afraid I don't."

"Okay. Whatever. Just give me to Smitty."

"You've called the security office, sir. There's no one here by that name."

Remo frowned into the phone. "Look, this isn't a good time to be yanking my chain. I need an ambulance here."

Remo heard the connection change as he was speaking, and another voice came on the line. "Remo, what's going on?" It was Mark Howard.

"Hey, Junior, what's with Sarah?"

"What do you mean?"

"She's giving me attitude," Remo said.

"When?" Mark asked.

"Just now."

"What? Remo, that wasn't Sarah. It was the voice-analysis routine."

Remo frowned again. The voice-analysis system that Mark Howard was talking about was designed to simulate a real human voice on the other end. The caller's responses would be assessed by CURE's supercomputer phone-answering machine to determine if the caller really was the one of two people who were allowed to call CURE headquarters via that special line. Remo was one of those people.

The computer had quizzed him in a number of different voices and they sounded amazingly realistic most of the time—but they had never sounded like somebody he knew.

"Junior, that was Sarah."

"I don't think so, Remo."

"It was. Believe me. My hearing's pretty good. It was Sarah."

"The computer must have generated a voice that sounded like Sarah," Mark Howard said impatiently. "The real Sarah's at home."

"In Providence?" Remo asked.

"At our apartment," Mark Howard said wearily. "In Rye."

"Oh." Remo recalled hearing that Mark and Sarah were getting a new place together. But that was beside the point. He'd heard Sarah Slate answer the phone. It was her. He knew it was.

"You said you needed an ambulance," Mark added.

"Yeah. I'm at some hotel."

"Silent Shores Beach Suites, Myrtle Beach, suite 104," Mark Howard informed him.

"Yeah."

"Did you identify the drug dealers who're running off the college kids?"

"Found drug dealers. Snuffed same."

Click. It was another connection coming on the line. "Remo," said a voice as sour as fresh-squeezed lemons, "you were not instructed to kill the drug dealers."

It was Harold W. Smith, and Smith was irritated. But then, Smith was always irritated.

"You didn't instruct me on anything, Smitty. This was my little mission, remember?"

"I remember it was ill-advised," Smith answered.

"In fact, it wasn't on the CURE dollar. Call it a personal job. This is on my own time. Junior, would you mind adjusting my time sheet to show this was on personal time?"

"They're just drug dealers, Remo," Mark Howard said. "Maybe they're bad guys, but they're not killers."

"In fact, they are killers. They owned up to two fatal overdoses in the past two weeks. I'll give you the names. You can check them out."

"I'm trying to verify. There've been no overdoses of college-age women in Myrtle Beach in the past two weeks," Smith replied.

"They were in Daytona until Monday," Remo said. "This is a well-organized business enterprise. They move from one hot spot to the next, satisfy local demand, then change venues before the body count gets too high. I found one underage victim in the room with the ringleader. That's the ambulance I told you I needed. She's in teenage wasteland, but I think she'll survive. I don't want to be the one to watch over her all night and make sure she doesn't swallow her own tongue."

"We can't send an ambulance with all those bodies there," Smith said.

"Then I'll call the ambulance myself. What's that number again? Nine-one-something?"

"Think what'll happen if the paramedics find a hotel room full of dead college kids," Mark Howard told Remo. "There'll be a panic."

"Like I care."

"Vacationers will flee Myrtle Beach," Smith added.

"Oh," Remo said. "I hadn't thought of that. Fine. I'll get rid of the bodies. You call the ambulance."

He slammed the phone and didn't bother wiping off his own fingerprints. If the place was dusted, if his prints were lifted, if they were fed into the crime systems that identified fingerprints, they'd come back without a match.

Remo Williams had been fingerprinted, back when he was a soldier and again when he was a beat cop in New Jersey, but that was in another life—literally. Remo had been executed for murder. The murder was real, but Remo hadn't committed it. The electrocution looked real, but Remo didn't die. He vanished into a strange underworld—and all records of him vanished at the same time.

Remo rifled the pockets of the corpses. He found the keys to a BMW, then high-tailed it to the front lot where he found the BMW itself. He inserted the key to unlock the steering column, but didn't start the engine. Instead, he used one foot to roll the car silently into the sand, around to the beach side of the hotel, then backward to the sliding glass doors of the drug dealers' suite. The drug dealers were arranged in a neat row in the trunk.

"How you feeling?" he asked the girl on the bed.

She didn't answer, just stared through glassy eyes at the ceiling, her breathing shallow.

Just a kid, and look what had been done to her.

Remo wished there were more drug dealers to assassinate.

REMO WAS AN old pro when it came to cadaver disposal. He wasn't repulsed by it, only mildly annoyed. He scooped sand with his hands and his thoughts were occupied by other things.

What was the deal with the phone system at Folcroft and why had it answered in the voice of Sarah Slate? It was supposed to come up with some anonymous character. A bricklayer from Pasadena or an investment broker from Evansville. It was a part of the whole elaborate scheme to make sure CURE stayed invisible. Putting Sarah's voice on the system was the wrong thing to do.

Not that it was a risk, really. Even if one of the wrong-number phone calls happened to get into the CURE system and happened to hear the simulated voice of Sarah Slate, it wouldn't tell them anything. It wasn't a security breach as far as Remo could see. But he knew Smith and Howard would see it in another way. Those guys were anal-retentive security freaks. They'd see it as a breach in the system.

So, wouldn't they have made the system so it couldn't do things like that? Sure they would have. It had to be an error. Even Mark and Smitty were sort of human.

But Remo had been convinced at the moment he heard that voice that he was talking to the real, living, breathing Sarah Slate, not a simulation, only to be told by Mark that she wasn't even at Folcroft. She was at the Rye apartment.

That was a temple-scratcher, but what was really confusing was why Remo was bothering to dwell on it. No matter what the explanation, it didn't matter, right?

He stopped what he was doing, only to discover his

hole was now twice as deep as he was tall, which was deeper than it needed to be. These guys weren't going to be found in this remote section of weeds and sand—not until the spot was bulldozed for condos, anyway. Remo silently stepped up the steep sides of the hole to the surface.

Where he landed, the loose sand was unblemished. No footprints. A gentle breeze would have disturbed more grains of sand.

Remo tossed in the bodies without a second thought. This bunch deserved nothing better than to be piled together in an unmarked grave and left to rot.

The open pit was surrounded by a near perfect ring of excavated sand. Remo scooped it back into the hole in a matter of minutes, then carefully compressed the bulge to make it level with the surrounding land. He gathered dry sand and sprinkled it over the moist sand of the grave, which was probably unnecessary. An hour after the sun came up, the top layer of grave sand would have dried anyway.

But Remo wanted to take no chances. What Mark Howard had said about a bunch of murders scaring off the vacationers had been correct. That was exactly what Remo was trying to prevent from happening, because no vacationers meant no customers at the beach stands. No customers meant no sales at the stand that sold silk Koh-Mo-Nos—and Remo's quality of life was directly tied to the sales of silk Koh-Mo-Nos.

Remo walked away from the grave without a backward glance. Again, his feet left no impressions in the sand. None of the weeds were bent where he walked among them. No one ever knew that Remo Williams had been to this place. A nearby lizard, devouring a cricket, was momentarily alarmed when the moonlight directly above him was momentarily darkened, but by the time it glanced up there was nothing there.

4

Turbo-charged with their latest upgrades, the Folcroft
Four churned away in the basement of Folcroft Sanitarium with ever greater efficiency at their core tasks:
gathering data and processing data. It was a simple pair
of assignments, really, until one considered the vastness
of the target domain and the amount of data to be analyzed.

The analysis of the data required millions of lines of
code, but even it could be broken down into two basic
parameters. Note occurrences of all predetermined
places, people, locations and key words of interest.
Note each aberration.

An aberration was a deviation from what was normal. Aberrations could be trouble.

But how could "normal" be quantified? What level
of deviation qualified as an aberration? Most of the
millions of lines of CURE's operational code were dedicated to answering those questions. A substantial por-
tion of the programming was dedicated to learning from
past aberrations to identify new aberrations, because

usually it was a subtle change in the behavior of the system in question that signaled the aberration. For example, two tornadoes hitting the same town in the same year was a subtle meteorological aberration.

Sometimes, the aberration wasn't subtle at all.

"Six microbursts, all three to eight days apart, all causing property damage and loss of life. All occurring during overnight hours."

"That seems highly unlikely," Harold W. Smith observed, looking across the small office to his assistant, Mark Howard.

"What's even more unlikely is that they're heading cross-country," Mark added. "Idaho, South Dakota, Wisconsin and all along I-90."

Smith frowned. "The microbursts are taking the interstate?"

"They headed south from there. Knoxville, Tennessee; Macon, Georgia. Madeira Beach, Florida. The motive was robbery."

Smith said, "Mark, microbursts are weather phenomena. They don't have motives and they don't commit robbery."

"Yes, that's what I thought," Mark said. "But these microbursts have committed felony theft of cash on several occasions. That is, whoever is responsible for the microbursts."

Smith considered this without enjoying it. "Without having seen the data, I believe it is premature to ascribe these events to true climactic microbursts. It is far more plausible to suppose they're the result of cleverly deployed explosives. Don't you?"

"Of course," Mark Howard said. The young man stopped to look at him. "My first assumption was exactly that. But that's not the case. Let me tell you why."

"Please."

"Six investigations. All in different police jurisdictions—in fact, they're all in different states. The first four occurred before the investigators had knowledge of the other events. Mistakes might have been made in the crime-scene detail, but not the same unusual mistake in every crime scene. They found no evidence of high temperatures, singed metal, melted plastic or other heat damage. None of the victims died of smoke inhalation and none of them showed evidence of burns to their bodies. What was found was evidence of traumatic impact."

"Suicides?" Smith asked.

"The damage to the bodies looked like the injuries sustained by building jumpers, but there weren't any buildings for them to have jumped from. In fact, two of the victims were armored-car guards who died in a parking lot without any buildings in the vicinity. Their truck was on its side, the money taken. In all cases, there was significant local damage consistent with a microburst."

Smith didn't like it. "I think we're jumping to conclusions. Let's look into the veracity of these investigations. Who labeled the events microbursts, meteorological scientists or weathermen on the local news?"

"We're way ahead of you."

"You are?"

"The system documented the credentials of the investigators in all cases."

"Why?" Smith asked.

"I guess because it assumed you would want it to. It probably identified that behavior earlier."

"Based on what variables?"

Mark said, "I don't know. Do you want me to find out?"

"No," Smith said. "It's just that I've never noticed this sort of responsiveness before. Your memory upgrades enable it?"

Mark said, "I imagine the upgrades are giving it the speed it needs to do what we programmed it to do—explore all the possible scenarios among all its input data to look for the patterns that match what it thinks we'll want."

Smith understood that easily enough. "Like a computer playing chess," he said. "The computer will think ahead to every possible outcome of the game based on every possible move it could make. The number of possibilities it has to analyze increases exponentially with every extra step ahead that it thinks. That's why early computer-chess programs took hours or days to decide on a single move."

"Right. But we're analyzing so many variables and

so much data, it's sort of like working on a chessboard with a million squares and a hundred thousand playing pieces. The mainframes could never crunch the data fast enough to give us good proactive advice until now."

"You're going to put the chaos theorists out of business, Mark," Smith said, nodding thoughtfully. "Let's see what the pattern matching can unearth about the microbursts. Have it look for patterns. Expand its search criteria to include any sort of pattern, regardless of relevance."

Mark grinned. "You're really going to push it."

"It's not like we can bog it down. It won't let its CPU be dedicated to the task," Smith said. "I'd like to see where this leads us."

"Got something."

"Already?" Smith said. "Let's have a look."

Smith and Howard both pulled up the results on their own displays and pored over the pattern match the mainframes had provided.

"Bull's-eye, Mark," Smith said after a moment, "I think you're going to put us out of a job, as well."

REMO DUMPED the BMW and strolled home along the Atlantic shore. It was a long walk back to Piney Point, but he didn't mind. His problems were taken care of. With nothing more on the agenda, he could get back to his lazy summer vacation—rest and relaxation, strenuous daily exercise routines and hours of scroll study. This was the life. He took the time to enjoy the still, calm night.

Why couldn't more of his time be like this? It seemed like he was always rushing around, flying here, assassinating there. Even when he wasn't busy, he was in a state of expectation for the next crisis.

The place made the difference. He had been unsettled for months after he and his mentor more or less gave up their two-flat residence, which had never had the feel of a real home. His last real home had been a converted church in Boston, which burned to the ground.

Living in a suite in the Doom and Gloom Wing at Folcroft wasn't good for him. It was too close to work. No wonder he was always poised for the next assignment, living just a few floors under Upstairs. Remo resolved he wouldn't live in Folcroft anymore.

Piney Point was just fine. Even the Airstream camper was growing on him. He could live with it for the foreseeable future.

But when he arrived at the campground, a taxi was idling in his remote campsite, headlights shining on the polished aluminum skin of the old Airstream camper and reflecting into the trees like spotlights.

The taxi driver saw Remo appear from the woods. He mouthed the words, "Help me."

"What's up, Little Father?" Remo asked the small figure in the back of the taxi, who sat with the window open.

Chiun said, "I am up, Remo, for hour after hour, waiting for my dawdling son. The Emperor has summoned us." The small singsong voice spoke to Remo in Korean.

"Called when?" Remo asked, also in Korean. "I just talked to them a couple of hours ago."

"Yes. So said the Prince Regent. He said he wished that you carried a phone so that he might have alerted you of the news, for you had just departed from the hotel room you shared with an underage girl."

"That's not exactly the situation."

"Was she of child-bearing age?"

"Please, save me," the cabdriver mouthed without actually making a sound.

"I guess so. But she wasn't my girl. I mean I didn't go to the hotel to be with her. She was with another guy."

"You were simply there to observe their activities?"

"Come on, you know why I was there. She was a victim," Remo said, then he disappeared into the camper, emerging again a moment later with four trunks, hand inlaid and beautiful. "I found the guys who were causing all the trouble on the beach and she was tonight's entertainment. She's in the hospital now."

"And the troublemakers who interfered with my sales?"

Remo opened the trunk of the cab, stowed the wooden trunks carefully inside and closed it again. "Having their eyes chewed out by crabs," he said as he entered the cab.

The driver was shaking his head mournfully. "Please," he mouthed.

"What's with our driver?" He read the name from the taxi license. "George W. Bhupendra?"

"He has many personality flaws, most especially his impatience. He wished to leave this place, collect more fares, with a promise to return later after you arrived home. I convinced him to wait." The tiny figure in the seat next to Remo reached over the seat and gave the driver's spine an adjustment.

"Okay, we're all set," Remo said in English.

"Yes, drive, cretin!"

"What'd George W. ever do to you?" Remo asked as the taxi rolled out of the campground.

The small figure pursed his wrinkled mouth. "He assumed that I did not speak Awadhi."

"And he said something insulting about the elderly?"

"He insulted me, personally, in his swinelike mumble. He claimed I had no understanding of the economics of taxicab driving."

"But you do," Remo said.

"I, who have counted the gold of Sinanju and negotiated with emperors, know more about the science of finance that he can ever dream of understanding."

"Surprised he survived the night."

"I showed him mercy, since we could not spare the time for you to dispose of his filthy remains."

"We're grateful, George W. and I," Remo said.

5

The afternoon was sweltering, and the air-conditioning wasn't doing its job. The swarthy man had deep lines of concern on his face. He was in crisis. When the phone range, he snapped it up.

"Alirio?"

"Is this Christophe Fortoul, the famous drug lord?" asked a man who spoke American English.

"Who is this? Give me Alirio."

"I don't talk to anybody but Christophe Fortoul, the famous drug lord. I'll hold until he is available."

The swarthy man was alarmed now. The call was from Alirio's cell phone. "This is Fortoul. Who are you?"

"Call me the Hurricane."

"Give me Alirio."

"The boat driver? He's dead. All of them are dead. You think Alirio would let me use his phone if he wasn't dead?"

Christophe Fortoul said nothing.

"I killed them, by the way."

"Who are you?"

"Already told you. I'm the Hurricane."

"What do you want?"

"Money. I have the cocaine. All of it. I'm offering to sell it back to you."

Fortoul broke out into harsh laughter. "This is a joke! You did not kill Alirio and all his men."

"And a bunch of guys in dreadlocks and a bunch of DEA agents, too. The DEA sprung a trap while your boys and the Bahamian boys were transferring the coke right off of Unreliable Island. The DEA would have got them, too, if I hadn't blown their helicopter into tiny bits."

"Liar!"

"Alirio is probably late checking in. You do what you need to do to confirm my story, then call me on Alirio's phone, okay? I'll give you all the time you need as long as it isn't more than twenty minutes. In twenty minutes I call Pedro Digna in Miami and sell the coke to him direct."

Christophe Fortoul sputtered. "Listen to me, you are asking for a long and painful death. This had better be a joke."

"No joke. Business. You now have nineteen minutes."

The phone went dead. Christophe Fortoul stared at his receiver, then shouted out the gold-gilded double doors of his luxurious office.

"Any word from the Bahamas? I must know at once!"

"Bad news, Papa." A stern-looking man strode in. His face was Christophe's face, minus twenty years. "It looks as if the American DEA got involved and everything went to hell."

The young man handed him a printed story from a Spanish-language newswire. There was a grainy photo of wreckage floating in the ocean. Christophe scanned the report.

"They are all killed. The cocaine is missing."

"There is almost nothing left of the boats or the bodies. The cocaine could be spread all over the ocean," the young man said unhappily. "It looks like the DEA started a shooting war. Everyone was killed. Even the DEA. At least Alirio took some of the American scum with him."

Christophe shook his head. "No. It was pirates. The thieves just called using Alirio's phone."

The younger Fortoul's eyes blazed. "Then we can get the shipment back!"

The senior Fortoul nodded. "And make an example of the fool who took it from us."

Fortoul called the phone that belonged to the now-deceased Alirio.

"The Hurricane speaking. How may I help you?"

"This is Christophe Fortoul. How much will it cost me to get back my property?"

"A million bucks U.S. You have more men in the Bahamas, right?"

"Not men who have a million U.S. dollars on their person."

"I'm not worried about the money. You'll find a way to get the money. Right?"

"I will find a way to get them the cash," Fortoul replied. "You shall meet them at a private club called the Nassau Sands at four tomorrow afternoon, and you shall have my property with you."

The Hurricane laughed. Fortoul looked at his son. His son was balling his fists, and the veins were standing out from his neck.

"You crack me up," the thief said, then spoke in an unflattering imitation of Christophe Fortoul. "You shall go to my snooty golf club. You shall bring me cocaine in a wheelbarrow." He laughed again.

Fortoul held his hand up to prevent the explosion that was about to come out of his son.

"Okay, listen y'old Colombian clown. You shall send your little flunky clown to Practice Cay at eight o'clock in the morning with the money, unarmed, or the cocaine will be sold to that Mexican dude, Digna."

"We cannot produce that much cash before the Bahamian banks open," Fortoul said reasonably.

"See, I could sell this stuff to Digna for twice as much. He'd think he's getting the greatest bargain of his life. You be at Practice Cay at eight. Think you can handle it."

"My men will be there."

"Tell them to bring along some extra fuel. I'm not gonna actually be at Practice Cay you know. When I learn of their arrival at the cay, I'll call you and tell you where to find me. They might need to do a little traveling around the Bahamas."

"I see no reason to play stupid games with a thief," Fortoul said.

"I do. If you want your drugs back, you will play the stupid games with me. And you will refer to me as the Hurricane."

"All right."

"All right what?"

"All right, Mr. Hurricane."

The Hurricane laughed and laughed.

THE SWEATING, HOT COLOMBIANS heard an engine sputter from the far side of the little island. One of the sand dunes began to move, and a sheet of tan camouflage was released. The lightweight fabric fluttered away, and a vehicle emerged from behind the little peak, spraying sand, then coming to a halt twenty yards from where Begot and his men waited.

The vehicle was some sort of 1960s retro sand-crawling dune buggy. Begot didn't like it. It was juvenile and flippant and made this enemy all the more strange. His patience was already at its breaking point. The thief had sent him and his men boating from one Bahamian speck after another for hours, until the sun was baking them.

The dune buggy was outfitted with heavy roll bars, bug-eye headlights and bulging wheel wells. The big balloon tires had large treads for scooping sand. This was all standard dune-buggy equipment. The hornlike loudspeakers weren't standard equipment. They looked like trumpet horns or public-address speakers, and there had to have been ten of them clamped to the overhead roll bars.

Each funnel-shaped, stainless-steel device was about the size of a two-liter bottle of soda. The large end was covered by a stainless-steel dome with tiny perforations, and the whole thing looked like a chrome trumpet with a trumpet hat. Heavy-duty electrical cables were bolted directly into each funnel.

At least one of them was, in fact, a public address speaker.

"Welcome. I am the Hurricane. You're unarmed, as I instructed, right?" said a piercing, amplified voice.

"We are unarmed, just as you asked," Begot called politely. "Where are the goods you stole from us?"

"The cocaine, you mean?" the man who called himself Hurricane asked, then laughed like a hyena. The brassy amplification of the public-address horn made it extremely abrasive.

Begot exchanged a glance with his men. This Hurricane was clearly an idiot. He's showing what an amateur he is, Begot thought. He doesn't understand how powerful is the enemy he has made. Begot couldn't wait to see his body riddled with bullets.

"Show me the cash," the Hurricane commanded.

Jose Begot nodded to one of his companions, who raised a suitcase from the sand.

"Open it," the man commanded.

The Colombian opened the suitcase and showed that it was neatly packed with cash.

"Bring me the suitcase," the Hurricane ordered.

"No," Begot said. "You will give us our shipment first."

"Nope."

Begot cocked his head. "I do not believe you even have what belongs to us."

The Hurricane pulled the dune buggy in a tight U-turn, then he stood in his seat and pulled the tarp off the cargo. There were several jumbled packages.

"Mauricio," Begot said.

One of his men was already examining the packages through binoculars. "The serial numbers are correct, Jose, but I see only a few of them."

"It is good enough," Begot said.

"You satisfied?" called the dune buggy driver.

"Quite satisfied," Begot called. "Now let us show you a real hurricane. A Colombian hurricane."

Begot flicked his hand toward the dune buggy, and his seven companions armed themselves. Begot didn't bother pulling out his handgun.

"Now you shall step out of the car."

The man called the Hurricane was silent for a moment, then he laughed. "Or what? You'll shoot me dead?"

"Exactly."

"I'm so pleased you've decided to betray me!" the Hurricane answered with true delight.

Then the wind started to blow.

THE GO-FAST BOAT PILOT took the phone absently. "*¿Sí?*"

The caller was the big boss himself, Christophe Fortoul. "What is going on? On the island?"

The driver released his fright. "I do not know—I only know it is something terrible."

"Well, what do you see, idiot? "

"It was a sandstorm, "the pilot said. "It broke their bodies and killed them all."

"What? They're dead?" Fortoul said.

"*Sí.*"

"There was a sandstorm?"

"*¡Sí!* It sounds unbelievable, but it is true. The one who is called the Hurricane—he made a hurricane come and strike the men and it killed them all. It broke the bones and tore their flesh. All are dead!"

"Imbecile!" Fortoul snapped. "Circle the island and look for the men. As soon as you get them on board, tell them I want to talk to them immediately."

"But the men are dead. I see their bodies broken on the beach."

"Begot is dead, too?" Fortoul demanded, as if he was beginning to believe the pilot.

"Begot, too. The man killed Begot and the others with his hurricane, and now he is taking their money."

"That is my money!"

"The Hurricane is taking it for himself."

"Stop him!"

"How can I when so many men have been killed already?" This seemed to make perfect sense to the pilot, but Christophe Fortoul wasn't thinking clearly.

"Get close to the shore and tell me what you see," Fortoul ordered.

The pilot steered the boat nearer to the little sand-pile and allowed himself to drift offshore. The water was clear and deep and turbulent on this side of the island, perpetually stirred by the crosscurrents that built the sand up and washed it out again and again.

The man called the Hurricane was too busy to pay much notice the go-fast boat pilot.

"What is happening?" Fortoul asked impatiently.

"The man has the case that he took from Begot. He is collecting some dollars that escaped in the winds"

"What is Begot doing about it?"

"Nothing," the pilot said simply. "Begot is dead."

"Still?"

"No man can come back from the dead except for our Lord Jesus Christ."

"I didn't mean he came back from the dead. I meant, does he still look like he is actually dead, now that you are closer to where he lies?"

"Oh, yes, he is most clearly dead, Mr. Fortoul. He is a mess."

"He was my nephew. Speak of him with respect."

"Your nephew is now twisted like a dishrag. His eyes are protruding from his skull, and it is hideous and disgusting."

"Enough. What of the American?" Fortoul demanded.

At that moment, the American whooped and laughed.

"What is that? Are my men attacking him?" Fortoul asked.

"No. The Hurricane is shouting for joy and throwing your money in the air. The men continue to lie silent and bloody."

THE SCRUFFY, SCRAWNY, twenty-something man had a scraggly goatee. He was dressed in a sweat-smelly T-shirt and baggy jean cutoffs, wearing flip-flops. His skin was fish-belly white, already burned red where it was exposed to the sun. After he finished distributing the dollars into the wind, he pulled out his phone and leaned his behind against the dune buggy.

"Fortoul," he said, and the phone dialed the home of Christophe Fortoul on his estate in rural Colombia.

"Hello?"

"Is this the head cheese himself?"

"This is Christophe Fortoul."

"Hurricane here," Harry Kilgore sad. "Your men tried to pull a fast one, as the boat driver has been telling you, I'm sure."

"The pilot's reports are confused. He claims my men are all dead."

"Well, then, the pilot's not confused at all. Your men are all real dead. One of them was your nephew, from what I understand. I'll bet you're relieved to have that loser out of the gene pool."

"My sister's son is truly dead?"

"Those losers were so greasy I don't know how they managed to even hold on to the knife when they tried to stab me in the back."

"He was of my family!" Fortoul ranted into the phone in Spanish. Harry Kilgore pulled the phone away from his ear and snapped it closed. He turned off the ring tone.

Harry rustled in the dune buggy, pulling out a plastic cooler. Inside was a mountain of crushed ice over a six-pack of bottled beer. Kilgore sucked on a frosty bottle, rubbed the cold glass on his forehead, then phoned Colombia again.

"No one hangs up on Christophe Fortoul," the old man hissed when he answered.

Kilgore closed the cover and finished the beer.

He phoned Fortoul again.

"You finished with your temper tantrum? I'm still willing to deal, old man, but the price just doubled. Two million dollars U.S. You interested?"

"I am interested."

"Good self-control you got going on there. How soon can you have the cash ready?"

"Within the hour."

Kilgore smirked. "Really?"

"They will come to you. Stay where you are."

"This isn't going to be another sleazy Colombian knife in the back, is it? I've heard you Latino losers would betray your own mothers to get your oily palms on a few American greenbacks."

"I give you my word."

"Good enough for me."

Kilgore hung up the phone, secured a sunshade to the roll bars and took out another ice-cold beer. He raised it in a salute to the uncomfortable-looking pilot in the boat, who had apparently been ordered to remain on-site. The man was frying in the late-morning sun and hadn't had the foresight to bring refreshments.

Kilgore heard the propeller whine and spotted a twin-engine aircraft closing in on the island. He pulled out the phone and dialed Fortoul.

"Hurricane here. I see your people coming. I thought you were sending a helicopter. There's no place for them to land in a plane, you know?"

"It is an amphibious plane," Christophe Fortoul explained, his voice much more relaxed than it had been.

"Can't be amphibious," Kilgore said. "There are no pontoons."

Before Fortoul could answer, the plane started firing. The machine gun turret was mounted under the fuselage, so the rounds shot out under the propeller and into the sands of the little island, where they made tiny craters that came closer and closer to Harry Kilgore's dune buggy.

"Hold on," Kilgore said with irritation. He powered up the manual systems, although his automatic defensive cannons had began delivering small, localized airbursts on their own.

The machine-gun fire veered away from the dune buggy.

Kilgore adjusted the muzzle of the manual air cannon pointed the trumpet end at the aircraft and triggered it.

The particle entangler inside air cannon made a rude *poot*.

The entanglement traveled at light-speed from the trumpet, then stopped being entangled. When it came untangled, the atmosphere changed position suddenly. The entanglement was a totally new process. Kilgore was the only person on Earth who had ever figured out how to make it actually happen outside of a laboratory.

What it did was take air from all over the place and compact it in a different, much smaller place. Nature didn't like this one bit, and allowed the pressurized air to release in a direction away from the unnatural disturbance.

The gentle Caribbean breeze transformed into a 300-mile-per-hour microburst that slammed into the underside of the twin-engined airplane and tore the wings right off. The fuselage tumbled end over end.

"I just blew its fucking wings off," Kilgore informed Fortoul.

"You lie."

"Why not ask the guy in the boat?" Kilgore suggested. "It's going down. Down. Down. Splish. All gone."

The phone went dead. Kilgore rewarded himself with another frosty bottle of beer and waited for the pilot in the boat to report on his telephone. Kilgore waved his hand over his face. Flies. Where were they coming from? He'd had enough of this little sandpile. His phone rang.

"Guess the plan was to gun me down, then come pick up your stuff," he told Fortoul. "You know, I'm starting to think you're sanctioning these attacks."

"I am not."

"Then you must be a real lousy leader. None of these people respect you."

"That is not so. I am respected and feared throughout the Americas."

Hurricane Harry snorted. "Old man, from where I'm sitting you look like a senile old coot who can't tie his own shoes."

Fortoul was breathing fast.

"You're either planning these attacks yourself, or you've got no control over your own operations. Either way, man, you do look like a loser. Anyway, the cost just doubled again. Four million dollars."

"That's ridiculous!"

"Now, don't you feel stupid? You could have had all your stuff back for a million. Now you've lost a plane and a boat and a nephew and a bunch of greasy goons. And you've quadrupled the cost. Wow, did you screw up bad."

"I will not pay four million dollars!"

"Then I get to keep the cocaine."

"It's my cocaine!"

"For a mere four million it will be. But not cash. You

know how big and bulky four million dollars of cash would be?"

"Then what? What do you want?"

"Well, Mr. F., I've been reading about you. It seems you've got a real nice collection of gemstones. Emeralds, diamonds, rubies. I hear you collect only the finest gems. Lots of value in a little package."

"I will never give you my precious stones."

"I'm pretty sure Pedro Digna in Miami won't be nearly such a pain in the ass. You think about giving me some of your rocks if you ever want to see your cocaine again."

The drug lord began shouting in Spanish again, almost hysterically. "I'll call you later," Kilgore said loudly, and closed the phone.

He started the dune buggy. He'd head back to his rented car-carrier on the other side of the island, but first he waved goodbye to the Colombian in the boat. The Colombian glared at him. He was talking on the phone again, and Kilgore aimed the air cannon right at him.

The pilot stood up, shook his head, raised his hand. "No! No!" His cries carried over the water.

Harry Kilgore emitted a particle entanglement— *poot*—and it created a microburst that blew the boat to smithereens.

"HE EXPLOITS A TRIAL physics procedure called quantum entanglement," Mark Howard said. "It's being used in physics labs for teleportation experiments."

Smith pursed his wrinkled, dry old lips. "That is alarming in itself."

"It's strictly a parlor trick in the physics lab at this point," Mark Howard added. He knew that CURE had encountered successful human teleportation of a type in the past. It was a devastating weapon. "Experiments are restricted to the transport of laser light particles. There's not much in the way of useful technology coming out of the experiments. But Harry Kilgore found an interesting use for one of the side effects of quantum entanglement. I'm scanning from his doctoral thesis research progress reports here—he developed a method of squeezing and focusing a laser beam that's similar to the earliest theoretical attempts at laser teleportation."

There was a silence. "I'm afraid, Mark," Smith said, "you've already exceeded my understanding of the subject."

"I don't get it myself," Mark Howard said, "but I've heard of a principle of physics called Heisenberg Uncertainty Principle. It says that the more precisely you try to measure or read an atom's quantum state for the purpose of replicating and teleporting it, the greater disruption you cause to its quantum state."

Smith frowned. "So teleportation is impossible?" He knew that wasn't true.

"No. They've figured out ways of using photons for transporting, and that gets around Heisenberg Uncertainty, but that's beside the point. Twenty years ago, they knew about Heisenberg and at that time they didn't yet know how to get around it. Almost on a lark, some physics students tried to perform atmospheric teleportation anyway, just to see what happened. What they achieved was a localized disturbance—miniaturized microbursts that were the result of high-energy, imperfect red laser replication techniques. They published their results just for a few laughs, and nobody paid any more attention to it until Harry Kilgore came along. He worked to make the flawed results of the experiment more extreme, and created a way of making high-level microbursts. Testing his theory was expensive, but he made them the subject of his doctoral thesis while at the college of engineering at the University of Oregon, Goodrich Campus. The program mentors let him get halfway through the development and writing, then they said his line of experimentation was an expensive folly. Pulled the rug right out from under him. They wouldn't give approval for him to continue work on the thesis topic, which made it impossible for him to get a funding grant."

Smith nodded. It sounded like the story was over. "And what happened?"

"There's records of all kinds of official requests from Harry Kilgore. He wanted his thesis approval reconsidered. He was denied, and next there's an official complaint of misconduct by the tenured staff of the college of engineering. He claimed they were negligent in approving his work on the thesis in the first place if in fact the work was without merit, but that he believed the work did have merit and should be allowed to continue. There are several statements from the engineering staff, very stuffy, and they're hinting that Kilgore overstated the results of the tests he performed prior to getting his first approvals on the thesis."

Smith nodded. "I see." He was wondering where the narrative was headed, but Mark Howard kept talking.

"Anyway, Kilgore never received approval for another thesis topic, and that's about the end of his school records. But he did retain a patent attorney to help him patent the device. He called it an Energy Generation Technique in the patent applications. But he was too late. A patent was already applied for. Frederic Laft, director of the Goodrich Campus college of engineering, made the application. Kilgore's own professor was stealing his idea."

Smith frowned. "I understand. What measures did Kilgore take?"

Howard wore a grim but satisfied smile. "Laft was the first known test of the Kilgore Air Cannon used as an offensive weapon. Look."

Mark Howard shuttled a report prepared by the Folcroft Four, starting with autopsy photos of Professor Frederic Laft.

His back was crushed and broken. His face and chest were unharmed.

"There was just minor bruising on his front legs, abdomen, chest and face," Mark Howard said excitedly.

"The medical examiner said it was as if Professor Laft was cushioned in a pillow, which was used to propel him into a brick wall at something between 150 to 200 miles per hour."

Smith nodded. "I see."

"Not a fall," Howard added before Smith could ask the question. "He was found adhered to a one-story administration building on campus, along his regular walking route from his office to his home. Impact marks on the wall. Death occurred not long after two witnesses reported him leaving his office. The Goodrich Police Department treated it as a hit-and-run. Officially, the cops assumed a car hit Laft and drove him into the wall. It was only during postmortem that there was any hint of strange circumstances—notably, if a car drove into him hard enough to push him into a wall, there would be damage on the front of the body, as well as the back. Not to mention the practical problems with any car going fast enough to launch a human body 150 miles per hour into a wall and yet not go into the wall itself."

Smith was intrigued now. "All right, Mark, what links the other attacks?"

"Each one has been explained away as a hit-and-run or gang activity using conventional explosives," Mark said. "There have been bank robberies and armored-car attacks. In each case there is evidence of violent damage done to blast shields, bank vaults or the armored cars themselves. So far, he's taken a cool 3.2 million dollars in cash. Here."

Harold W. Smith found himself facing a photo of the remains of an armored car, on its side in a parking lot. The metal was gashed open. The thick steel plate was sliced in as if by a powerful machine. The uniformed guards were flat on their backs and smashed like bugs.

"Have the police put the pattern together?"

"There's rumblings about the similarity of the attacks and some mention of microbursts," Howard said, "but nobody in law enforcement wants to go on record as claiming that someone is using a microburst for armed robbery. No official pattern, no official cause to get a multistate task force together."

"And what of Kilgore?" Smith asked as he perused the crime-scene reports that the nation's law enforcement refused to link together for fear of looking foolish. "Any sign?"

"He was legally evicted from his apartment two weeks ago for back rent. The place was dusty when the eviction was served. His patent attorney filed a small-claims complaint against him. No trace of the man himself in at least four months."

"Good work, Mark."

"Thank you, sir."

Smith raised his gaze from the display below the glass of his desktop. "For what?"

"For saying 'good work.'"

Smith nodded his head slightly. "Oh. Yes. Good work. And not for these reports alone. It's already clear that you've made great improvements to CURE's computer capabilities. Who knows how long it would have taken us to get a line on Harry Kilgore without the upgrades."

"Thanks," Mark said. "It's sure a one-of-a-kind piece of work, if nothing else. I can guarantee you, nobody else has anything like it."

6

The Pentagon's unique layout required a one-of-a-kind system just to keep employees from getting lost.

The halls of the Pentagon looked so much alike that security false alarms triggered by lost employees had become a line item in the budget. It was embarrassing. A task force was convened to determine a solution—it was a black-budget special project that appeared in subsequent accounting as Pentagon Security Project 6152A. The official recommendation of Project Leader General James Farabee: color coding. Each Pentagon staffer was provided with a personal security spectrographic designation, which provided a custom color-coded map to the individual's office. The security rainbow was printed on each security badge. All a Pentagon staffer needed to do was take the color-coded passages in the same order as the color coding on the badge.

There were problems with the system. First, General Farabee was surprised to learn that, among the twenty-three thousand military and civilian employees at the Pentagon, there were some who were color-blind. The general filled out Mass Termination Form 61-B, only to have the form rejected by the Public Relations Decision and Action Evaluation Department, who claimed that the Pentagon might be perceived as politically insensitive if it fired 342 staffers simply because they were color-blind.

Pentagon Security Project 6152 B, after another year of careful reevaluation, issued color-blind staffers an electronic mapping device to guide them through the halls—at an obscenely high cost to the U.S. taxpayers, in General Farabee's opinion.

Thomas J. Shep, CPA, ABV, was one of the civilian employees of the Pentagon who loved the color-coding system, because he could use it to his advantage in significant ways. Some time ago, an auditor of activities started sticking his nose into Shep's business, and Shep solved the problem by making use of the color-coded hall signs. He replaced them with cards of his own making—the colors changed when hit with narrow-beam light of a specific spectrum. Shep followed behind the auditor and shone his special flashlight on the fake signs, and the auditor ended up following incorrect routes without authorization. The fifth time the auditor was apprehended in off-limits wings without a reasonable explanation, he was sent away—to Guantanamo, where he was in his seventh month of interrogation.

Shep checked on the man each morning, using his

access to the Guantanamo Webcams. Access to these secret Webcams was exactly the kind of the thing that a civilian accountant should not have and should never need. It was just the kind of thing the auditor would have been looking for if he had ever actually made it into the inner workroom of Thomas Shep's Suboffice for Equitable Distribution of Departmental Authority.

The Webcam was highly illegal. What would have worried the auditor the most was how the Webcam could have been put in place, what it was used for— and what, in fact, all the other Webcams and microphones were used for. There were hundreds of them, all around the world, feeding data to Thomas J. Shep.

The purpose was simply to feed Shep intelligence of the most unorthodox kind. The reason he needed such intelligence was so he could monitor the goings-on of other intelligence agencies. That was the simple, traitorous truth. What was most extraordinary was that Shep had put the system in place using his own authority—as a civilian certified public accountant in the employ of the Department of Homeland Security.

Federal U.S. intelligence agencies were being combined and merged and controlled like never before, all on the basis of recommendations of amateurs who had no real understanding of the culture of these agencies. Nobody who understood U.S. intelligence thought it was wise to merge under a single intelligence boss the FBI and the CIA and the NRO and all the other offshoots and independent offices. This was a period in history that demanded heightened governmental secrecy, not less, and that required more autonomy for every intelligence agency. The administration knew this, but acquiesced to public demand.

Those who spoke for the federal agencies—the figureheads of the FBI and the CIA, especially—kissed ass and played along and pretended they were okay reporting to the new intelligence czar. Below the surface, they bristled and the true power mongers didn't hesitate to start up their own intelligence-gathering programs. The FBI recruited more CIA agents to feed it intelligence on CIA activities and the CIA planted extra moles in the Bureau and the Pentagon had at least two competing military intelligence suboffices whose secret mission was find out what all the other agencies knew.

It was all a matter of protecting turf—which was what it had always been about.

Thomas J. Shep was one of the necessary evils of the trend to make all the intelligence agencies into one big happy family. His job was to look for power imbalances, report them to the DOHS and recommend changes. The Pentagon gave him an office as a way of brownnosing to the intelligence czar, but Shep was a pariah. That was fine with Shep.

Thomas J. Shep's little bureaucratic accounting role led him unexpectedly into new roles. Today, he was the world's ultimate intelligence gatherer, monitoring all the other U.S. agencies and answering to none of them. He was pretty sure he was now the most powerful man in the world. All this came about because, one day as he pored over documents in his office in the heart of the Magenta Suite of the Forest Green Wing, he discovered the greatest loophole in history.

It was in the new Interagency Information Exchange Protocol, and at first glance it looked like most other loopholes. It seems that the protocol allowed for certain personnel in certain agencies to issue orders to certain departments of other agencies. The protocol was for emergency use only, of course. To prevent abuse, time-limit restrictions were in place and investigations were immediately triggered by the issuance of such orders—all designed to prevent someone from, say, the FBI, bossing around people in the CIA and vice versa without a very good reason, like an immediate threat to national security.

The loophole was this: the personnel from Agency A could also issue orders to Agency B that would direct it to ignore the time-limit and investigative alert procedures. It was a classic loophole created by a typical lack of oversight. What was different about this loophole was that it was imbedded in the Interagency Cooperative Directives. It meant, theoretically, that anyone who exploited it, if they exploited it judiciously, would have virtual carte blanche and unlimited authority to pull strings throughout the U.S. intelligence network.

It was too good to be true—but it was true. Shep worked it perfectly.

First he quietly raided the CIA. He issued Pentagon orders to allow him access to the CIA data nets. As soon as he got in, he issued further orders to redirect the reports of his use of cross-agency authority. The reports went to the dead-letter office of the CIA.

Shep used his short-term CIA authority to grant himself CIA clearance. Now he could get whatever he wanted from the CIA whenever he wanted it. It was like getting one wish from a genie in a bottle and wishing for unlimited wishes.

He even created Company employment status for himself, with a CIA salary.

Next he pulled the same trick over at the Federal Bureau of Investigation. Soon he had highest-level security clearances for all the various branches of the FBI, and he had an FBI paycheck, as well. Next he branched out to the NRO and the Secret Service and all the others. He couldn't believe it was working—but it *was* working. In a matter of days he had secretly infiltrated and established a permanent data pipeline to all the other agencies.

Next, he used the leverage of his new CIA rank to deliver some orders to the Pentagon itself, creating a new intelligence channel that took data out of military intelligence at the highest levels, fed it to a CIA sub-suboffice that the CIA was not even aware existed and shuttled it directly back to Shep's Pentagon accounting office.

The trick was to keep the human beings out of the

picture as much as possible. When the help of human beings was required, deliver an order here, an order there, a directive to someone else. Give someone one small task, then don't bother them anymore. They'll forget all about it. Carefully assemble the jigsaw puzzle from pieces of bureaucracy.

By the time he was done, Shep had data coming in from all over the world, from all the secret sources belonging to all the agencies. They all spied on one another, but Thomas Shep was the only one who watched all of them, all at once, all the time. Like the Webcams. Nobody except him had access to all the Webcams.

But then came the disappointment. Now that he had all that power, what would he do with it? Make money? He didn't need more money; he was already collecting a dozen government salaries.

Then he remembered the reason he had been drawn to the field of hierarchical influence measurement and adjustment in the first place. Not just the chance to have a power base of his own, but the gratification of using his power to deny other people power.

Thomas Shep was now the ultimate power broker. In his field they had a term for it: state of morbidly inequitable influence, and it was considered the ultimate evil to those who studied the accounting methods of hierarchical influence, but it didn't bother Shep. He had always been into hierarchical influence for the glory, not to soothe his sense of ethics.

And now he would use his skills to keep himself at the apex of federal power while diminishing everybody else's power.

It was easy enough. There were more secret subagencies than anybody guessed existed, and they all spent most of their resources defending their own turf. The public agencies did so, too. They were always fighting and finagling and pulling strings behind the scenes to keep the other guy down. They all stayed down, all of them, all the time. All Shep had to do was help the process along. Feed the agencies secret data that got them tearing at one another's throats. Especially important was the need to shut down the truly powerful secret subagencies and black-budget operations. Since they were so secret, you could make them go away simply by revealing their existence to the right set of eyes. He had erased nine officially nonexistent agencies so far, and the thrill never went out of it.

But eventually, as his skills improved, Thomas Shep began noticing untraceable anomalous multihierarchical influence events.

He investigated. He found more secret sub-subagencies that he had never known about, but none of them could be tied to the anomalies he witnessed. The anomalies were too far-reaching. They crossed international and governmental boundaries.

He delved deeper, using his CIA rank to issue high-clearance probes into one chain of events after another. There was the defense-technology crisis of a couple years back—what had happened there? Many of those events remained unexplained. What about the bizarre misuse of military intelligence technology in the Southwest? Who had *really* stolen that stealth spy drone airship? The orders deploying it went through the proper channels, but when Shep tried to trace them back to their source, he became lost in a morass of misleading electronic paperwork.

Whom had the drone airship been used to spy on? Why was the airship sent on an uncontrolled joyride through a major southwestern city? How could it have tied in to the strange travel camper that made a spectacle of itself on the highways that morning, only to be snatched away by the U.S. military under orders that were once again untraceable. And who took the prisoners from the camper? They vanished within hours, along with the camper itself.

Thomas Shep issued secret bulletins across the intelligence networks, until every federal agency was involved in the hunt for the lost camper. It was a tiny CIA office, secretly charged with responsibility for monitoring FBI activity inside the United States, that got a line on the camper as it went through a series of identification changes and facelifts. Shep gave the little CIA office a mandate to track the camper to its owners. They even managed to get a mole into the driver's seat when the Airstream was to be transported cross-country. The camper was restored to like-new condition. No more strange body lines. Nothing to make it stand out among the thousands of other restored Airstreams on the highways of America.

Somebody was doing a witness protection job on an antique camper trailer, and that made no sense whatsoever.

The camper was hijacked on the interstate by the very agency that had commissioned its facelift, with the CIA mole still inside. The hijacking was a ruse designed to confuse the agency monitoring of the camper, in theory, but the hijacker made the CIA agent and dumped her along the roadside.

But what was so special about the camper? There couldn't be anything hidden in it, as it had been ripped apart and rebuilt again and again. It was just another restored Airstream like thousands of others.

Whatever it was for, there was no expense paid in retrieving it. A high-bay transport plane, later traced to a Missouri Air Force base, was deployed to land on the interstate and whisk the camper away. The CIA agent driver was left behind, telling stories about an unarmed assailant who paralyzed her with a touch.

Shep scurried to track the transport plane. Every record he could find told him it flew nonstop to Bismarck, delivered its cargo to unknown personnel, then flew back to its base in Missouri. FBI agents deployed by Shep in Bismarck reported no such aircraft. In fact, maintenance records showed the transport plane was back in Missouri too quickly to have flown that far north.

Shep didn't like it. Somebody out there was making a fool of him. Somebody out there was doing what he had done—achieved the coveted state of morbidly inequitable influence—but was using it even more effectively than Shep was. Which meant they were more powerful than Shep was.

And that was simply intolerable.

Thomas Shep dedicated himself to this one, Herculean goal: figure out who had more power than he did, and take it away from them.

7

The Korean man was extremely old. If he happened to be holding still—and the old Korean could make himself very still when he wanted to—one might be tempted to give him a poke, just to see if he was still alive.

Poking the old Korean man was one of the worst ideas one might ever have.

His Asian features were etched with wrinkles, and the ancient flesh was transparent enough to show the veins under his skin. He had little hair except for wisps of white, turning yellow, over his ears. His beard was the same yellowish-white, and so sparse that one might be able to count the whiskers. Attempting this, however, was another extremely bad idea.

In the dingy office with the wide picture window, the ancient Korean stroked the beard thoughtfully, then put his hand back into the sleeve of his beautiful embroidered robe. He was listening to the words of Harold W. Smith and trying to find a fragment of meaning in them.

There was a curious contrast between the two men.

Harold Smith was decades younger, but he looked old, his skin wrinkled and sallow, his eyeballs an unhealthy yellow. His prim suits were beginning to look oversized as his body, year after year, diminished.

But the old Korean man was Chiun, Master of Sinanju Emeritus. His back was iron strong. His slender hands contained the strength of ten healthy men, maybe a hundred. His eyes were the eyes of a vibrant, healthy child.

"Teleportation is not as outlandish as the popular public perceives," Smith said.

"We know that well enough," Remo Williams agreed. He was sitting in one of the guest chairs in front of Smith's desk. Chiun had opted to stand. "All you need is a telephone and a remote control and bingo," Remo added. "Beam me up, Scotty-san."

"Essentially," Smith agreed. "The Nishitsu Corporation technology did require much more than just a standard remote control to allow teleportation. In addition, they did not beam, nor move directionally."

Remo wasn't about to get into an argument about it. "Whatever."

"The point is, modern physics has been playing with the concept of teleportation for years. Publicly, the best successes came in the form of the teleportation of laser photons over a distance of two miles—without a receiving mechanism. This was achieved after a breakthrough work—around of the Heisenberg Uncertainty Principle."

"The principle stipulated that the more accurately you tried to scan the atomic structure of an object for teleportation, the greater you corrupt the original structure's quantum state," Mark Howard explained.

"I've heard that before," Remo said. "It's just an excuse."

"What?" Smith was distracted from the flow of the conversation. Remo had a way of doing that—throwing rocks in the road of an important discussion. "Are you saying you know the principle?"

"I know that so-called geniuses are always saying things like that," Remo said. "When something looks too hard to figure out, they say you can't do the thing because the closer you get to overcoming Problem A and doing Thing B, the worse Problem A gets. Like the speed of light."

"Remo," Master Chiun said, "hush. The Emperor speaks of the enigmas of science. It takes the mind of a bent savant to grasp the idiotic intricacies."

"No, I know about this, Chiun," Remo said. "Albert Einstein had the theory of going as fast as light, right? He said the faster you go, the heavier you get, until you reach light speed and you become so heavy you become too heavy to move, which keeps you from actually reaching light speed—so why bother trying? He only said it because he couldn't figure out how to make it happen."

Smith stared. "Are you saying the Theory of Relativity was Einstein's deliberate attempt to disguise his own ignorance?"

"Hey, who am I to point fingers? All I know is smart guys say some stuff can't be done and then five years up the pike you hear about somebody actually doing it."

Smith shook his head. "In point of fact, the Theory of Relativity has never been disproved."

"Yeah, right. Neither has the Isengard Uncertain Theory. Oh, wait, you were just telling us about how they disproved it. Is this what the cocaine kook is using, Smitty?"

Smith shook off the abrupt shift in subject matter, only to realize they were back on track, and said, "Not at all."

"So why are we talking about it?"

"Remo, listen for one minute without speaking," Chiun admonished. "The Emperor often has a relevant point to his ramblings, and he shall arrive back at his true intent eventually."

Smith didn't take offense—much. Was it his imagination or was Master Chiun becoming more openly insulting these days? Now Remo was leaning forward with a condescending, doglike look of expectation.

"Harry Kilgore was an engineering doctoral student with a physics minor," Smith said. "He began incorporating some of the quantum entanglement exploitations techniques used in the teleportation experiments, but his purpose was practical application. He developed methods for causing particle entanglement in the lab, but the results were explosive. The lab was damaged. He studied his results and came up with a method of controlling and causing localized quantum entanglements and resulting energy bursts."

Remo's dog smile was fixed and his eyes were very glazed. Chiun nodded seriously, but his attention was clearly not with Smith.

"He made thunderclaps," Smith said. "He displaced air. He caused small deviations in the atmosphere. Now he's using it as a weapon."

"Gotcha. He's a geek with a leaf blower."

"The Kilgore Air Cannon is clearly deadly technology," Mark Howard added.

"I get the picture. He's a geek with a kick-ass leaf blower," Remo said. In his mind he tried to match his mental picture of the leaf-blower geek with the reports CURE was getting from the Caribbean. First the DEA invited itself to a drug swap in the Bahamas. Then a fourth party showed up, slaughtered the DEA and the smugglers and made off with the cocaine. Now the party of the fourth part was negotiating to return the coke to the party of the first part, a Colombian cartel kingpin named Christophe Fortoul. CURE listened in on their phone conversations in the same way the DEA had homed in on the drug exchange in the first place—a satellite phone with disabled encryption. Lot of good that had done the DEA.

Fortoul, unsurprisingly, had tried to use force against the drug thief, who liked to call himself the Hurricane. He purportedly wiped out two sets of cartel enforcers sent to take him down, and yet the Hurricane was still willing to negotiate with Fortoul.

"What's the windbag's purpose?" Remo asked.

"That's not clearly understood," Smith stated, glaring at his desktop.

Remo nodded. "What do you mean?"

Smith looked up, eyes narrowing. "I meant what I said. His intent is not apparent."

"Are you telling me a fib?"

"Remo!" Chiun exclaimed. "Allow the Emperor his secrets."

"What do you mean by that, Master Chiun?" Smith asked.

"I mean nothing, Emperor. We accept your denials."

"I'm not denying anything, Master Chiun."

"Of course."

"Do I smell smoke?" Remo asked. "Oh, it's your slacks, Smitty."

"I beg your pardon?" Smith raised his lemon-sour voice.

"You're being less than truthful. I can tell."

"You are mistaken."

Remo glanced at Chiun. Chiun glanced at Remo and raised his eyebrows, not quite raising his shoulders.

"I have to hand it to you, Smitty, you're a really wonderful liar. I can't tell half the time when you're telling the truth or not. Right now, though, you reek of fibbery. Come clean and tell me what Harry Kilgore is up to."

Smith put his hands flat on the surface of the desk. "As I said, it's unclear." He added, "In my opinion."

"Ah," Chiun said quietly, almost to himself.

"Oh. Uh-huh." Remo looked around the room, searching for another opinion, and eventually he discovered Mark Howard. "Hey, you, over there at the desk. What's your opinion?"

"Uh, well." Mark Howard's trousers were apparently overheating, as well. He wriggled uncomfortably. "It's my feeling that Harry Kilgore is on some sort of a power trip. His psychological profile describes a social misfit. He was rejected by his blue-collar family and friends for his genius and he grew up a loner. He severed all ties with his family as soon as he could go away to school—which they disapproved of and refused to help pay for. His brains got him scholarships throughout college, but his records hint that he was an outcast even among his college peers. I think he thought he finally found a place to fit in, and it was a shock when he realized he was still considered a weirdo."

Mark Howard trailed off. For a moment, there was silence. Remo waited for him to continue. No smart-mouth remarks.

"To make matters worse," Howard said, "he finally achieves something of merit. He thinks it might even make him some money, which would be a real triumph after living off dorm cafeteria food and dry noodles for eight years. But, first the people he admires tell him that all his work is junk. That's bad enough. Then he finds out his work was good, but the people he admired actually despised him so much they didn't think he deserved the rewards of his success and tried to steal it away from him. This guy's getting even for a lifetime of ostracism."

"Makes sense to me," Remo said. "Assuming ostracism has nothing to do with giant, flightless birds."

"It means socially unacceptable," Mark explained.

"Understood," Remo said agreeably.

Smith frowned deeply. "I must say I fail to see the connection. Why would a life of social unacceptability lead Kilgore to seize drugs for ransom?"

"Normally it wouldn't," Remo said. "But think about the chain of events and it makes a kind of sense. Kilgore was an orphan, in a way. He didn't have a family, really. Worse, he did have a family and they were so awful in his mind that he disowned them. So his entire family is composed of his peer group. The other geeks at Yoo-awg."

"Pardon me?" Smith asked.

"The place he went to college. UOG. *Yoo-awg.*"

"I see."

"That's his orphanage. Maybe he was counting on the school to accept him, so he burned bridges with his family. When the Yoo-awgs turned their backs on him, it was really hard to take."

"You speak as one who knows," Chiun said.

"I do know," Remo said. "Believe me, being an orphan sucks the big one, Chiun. You're lonely. When you're on the outs with the other orphans you feel *really* lonely. It's a shitty, shitty place to be."

"Watch your language."

"Hmm. Nope. *Shitty*'s the only word that works. I got the other kids pissed off at me more than once for whatever reason, but my friends always went back to being my friends eventually. Being friendless all the time would have been unbearable. I can see how it would affect a guy's outlook."

"You have an empathetic viewpoint," Smith allowed.

"When you're in that place, you get mad at everybody. You wanna get back at the whole world somehow. First he gets back at the people who did him wrong— the school people that tried to rip him off. Then he goes after what he thinks he's got coming to him. Money, first of all. But he's also been an irrelevant weakling forever, so he's going to prove just what a hard-ass he is now. He's gonna make big money, he's gonna go up against the worst bad dudes he knows how to find, and he's not going to be taken advantage of. A Colombian drug cartel satisfies all the items on his to-do list. He goes and steals the drug cartel cash because he knows he'll get a huge ransom for it but also because he actually wants them to pick a fight with him. Nobody more brutal out there than Colombian drug cartels."

"This is how you see it?" Smith asked Mark Howard.

"Well, yes, pretty much," Mark admitted. "I guess Remo said it better than I did."

Smith nodded. "If this is truly who Kilgore is, then this is just the beginning. He won't be satisfied with extorting Fortoul. He'll escalate his power grabs, and we can presume he'll kill as many people as get in his way. That was an incisive psychological profile of Harry Kilgore, Remo."

"Hell, I know how the poor guy feels," Remo replied. "Now, where is he so I can go kill him?"

8

The Colombian crew was tense. They stood around on the decks of the *Fortoul IV* watching the turquoise sea, watching the swaying palm trees, glaring at the pedestrian traffic on the dock. The call was supposed to come at nine o'clock in the morning, but it didn't come until eleven.

"Hello. This is the Hurricane. To whom am I speaking?"

"You're late," snapped Dominguez, determined to put this lunatic gringo in his place, right at the very start. He wasn't going to screw this up—as so many others had screwed up when dealing with the lunatic who called himself the Hurricane.

"To whom am I speaking?" repeated the nasal American voice.

"You know who I am."

"To whom am I speaking?"

Dominguez bit the inside of his lower lip. "Jorge Dominguez."

"Fortoul's bastard boy?" The American giggled.

"Señor Fortoul wanted me to be in charge of this meeting," Dominguez growled. "He wanted no more misunderstandings. That is why he sent his best man and his son."

"Yeah, right. They still don't let you sleep in the family wing at the big house, do they, Dominguez?"

Dominguez bit hard on his lower lip to stifle the battery of profanity he wanted to level at the idiotic American. The truth was, Dominguez did not have rooms in the family wing in the Fortoul mansion. It was a badge of shame, a public denouncement of Dominguez's out-of-wedlock status. His burning desire was to be accepted by the family as one of them, and eventually to take his place as the head of the family.

Making himself accepted required success in all his family undertakings. He had to prove himself to be their good little shepherd, and that meant playing this American perfectly—even if the American baited him.

"You didn't answer the question."

"There is no need for me to answer the question," he said evenly.

"There is. Call it a test, Jorge. I know the answer. It will prove to me that you are who you say you are."

"Who else would I be but Fortoul's man?"

"Answer the question or I hang up the phone."

Dominguez's face burned, but he answered quickly enough. He couldn't afford not to. "It is true. I do not yet have my rooms in the family wing." Silently, he added, "But someday I will, and someday I will find who you are and I will tear out your throat with my own fingers."

The American was giggling like an ugly, mean little girl. "That must have hurt, but at least you know how to cooperate. Maybe we can actually make this exchange without me having to kill a whole bunch more of you narco-goons." He read out a set of GPS coordinates for the rendezvous.

"You will be there when we get there?" Dominguez demanded.

"I'm here now. Been sitting here for hours getting some sun. This is sort of a working vacation for me, see?"

DOMINGUEZ SNAPPED OFF the phone and unleashed a stream of orders as he climbed from the front deck to the deckhouse. The engines were being started before he entered the air-conditioned comfort of the computerized bridge. He relayed the Hurricane's coordinates to the Colombian captain.

The captain was a respected sailor with many long years in the merchant marine. He knew he worked for a drug lord, but he never made illegal shipping runs. He was charged with captaining the personal yacht of Christophe Fortoul, and the cartel kingpin never allowed drugs to come anywhere near his person when he was beyond the boundaries of his Colombian estates. The DEA had stopped Fortoul's yacht a hundred times to search, and never found a single grain of any controlled substance aboard.

The U.S. Drug Enforcement Administration would have loved to have an excuse to nail Christophe Fortoul.

The old captain of the *Fortoul IV* liked to keep a clean ship. This run was different. Fortoul had had no choice but to send his precious, million-dollar *Fortoul IV* yacht—those were the terms of the blackmailer. The captain would do his duty, but he was thinking that maybe working for one of the world's biggest cocaine suppliers had its drawbacks. He might take early retirement.

"How soon until we can get to this spot?" growled Dominguez, the son of one of Christophe's whores.

"Depends on the currents around these breakers," the captain said, pointing to the hazard symbols on the electronic marine display of the route. "Maybe forty minutes, maybe sixty."

"Make it thirty-five minutes."

"And risk damaging the ship? You can't have it both ways, sir. Go too fast and I might hit coral."

"Just get us there," Dominguez snapped.

"Yes, sir," the captain said, and with a nod to his first mate they began operating the controls that nudged the *Fortoul IV* away from the dock. Once they had a few feet of clearance, the engines rumbled, and the vessel hurried away from the private yacht slip near Belize City.

The tense Fortoul staff were glad to be under way finally, but they still had nothing to do as they journeyed toward the rendezvous, and they lounged nervously on deck. They never saw their pursuers. They never even knew that they were being followed. It would have been hard for them to understand the nature of their pursuit, had they even seen it. Just a colorful flash that seemed to jettison from the wharf and skim across the surface of the Caribbean. Nearby, another streak of less vibrant colors moved just as effortlessly over the ocean.

The pursuit made no sound. It whisked alongside the *Fortoul IV* and the strange, silent shapes scampered up either side of the hull like quick spiders. And then the shapes were gone from sight.

THE YACHT MADE ITS way swiftly but with all due caution into the open ocean, out of sight of the shore of Belize on the Yucatan Peninsula.

Dominguez kept his eyes to his binoculars as they closed on the coordinates provided by the one who called himself the Hurricane. At last, Dominguez spotted a craft. It sat alone on the vast, calm turquoise water, a catamaran without a mast for sails. Dominguez alerted the armed men gathered on the aft deck, below the pilothouse. Every man hunted the open sea for signs of another craft. They found nothing. The catamaran was all alone.

Dominguez phoned home and reached Christophe Fortoul, whom Dominguez was not allowed to call his father.

"We are almost upon him," Dominguez reported. "It is a twin-hull, twin-engine catamaran, no sails, big and boxy, perhaps fifty-five feet. It appears to be second-hand junk. It is alone."

"What of aircraft? "

Dominguez was watching the bridge radar. "We've seen nothing in the area," he said. "Just the catamaran."

"I see," Fortoul replied.

"How will this be played?" Dominguez asked.

"Is there evidence of the weapons?" Fortoul asked.

"We see no usual weapons, but there are horns mounted on the deck rails, and on the deckhouse. They look like the horns that were described on his dune buggy yesterday."

"Do these look like weapons to you?" It was almost a challenge.

"They do not," Dominguez replied.

"It is your judgment," Christophe Fortoul said. "You will approach this one in whatever way you decide is best."

Dominguez understood completely. Christophe Fortoul was placing all responsibility on his shoulders. Bitterly, he understood that he was being placed in a situation that would make or break him.

Fortoul was allowing Dominguez to best assess the level of risk to his crew and Fortoul's precious yacht. But how could he assess the risk? Dominguez only knew that the little catamaran posed some kind of special threat that none of them understood.

Fortoul had given him the option of capitulation, but Dominguez couldn't capitulate. If he did, and even if he succeeded in buying back the shipment, a question would forever linger in Fortoul's mind and the minds of all the others. Was it truly necessary to surrender a huge ransom to an American thief?

The strangeness of yesterday's massacres would fade with time. The slaughter would be explained away as happenstance or weakness. If Dominguez surrendered to an unarmed man in a little catamaran and gave away a valuable ransom without even putting up a fight, he would be marked for all his life as a coward. It would hamstring his advancement and quite probably insure that he never became accepted as one of the family.

Dominguez's only real choice was to go on the offensive. If he succeeded, then all would be well. But there was a real and little understood danger here, and if he should fail, then that too would be his responsibility, and his undoing.

Dominguez had no true choice, but such was the way of things. He would make the best of it.

Dominguez issued his orders to the captain.

The sleek, white, 152-foot *Fortoul IV* bore down quickly on the power catamaran, which was faded from its original white and was mounted with black instruments that made it look ugly and crippled. The yacht made a large circle around the catamaran, which was stable in the water and rode the wake swells sullenly. A figure emerged from the cockpit, gripping the rail tightly with one hand, and waved to the Fortoul craft as if greeting a yacht buddy who was arriving for cocktails. The yacht finished its circle, then adjusted its great girth to face the catamaran, nose-to-nose. It edged forward to within a hundred feet.

Two rigid inflatable dinghies were lowered from their braces at the rear of the yacht and Colombian gunmen piled into them, then they motored quickly across the open space to the power catamaran. The figure on the top back of the catamaran could be seen making a phone call.

Dominguez answered it.

"Hurricane calling. Excuse me, Jorge, but the deal was for just one man to make the transfer. Call back the goon squad, or else."

"I think not," Dominguez snapped, and he thumbed off connection.

The figure on the power catamaran folded his arms and tapped his foot in a broad display of annoyance, then dialed his phone again. Dominguez let the bridge phone buzz, until it began to annoy him and he turned the sound off.

The two launches reached the power catamaran, and armed men began quickly climbing onto the broad deck. The man in the cockpit waited for them to come. Dominguez didn't like this exhibition of inexplicable confidence.

As the boarding party assembled on the deck of the power catamaran, the man in the cockpit calmly put on a backpack. A thick cable ran around to the front, where it attached to a metallic tube with an open end that looked like nothing more than an old-fashioned musket muzzle. It was a ridiculous contraption.

The boarding party responded by covering the Hurricane with an arsenal of firearms. The Hurricane shouted at the intruders, but the intruders didn't respond save for a few terse words. The man on the top deck shrugged and began to fire his weapon. Simultaneously the intruders fired their own weapons, and the crack of gunfire came across the water.

Dominguez was astonished to see the effects. The gunfire should have shredded the man in the cockpit and damaged the boat itself. And yet, watching through his binoculars, he saw no evidence that a single round had even reached the man or the cockpit.

Meanwhile, with a burst of sound like isolated thunder, the intruders on the wide catamaran deck were shoved around. A louder burst sent them staggering against the rails. With another burst, bodies seemed to be ejected from the deck and they flopped in the air like broken dolls before splashing into the sea.

Now the deck of the catamaran was empty. No one remained except for the man with the backpack. He stood there in khaki shorts and a sloppy flower-print shirt, and gave Dominguez a wave. The Hurricane made a show of dialing his phone. Dominguez turned on the bridge phone and it rang.

"I told you," the voice from the phone said, and then there was that ugly, girlish giggling again.

Dominguez stared across the ocean to the man on the power catamaran, unable to believe what he had just seen. His men floated lifeless in the water, several of them clearly shattered.

The man on the power catamaran made another phone call, and this time it was not to Dominguez. Dominguez felt cold horror as he realized who it was that the man on the catamaran was actually calling. A moment later, the man on the catamaran hung up, and Dominguez's phone rang.

It was Christophe Fortoul.

"Is this true?" Fortoul demanded. "Has he killed all those men?"

Dominguez didn't know what to say. "He killed many," he admitted at last.

"I do not need any merchandise back so much as I need this enemy squashed," Fortoul said icily. "You will kill him, even at the risk of losing my shipment."

The words were music to Dominguez's ears. "Yes, sir."

Dominguez issued a few curt orders, and his best sniper took a position at the aft rail. The sniper carefully adjusted his rifle on a deck-mounted tripod and peered down the sights, searching for the opportune moment to trigger the weapon. It was a difficult shot, taking into account the rise and fall of the yacht, as well as the rise and fall of the victim's boat. Still, the sniper was a professional, with many years' experience, and he made an expert shot. The sniper rifle thundered, and Dominguez observed what happened next to the man on the catamaran.

The man on the catamaran, this Hurricane, was examining his fingernails in a display of boredom as the crackle of rolling thunder reached the yacht from across the water. The sniper bullet, so it appeared, missed. The sniper fired again and again and continued to miss the Hurricane.

The sniper loudly defended his skills, and Dominguez ordered more firepower turned on the catamaran. From belowdecks came men with grenade launchers and a deck-mounted machine gun. The hot Caribbean afternoon was filled with the blasts of the weapons while the noise of constant thunder continued coming from the catamaran without a visible source.

REMO WILLIAMS WAS BORED as yet another shoulder-fired grenade arced through the sky, came down precisely on the catamaran, and once again went spiraling off course until it plopped into the ocean or detonated harmlessly.

"Okay, we've seen enough," he announced. "Come on, Chiun. Let's go visit the big windbag."

Chiun remained seated cross-legged on the roof over the bridge of the big Fortoul yacht. Although his eyelids were almost completely closed, as if he was meditating, Remo could see the green glimmer of his eyes and knew the old master was interested in the goings-on.

"It's just a guy with a gizmo," Remo said. "Let's go take the bluster out of his sails."

Chiun asked in a singsong voice, "You wish to save the smugglers of drugs from more inconvenience?"

"Come on, Little Father," Remo said. "You know that's not the way that it is."

"Then what way is it?" Chiun asked.

"We promised Smitty we'd observe. So we've observed. Let's do something."

"He comes to us," Chiun said with a nod as the catamaran's engines buzzed to life and the boat headed for the sleek Fortoul yacht, three times its size.

This interested Remo. "Somebody's in trouble. I just don't know which one of them it is, the Colombians or the blowhard."

The thunderlike booms from the catamaran became more intense and more rapid-fire as it closed in and the fire from the Colombians became constant. The machine gun was rattling off rounds nonstop, as if the gunners simply couldn't get it through their heads that their barrage wouldn't reach the looming target. It did seem impossible to miss a fifty-foot, twin-hull craft with an extrawide light-colored deck, and yet not a single round was marring the boxy deckhouse or the twin hulls.

The man in the catamaran cockpit was grinning. The yacht captain started his engines, as if just now realizing he ought to be getting out of the area.

Remo cocked his head, listening for the softer sound that came under the thunder noise. There was a rude little *poot* that Remo thought came from one of the longest of the bugle-shaped devices mounted on the front rail. The air cracked and the water blasted apart within a few feet of the Fortoul yacht.

The yacht vibrated under their feet. A second charge detonated close enough to nudge the yacht unpleasantly.

Remo could see where this was headed.

"Maybe we don't want to be hanging around here all afternoon," he advised. The next blast shook the boat like a depth charge, too close and too near the surface to be strictly safe. Chiun opened his eyes and looked annoyed at being bothered during his meditation.

The next blast caught the aft end of the Fortoul yacht, and it sounded to Remo like a small earthquake had opened up nearby.

There was a sudden mess of crushed aluminum and a shower of fiberglass that ruined the perfect lines of the white yacht.

The yacht put on a burst of speed, and the catamaran suddenly fell behind. On the voyage from the Belize wharf Remo and Chiun had experienced the yacht's speed. It could sail at a nice clip on the open sea. The catamaran was strictly a pleasure boat with twin hulls for stability, not speed. It would never keep up with the *Fortoul IV* once she got going, and the pilot of the catamaran seemed to know it. He intended to take the Fortoul yacht down a notch before she slipped away.

The Hurricane scrambled with his controls and adjusted the bugle that extended from the front of the catamaran deck. The bugle dipped until it pointed at the rear end of the yacht, right at water level. He triggered the thing, Remo heard the small sound of the firing, and a moment later the deck lurched as if a bomb had blown in the bilge.

Belowdecks they felt the engine speed up uncontrollably, and Remo knew the driveshaft was disconnected from the prop. The prop was probably sheered clean off. The engine was revving uncontrollably until electronic safeguards turned it off.

The Fortoul yacht was abruptly silent, drifting without power.

"I guess he showed them," Remo said. "Now, let's go show him."

"What exactly shall you show him?"

"A thing or two."

Chiun nodded. "Let us go show him a thing or two. This is most illuminating and wise."

Remo was already gone.

REMO STARTED RUNNING, grabbed a rung on the hull and swung his body out over the ocean, then landed on his feet on the water's surface. He was running.

His expensive, handmade, Italian leather shoes slapped the ocean like a seal flipper. Remo's feet found the natural buoyancy of the ocean water, and his skills of speed and balance insured that he never exceeded this level of surface tension. It was a neat trick. A Sinanju trick. It relied on Sinanju senses, and honed instinct, and training, and Remo could not in a hundred years have a explained how he did it. So he claimed.

Walking on water was truly useful when one was in the vicinity of the Caribbean, which was a vicinity Remo had experienced far too much of lately. Remo sensed that Master Chiun was now at his side. The man on the catamaran was alone, his attention focused on the Colombian yacht. Still, Remo was feeling cautious.

Chiun alighted first on the scratched and chipped fiberglass hull, then Remo clung alongside him like spider monkeys hanging to the chicken wire of their cage.

They felt the tiny actuation of an unseen switch. Remo snatched at the nearest trumpet-shaped device and sent it flying into the ocean as Chiun struck another pair of the horns with his long fingernails. The horns separated from the hollow metal base, the metal neatly sliced through.

But there were other devices nearby, and all of them seemed to be doing whatever they did. There was a quick breath of air from each of them, and Remo felt something invisible and powerful blossom in the empty space all around.

Whatever it was, it wasn't something Remo knew how to fight. The tremendous pressure waves spread out from an empty point in the air—pressure waves like a powerful, compact explosion. Chiun retreated and Remo followed him over the water. The invisible ball of energy chased after them, so fast that Remo knew it would be all over them before they could get away.

Remo didn't know what would happen when it caught them, but he pictured the rear end of the Fortoul yacht. Master of Sinanju or not, a blast like that would be unpleasant.

Remo did the only thing he knew to do—ride it out. He leaped off the ocean surface with the arrival of the shrieking wind and allowed his body to be carried like a slip of paper or a tuft of down.

Then the thing that was chasing him burst underneath, and the gust became a wall of air that plowed into him and flung him over the water. He fought for control, to create stability with his arms, and at last the energy dissipated and he landed in the ocean.

"Most ungraceful," Chiun said nearby. He was neck-deep in the water.

"I bet you looked just as ridiculous," Remo said.

"I did not," Chiun replied simply.

"I don't like being made to look bad," Remo snapped.

"It is a wonder you are not constantly angry."

"Let's go back and show smart boy what for."

"I should hope your *what for* is more effective than your *thing or two*."

ABOARD THE POWER catamaran Kilgore had turned his attention to the Masters of Sinanju. He had not seen what happened, but his systems reacted automatically to the arrival of any intruders and his sensors alerted him at the same moment they took their defensive measures.

Kilgore was concerned, and a little amused. Two men were in the ocean a few hundred yards away, watching him, obviously victims of the air cannon.

What Harry Kilgore didn't understand was how they had managed to actually come into contact with his boat without his seeing them first. How had they acted fast enough to damage some of his emitters? How had they survived the blowback? The air-cannon emissions were not configured to leave survivors.

Then, to Kilgore's consternation, the two men stood up, on their feet, on the water, and ran across the surface of the Caribbean Sea.

Kilgore peered into the sea. There had to be a subsurface coral reef or sandbank they were walking on. Right?

They were coming fast, faster than a man should be able to run on land, let alone on a partially submerged reef.

But the crystal-clear waters showed Harry Kilgore definitively that there was no coral reef or sand just under the surface. So how were they doing that? Why was one of them dressed in a brilliant, multicolored Asian robe of some sort?

Too much for Kilgore to take in and he almost forgot to defend himself. But he came to his senses soon.

All the emitters on the ship actuated together.

There was a rush of air all around the ship, as blast after blast came in quick secession until they rolled together like thunder.

Remo and Chiun felt the swell of pressure waves headed their way. They could run faster than any track star, but they couldn't outrun a blast from an air cannon, with winds twice the speed of a typhoon blow.

They dived into the water quickly and sank well below the surface as the wall of air pushed away in all directions from the Kilgore catamaran. They pressure waves from the surface vibrated against their bodies— and kept vibrating. The air cannon just kept firing and firing. If they tried to surface inside of it, they'd be crushed.

THE FORTOUL YACHT was plodding along on maneuvering engines, and making a very slow escape of it, while the pair of surface walkers were nowhere to be seen. Kilgore would have plenty of time to catch up to the Fortoul yacht; it was the pair of water walkers that concerned him right now. He used his own high-power binoculars to scan the surface of the water in all directions. The bodies would float to the surface eventually.

For a long time the bodies didn't appear.

Then Kilgore's binoculars focused on them at some distance, in the water, holding their heads erect. They were both very much alive. They were riding the waves and watching him, and at the moment Kilgore spotted them the younger man raised his hand and waved.

Kilgore wondered how the man, so far away, saw Kilgore seeing *him*.

How had they survived not one but two air-cannon blasts?

Kilgore realized that the Fortoul yacht was heading out to sea, likely to rendezvous with reinforcements, while the two men floating in the water were making strong strokes in the direction of the Belize shore. At that point Harry Kilgore understood that the pair of water walkers was not with the Colombians. They had to be DEA. That was a troubling thought. He thought of chasing after the pair of swimmers or chasing the Colombians and pummeling them until the yacht collapsed and sank in the Caribbean—but then he decided on a third and wiser option.

He went in another direction entirely.

9

Remo and Chiun had a room waiting for them at small, ritzy beach resort on a secluded stretch of the Belize coast. Remo stripped, tossing his waterlogged Chinos and T-shirt into the waste bin, followed by a pair of hand-stitched Italian shoes, which had been brand-new last week. Another pair of new Chinos, an olive-green T-shirt still in the wrapper and an identical pair of hand-made Italian shoes were all nestled in a bag that had been delivered to the hotel along with Chiun's trunks.

Chiun didn't bother to change out of his sea-soaked clothing, but lowered himself into a cross-legged position on his mat on the floor of the resort room and closed his eyes. Steam began to rise from his kimono as he raised his body temperature sufficiently to evaporate the water. This was but a temporary measure; his valuable robe would require careful cleaning later to remove the salt.

Remo found a slip of paper in his bag, upon which were carefully written a series of numbers in Korean Hangul characters. It was the temporary direct-dial number for CURE, which was quicker than using the roundabout method of consulting directory assistance. However, it was an impossible string of digits to remember, and Remo could only use it when he had his cheat sheet. He dialed once, got a this-number-not-in-service message and dialed again.

The computer verified him with some nonsense about a rendering plant in Maine, then Harold Smith came on the line with Mark Howard. Remo related the altercation briefly, though Smith and Howard seemed to already know the basics.

"We're still intercepting some of the communications coming from the Fortoul ship. They're using an unsecured radio. It seems that their other communications equipment was damaged. They've already met up with a hired tug, and they're being towed to a Colombian shipyard."

"I don't give a rat's ass about the Colombians," Remo said. "What about Harry Kilgore?"

"Kilgore is also headed for Colombia, from what we can tell," Mark Howard said. "Now that we have a bead on his boat we can follow him via satellite."

"Yeah? And?"

"He's hugging the coast of Honduras as we speak."

"But what exactly is being done about him?" Remo asked.

"We are looking into military options," Smith said.

"That is unnecessary," Chiun piped up as he stood and took the phone. "Emperor, the war machinery of this nation is not prepared to take on a weapon of this nature. Allow Remo and myself to disable it."

"Chiun," Remo said, "we tried already. We got blown off. Remember? I'm pretty sure you were there."

"Silence," Chiun hissed.

"Master Chiun," Smith said, "I see no reason not to use an air strike to solve this problem decisively."

Chiun placed one small, dry hand over the mouthpiece of the hotel phone. "See what you have done? Your failure forces the Emperor to seek other means to solve his problems."

"Good thing, too," Remo said. "We didn't do much good out there."

"But it is up to the Master of Sinanju to solve the emperor's problems," Chiun said. "Must I remind you it is why you are paid much gold?"

"I am? How come I never see any of it?"

"Do not to encourage him to find other methods to enforce his arbitrary will. Are you so eager to make yourself useless in his eyes?"

"Of course not, but it makes more sense to have Harry Kilgore blown up long distance than for us to throw ourselves in front of his boomsticks again. Why should we take the brunt of Kilgore's attitude problem when Smitty can just send in a fighter jet?"

The tiny speaker from the phone was buzzing with agitation by this time. Smith was asking if anyone was still on the line.

Chiun said to him melodically, "Wise Emperor, Remo is addled from his experience and perhaps has vapors on his brain. Don't listen to what he says until the gas has passed. Rest assured that we shall handle the problem of the man that makes the thunder. You need not resort to the messy extravagance of dropping a boom."

"I disagree, Master Chiun," Smith said. "There is simply no cause for you to engage Kilgore again. We know his precise location, and we'll keep tracking him, then we can neutralize him with a precision air strike. The problem will be solved."

"Then we can go home now," Remo called.

"No," Smith replied sourly. "Not until we see this finished."

"If this man could dispel even a Master of Sinanju with his foul winds, it is doubtful that a simple flying boom will scratch his hide," Chiun said.

"I don't know about that," Smith said.

"Meaning what, O wise Emperor?" Chiun asked, and his voice was almost as sour as Smith's.

"I mean merely that an air-launched explosive will seek out and destroy large targets. Even a Master of Sinanju cannot crush a fifty-foot boat in one blow."

"Of course not. We do not engage in acts of gross vandalism," Chiun said. "Dispatch your imprecise rockets, and we shall be waiting to be alerted that the attempt has failed."

STRIKING AT A TARGET MOVING within the territorial waters of a foreign nation was not to be attempted lightly.

Harold Smith's added challenge was to order the hostile action to be taken by the U.S. Air Force while keeping it a secret from the U.S. Air Force. This was nothing new. He had perpetrated such machinations on the military time and again.

He had the procedure down to a science, and he never made mistakes. He didn't make a mistake this time, either.

Nevertheless, this time his intervention did not go unnoticed.

IT WAS THE DARK OF NIGHT, and the tiny village of Del Carmon on the Honduran coast was dark except for the muted lights in the taverns and other places of business, and the dim, rhythmic illumination of the Del Carmon lighthouse.

The lighthouse was actually nothing more than a tower of ugly, rusting steel anchored in concrete in the jumble of rock on the shoreline of Del Carmon. Harry Kilgore rested his eyes upon the glow of the lighthouse because there was almost nothing else in the pitch black for him to look at.

He really, really wanted to go ashore and patronize some of the Del Carmon businesses, but it was way too risky.

Here the shore was too rocky for nice swimming beaches and the water too unpredictable for fishing, but the town of Del Carmon had existed here for centuries, for reasons no one now remembered. The people had little money and no prospects, and so they did what many starving communities did. They looked for other resources among their people.

The people of Del Carmon had neither great warrior skills nor crafting skills, but they did have daughters. So they sold their daughters. Del Carmon was one of the busiest brothel towns on that stretch of coast, and the nature of the work made it preferable to keep the lights turned low. No streetlights blazed after dark. Only the welcoming beacons from brothel windows and the glare of the lighthouse.

Kilgore knew all about the whores of Del Carmon. He had read the Honduran sex-industry guides on the Internet a few weeks ago, about the time he started planning this little expedition. He had intended to use the lighthouse as guidepost on his journey, although mostly he would depend upon the accuracy of his computer guidance system, the GPS feed from the satellites and electronic marine maps. His boat had a very shallow draft, so he could run the shallows, as well as the open ocean. Kilgore wasn't much of a sailor, and he never intended to wander far from shore. Wave crests of more than a couple of feet concerned him greatly.

Following the shoreline offered other strategic advantages.

Tonight he would see if the advantages were truly worthwhile.

Tonight he knew the aerial bombardment would come, because he had planned for its arrival. He knew that the strange agents who attempted to board his vessel that afternoon during his interception of the Fortoul yacht would have reported back to their superiors in the United States government. The DEA now knew where he was. He had killed five or six of their people, and they'd be itching to off him. They would watch his position every second, from the air or from space, and they would attempt to neutralize him in the most efficient manner possible. That meant an aircraft would deliver a bomb that would blow him to oblivion.

It would be a true test of his engineering skills to see if he survived this night.

In the deep of night Kilgore activated the emergency lighting system, which consisted of hundreds of tiny lights implanted in plastic runners on the deck and stairs and in the cockpit. He paced the width of the deck as the hours crawled by. By three in the morning he was ready to drop from exhaustion. Still, he knew that any moment could bring the alarm that meant he was under attack.

At 3:02 a.m., the alarm sounded and Kilgore rushed to the cockpit, checked the small display screen and busied his fingers on the controls. He really didn't have anything to control. Everything was automatic, the bomb was coming, and all he could do now was trust his defensive systems were as effective as he had planned them to be. He tilted his head far back and gazed into the black night sky, seeing nothing.

Miles above him the bomb was indeed falling. It was a small, deadly, precision-guided device that had locked on to Kilgore's GPS location, created a digital profile of the boat and used laser guidance to keep its aim locked on that target all the way down. It was a long, long journey to the electronic brain inside the explosive device, but the journey was also uneventful until the last ten thousand feet.

THREE THOUSAND MILES to the north, Harold W. Smith watched in growing horror as the bomb guided itself away from the place where it had originally seen Harry Kilgore's boat and onto the shore, zeroing in on the poverty-stricken village of Del Carmon.

Smith snapped out a series of instructions that he already knew were too late.

The bomb's systems were haywire. It knew it was off course and it struggled to correct itself, but the fins were pushed all the way over and it still kept traveling away from its target.

Smith ordered the bomb to destruct—then its systems blinked out of existence. Had it followed his commands, or had the bomb blown up because it reached twenty feet above sea level, which was where it was programmed to detonate?

Smith gazed at the final data feeds from the bomb and saw that his command had not even reached the device. It blew itself up—right on top of Del Carmon.

THREE THOUSAND MILES miles to the south, Harry Kilgore laughed.

Kilgore's system, mounted high above him on a

weather balloon, worked perfectly. It created a power blast of aberrant air as the rocket entered its range, and the powerful wind sheer pushed the bomb away. It slammed into the shore and erupted into a firestorm.

Kilgore watched human figures race into the streets. He heard screams. He saw a dancing, human-shaped figure clothed in flame emerge from a burning building, cross the rocks and collapse into the tide with a visible wisp of steam.

It was gratifying to watch. Then Kilgore realized what he was not seeing—the lighthouse of Del Carmon. The structure had vanished and in its place were only smoldering ruins. Harry Kilgore laughed and jumped into the air and clicked his heels. That's just how delighted he was.

HAROLD SMITH DETACHED HIMSELF from the empty screens that signified the destruction of the brothel village of Del Carmon. He concentrated on what else it signified—his inability to destroy a flimsy little power catamaran off the shore of Honduras with a computer-guided U.S. Air Force missile.

Smith considered his backup plan. It was an extreme measure, even by his standards. It involved more human beings from the U.S. military infrastructure, and it required significantly more effort to cover it up once the deed was done.

Nevertheless, something had to be done. Harry Kilgore and his equipment needed to be snuffed out before more people were killed. Who knew how many were dying at that moment because of Harry Kilgore?

Smith began issuing new orders on the secure military channels, and almost at once, began covering up the evidence of those orders.

But again, unknown to him, his actions were being observed.

10

United States Special Reconnaissance Submarine *Rehnquist* received its orders and headed to its target. The cloaked stealth submarine and its crew of fifteen didn't question or discuss the mission.

It was an hour shy of dawn when they tracked down their target. The GPS coordinates were correct, and the general profile of the vehicle matched the description in the orders. It was a power catamaran, without a mast. It was the kind of boat used by vacationers, with lots of deck space for sunbathing and parties at sea. It was not the kind of boat used by drug runners very often, as it was too slow.

The captain of the *Rehnquist* tried not to think about the identity of the people on this vehicle, but he was curious. If not drug smugglers, who were they? The sub crept into the shallows along the Honduran shore in full stealth mode. The catamaran was crawling along the shore, and the submarine could use its near-silent electric engines to maneuver into position, making no detectable noise. Not that the Hondurans had an effective coastal surveillance system. Still, it was best to be absolutely sure their presence inside Honduran waters was not known.

The *Rehnquist* took up a position in the water in the path of the slow-moving pleasure boat, intending to strike using the most silent tactic in its arsenal. The sub had an artificial reef, made of floating barbs of plastic-coated ceramic-fiber. It would be easy enough to entangle the hull of the craft, then drag the thing out to sea. If the boat happened to sink along the way, through a self-inflicted wound or in the course of resistance, the barb cable would release from the sub, go down with the boat and disintegrate in the salt water. Within three days there would be nothing left of it except the litter of man-made ceramic fiber fluff.

The barb was deployed, leaving its dry tub in a torpedo-shaped bundle, then reached the end of its tow cable. The barb float automatically adjusted to neutral balance at about six inches below the surface of the ocean. The catamaran would drive straight into the trap. The spring-loaded barbs would close automatically, gripping the hull like the claws of a predator and never letting go.

The captain of the *Rehnquist* ordered a slight adjustment to the position of the sub, reversing for a mere three yards. The barb was five yards in diameter, which seemed big, but lining it from inside the sub was a tricky business.

The captain enjoyed the challenge.

The catamaran stayed on course, coming at a leisurely pace, and the captain watched it on the floating video pickup that served as periscope. He had the barb positioned perfectly, and he wished the boat would deviate, just to make it more exciting. But there was nothing more for him to do except watch the trap be sprung.

The catamaran closed to within few yards of the barb net, and then they heard the burst. The tension monitor on the tow cables showed a sudden drop in the tension level, as if the barb net had become unattached at the other end. The cable was dropping to the ocean bottom.

"Let it go," the captain ordered, irritated.

"Detaching tow cable," one of his crew answered.

"Any explanation for that?" the captain snapped.

"Some sort of armed defensive probe mounted on the bow of the boat?" postulated his second in command.

The captain frowned at the reading on his screen. The power catamaran had come to within seven feet of the barb net when the net was destroyed. Any sort of explosive measure capable of neutralizing the net should have also damaged the boat, but the boat continued on its course, almost as if its crew was oblivious to the attack.

"You sure this wasn't a malfunction on our end?"

"No, sir, Captain," the gunner replied.

"Looks to me as if we let go of the net," the captain added.

There was a rebellious silence.

"Let's surface," the captain said. "Prepare to board the target vessel. We'll do this the old-fashioned way."

KILGORE WAITED TILL he spotted the ominous black shadow breaking the surface. He twisted the wheel and drove straight at the sub.

The hatch on the sub deck whispered open. Military men in blacksuits, bearing shoulder-fired weapons, clambered onto the oily-looking deck and opened fire on Harry Kilgore and his pleasure boat.

Kilgore winced when the brilliant orange rocket streaked through the black night on a perfect trajectory, coming right at him. Not just on target to hit the deck of the pleasure craft but on Harry Kilgore himself.

He would never get used to being on the receiving end of rocket-fired grenades.

But he had nothing to worry about. The air cannon reacted with percussive blasts that deflected the rockets. Rifle rounds ricocheted, tracers throwing up billowing sparks, and they skipped across the black ocean.

The sub began backing slowly away from Kilgore's boat, but by then the gunners were losing their nerve. Kilgore targeted the front end of the sub and hit it hard using the same emitter that had blasted the barb net into powder. The impact shoved the nose of the sub down, and water reached up the deck toward the open hatch. Hundreds of gallons poured inside before the sub righted herself. By then all the topside gunners had gone into the water.

Kilgore's next blast jolted the sub to the side. More water flowed through the hatch.

There were shouts from inside. The *Rehnquist* crew was engulfed in water, and they were being battered by the air cannon. Just twelve inches of its low-profile deck was still above the gentle waves.

One more wallop was all it would take. The next blast bobbed the sub down, and up, and down again. Water surged through the hatch. It was too much water too fast. The churning pumps couldn't hope to keep up.

Wads of plastic burst from the sub's outer hull and began expanding into rafts on the surface. A sailor managed to drag himself out the hatch and he tossed himself into the sea. The gunners flopped into the rafts and unfolded plastic paddles. They began to row hard, eager to get clear.

The sub never quite managed to surface again. It listed just below the surface as it filled with salt water, then went down. One of the rafts was dragged with it, and the seamen fought to free the line. The raft stood up on end, flinging seamen out of it. The raft penetrated the water, straight as a nail, then shot back out again in a riot of bubbles from a gaping hole where the safety line had been ripped out. Most of the air compartments were still sound, and the thrashing seamen swam for it. They called to Harry Kilgore, promising to rip his heart out of his body.

Kilgore gave the catamaran a little gas, then he hit a raft with a blast just as strong as the one that sank their sub. Its effect on human flesh was dramatic. Their bodies were pulped, and two rafts burst apart. All that was left floating on the sea was pieces. The sailors in the only surviving raft couldn't tell the rubber scraps from the human shred.

This bunch of survivors showed less arrogance in their final, dismal moments of life. They tried to flee, but their little electric motors and their plastic paddles got them nowhere. Kilgore tailgated them, nudging them in the rear a few times for effect, then blasted them out of existence. He left nothing but stains on the surface of the ocean, with less substance than the crushed remains of a stepped-on ant on a city sidewalk.

KILGORE WAS EXCITED about his next experiment. The device had not been used yet. This would be its first field test.

He hoisted the small, airtight steel canister over the side and allowed the winch to run out forty feet of line. He watched his electric fish finder, looking for the submarine's resting place. He found it soon enough and maneuvered the steel canister, with an emitter encased inside a sealed, airtight environment, directly over the sub.

Kilgore activated it. The emitter blasted inside the canister to create intense shock waves underwater, which cracked against the hull of the small sub like a depth charge. The burst of bubbles made Kilgore laugh out loud.

Kilgore was having a wonderful time, and he was thrilled to spot two survivors floating in the ocean nearby. They had somehow missed out on the blasts that flattened their crewmates. Kilgore cranked the wheel and closed in on the men, who separated and swam in opposite directions with desperate strokes. Harry chose the one on the right and closed in on him.

The sailor didn't get far.

He dived under the surface and Kilgore snapped on floodlights all around the hull. It made wild shadows on the gentle coastal tide. Before long the sailor was forced to surface for a breath. The sailor took a huge breath, and Kilgore blasted him hard. The sailor's head was smashed down on his shoulders, spread like a mushroom cap.

Kilgore said, "Ha!"

He found himself hoping it would take more time to find the last sailor. It did. The man swam an extraordinary distance, and Kilgore spotted just a tiny black shape in the nighttime sea. Kilgore's lights had trouble pinning him down. Kilgore's patience ran out and his enjoyment evaporated. After a half an hour, he was afraid he had lost the man.

"Show yourself, you son of a bitch!" Kilgore shrieked.

He hated it when people took advantage of him or got the better of him, and people had been doing this to him *forever.*

But not anymore. Everything changed when he created his Kilgore Air Cannon. With that tool, he changed the course of his own existence and changed how he dealt with his world. Harry no longer allowed himself to be exploited. That was not who he was anymore. His entire existence was now dedicated to proving it.

And now this little worm of a sailor wanted to humiliate him?

He would not let it happen.

If it took a week he would follow this man across the very ocean. If the man got to shore and escaped, then Harry Kilgore would devote his life to discovering the man's identity and then tracking him to the very home he lived in and then kill him in the most horrible way that was possible because people did not take advantage of Harry Kilgore anymore.

It didn't take a week or a land search. It only required another ten minuets of Harry Kilgore's time, and then, in a lull in the rumble of his own engines, he heard a discordant splash from the ocean far to his port side. He peered into the night, and spotted a tiny dark ball among the high-contrast shadows of the ocean waves.

Kilgore turned toward it, and sure enough, the bobbing head of the gasping sailor appeared on the surface. He turned his wide, reddened eyes to see the catamaran closing in on him.

Like the sailor before, this one sought refuge under the waves, but Harry Kilgore had only to wait. The exhausted sailor couldn't hold his breath long. He came up, gasping for air, and he looked Kilgore in the eyes. Kilgore triggered his air cannon.

The last sailor deformed violently, and the mass of his broken skull fell into the water, and he drifted limp in the tide.

Kilgore should have been happy then, but he wasn't. The obstinate sailor had brought Kilgore's old feelings to the surface. The man had tried to take advantage of Harry Kilgore, but he'd learned his lesson, right? Harry Kilgore couldn't be exploited. He had just proved it—again. Why wasn't he happy?

Was it because of Fortoul? No. The cartel kingpin was getting his just deserts, and Kilgore was doling them out in just the way he had planned to.

The problem was the strangers. The two agents who had attacked his boat earlier today. They hadn't beat him, but he had not beaten them, either. They had survived his attack and it was an insult. It was evidence that he was still exploitable.

Nobody did that to Harry Kilgore. Nobody.

HAROLD W. SMITH FELT a sort of dreamlike déjà vu as the screen of vital information from the sub showed sensor readings that indicated a catastrophic attack. Water was coming in. The sub captain sent a mayday signal on the same encrypted channel as the data transmission, but the captain had to have known there would be no rescue. You couldn't mobilize a rescue for a sub that wasn't supposed to exist.

Then the data feeds flatlined. The only signal left was the tiny emergency locator ping. Even that would go silent as soon as it broadcast its final location to the impassive satellites.

Smith glared at the GPS readings of the sub's resting place. It hardly mattered. The crew was almost certainly murdered, and Harry Kilgore was almost certainly going on his way unharmed.

There would be many innocent dead in the town of Del Carmon and many dead sailors on the sub.

Smith allowed himself momentary regret, and then he made it go away.

The director of CURE couldn't afford to feel remorse. Ever.

11

Thomas J. Shep felt like one of those TV show directors who gets to sit in a room with all the different camera feeds, and he selects one camera angle, then another, keeping the attention of the audience moving all the time.

But really, Shep was director and audience both. He had all three of his computers going at once.

One of them was dedicated to tracking messages traveling through the military nets. Shep was watching them and he was tracing the orders as fast as he could. He had gotten way better at this. Somehow he knew tonight was the night. This business in the Yucatan seemed ripe for U.S. intervention of the cloak-and-dagger kind. Somebody would want to get their hands on that weirdo with the big wind machines, or kill him in retaliation for killing a bunch of DEA agents. Somebody would do something.

Then somebody issued an order for an air strike.

Nobody ordered U.S. air strikes in the Western Hemisphere without Shep's computer beeping him about it.

Shep logged in using his military intelligence all-access security pass and he read the order. U.S. Air Force Brigadier General Ian Crooksten ordered the strike. Shep knew the names of lots of brigadier generals, but this one didn't ring a bell. He moved to a second computer to call up Crooksten's service records. The records looked legitimate. Pages of biographical details. Photos. If this was a forged record, it had been forged by a master.

But Shep had found service records before that he was pretty certain were forgeries, and they always looked perfect. You had to delve a lot deeper to uncover the falsehood. Shep delved.

The bomber aircraft was in the air and heading for its target.

Shep checked the records behind the records. His university transcript looked legitimate. His tax returns appeared genuine. Everything about him looked electronically legitimate.

Then Air Force Brigadier General Ian Crooksten vanished.

One minute the record was there; the next minute the brigadier general was nonexistent in the military service records. The man who had ordered the air strike had ceased to exist before the bomb even fell off the airplane.

Shep smiled wide and said, "This guy is *good*."

The backup records were gone, too. His service biography and college transcripts and his driver's license—erased.

Another computer was providing data feeds on the secure military channels. Every bit of data had to be crunched through some sort of godawful decryption routine and Shep's poor desktop computer was practically smoking at the ears. But it was great stuff! Feeds from a bomb, in real time, right when it was coming down on its target. Then it goes crazy, off target, and somebody tried to take control of the damned bomb while it was falling.

Thomas Shep watched it happen as it happened.

"It's you!" he said aloud. "My rival. I *found* you."

Not found him, really. He still had no idea who the guy was—or guys. Probably a group of them. Shep wondered what they would do now that their air strike had apparently gone wrong.

"Nice. Nice!" he cheered when his system alerted him to a set of urgent commands for an at-once mission by a spy sub. It was the same secret agency that issued the orders—Shep just knew it was. He confirmed it by getting the name of the high-ranking official who supposedly issued the orders and then making a quick search of the service records. Another set of perfectly forged service records that went poof! Just like that, gone. Army General Dean Glenwillow had come into existence and gone out again in a matter of minutes.

Shep breathlessly watched the sub go into battle against a tourist boat off Honduras. The sub went to the bottom, presumably with all hands.

About that time Shep caught the intelligence electronic news clipping service, listing breaking news reports about a catastrophe in Honduras. A massive explosion. An entire coastal village in flames. The cause was a mystery, since there was no industry or fuel storage in the town.

Wow. The bomb struck civilians! Lots of them! Thomas Shep spoke out loud to his rival. "Whoever you are, man, you really screwed up tonight. Big time."

Shep had to figure out what it was that had led his rival into this very sticky situation.

He called up everything he had on the man who was wanted for the murders of DEA agents and destruction of Drug Enforcement Administration property.

There had been a DEA debacle a few days ago. A drug bust gone bad in a most unusual way. As the DEA attempted to seize a shipment and arrest the smugglers, another party intruded and overpowered the DEA and the smugglers both. The drug pirate stole the cocaine and slaughtered all the DEA agents and all the smugglers indiscriminately. This all occurred after the pirate had somehow caused the DEA support helicopter, which was waiting several miles away from the scene of the bust, to crash, killing everyone on board.

The DEA was monitoring ransom demands being made by a character who called himself the Hurricane. The Hurricane wanted the Fortoul cartel to buy back its cocaine. That took balls.

The Colombians had tried again and again to take back their cocaine by force. Well, what did you expect the Colombians to do? The amazing thing was that the cartel enforcers were soundly beaten, each and every time. The Hurricane was apparently impervious to whatever the cartel could throw at him. He would agree to an exchange, Fortoul would throw a bunch of Colombian hardmen at him, and the Hurricane would wipe them right out. Then he'd call up Fortoul again and double the price.

The Hurricane would take a stab in the back as his final answer. He was right now en route to Colombia. Apparently he was going to take the fight directly to the Colombians on their own territory.

Shep was getting overexcited and overwhelmed. There was so much going on, he didn't know where to concentrate his efforts. This Hurricane had some kind of crazy new weapon. What if Shep could get his hands on it? If the Hurricane was fighting off missiles and subs from a damned cabin cruiser, just think what soldiers in a tank could do with it.

So why was Shep's secret rival bent on blowing it up?

Maybe Shep should try to keep that from happening. Maybe he needed to get his hands on the catamaran before anybody else did.

But for that, he would need field agents. An team to enforce his will. It was risky, but he'd have to consider it.

12

The Folcroft Four were soulless and insentient. They could think furiously, but they could never be aware of their own existence. They didn't have emotions and they absolutely did not have a sense of humor, but sometimes it appeared as if they spit out random bits of information just to see what kind of a reaction it would get.

Mark Howard's reaction was to simply stop doing anything and stare at the screen, turning over the facts in his mind again and again until he was sure they added up to what he thought they added up to.

"I think someone is onto us."

Smith looked up. "Meaning?"

"I just got an alert from the back-tracer application we installed last year."

Smith scowled. "Refresh my memory."

"Actually, it was your idea. It's a benign tracer application that monitors activity in the federal nets regarding the false IDs we use for issuing military orders. It reports that the service records of two of these IDs were rerouted last night. What's worse is that it was the IDs you used to order the air strike and the sub attack on Harry Kilgore."

"That is unfortunate." Harold Smith felt an uncharacteristic sense of dread. "Those orders should not have been traceable to a single source," he pointed out. "The question, then, is how much this party knows about us."

Mark Howard didn't feel nearly as calm as Smith sounded. "I can think of a lot of other questions. I'd like to know who it is. What they're up to."

"I feel these are of less importance," Smith said. "It is likely to be some sort of monitoring agency in the federal intelligence system. Someone with an eye for anomalous activity. My guess is, there is someone with a high level of clearance who managed to isolate CURE activities by their common lack of traceability."

"You make it sound like an accident," Mark said.

Smith shook his head. "Not an accident, but let's estimate the depth of their knowledge about us. They know there is some party operating behind the scenes, with leverage enough to place highest-level military and intelligence commands. What more might they know?"

Mark was miserable. This fragment of news could be a disaster. "Who can tell?"

"Mark," Smith said, "there is no reason to think they have seen any more than the false records that we put there for them to see. What is worrisome is that they knew to look for the records at all. They suspect something. That is all."

"I wish I felt as confident of that as you do."

Smith thought about that. Mark wasn't as confident. Mark's judgment told him the problem might be more serious than Smith's judgment was telling him. Harold Smith had the benefit of many years' experience guarding the security of CURE.

But, come to think of it, the same could be said for Mark Howard. Though Smith still thought of him as a newcomer, Mark had been with CURE long enough to have mastered the security systems; in fact, he had developed many of their current security systems. He was intelligent and deeply intuitive.

Mark Howard, Smith realized, had developed into a world-class intelligence and information security expert. With his rare insight and his understanding of the dynamics of the technology of the twenty-first century, one could make the case that Mark Howard, and not Harold W. Smith, was the better judge of CURE's security. When somebody with that level of expertise had concerns about a breach, it was foolish to discount those worries.

For a moment, Smith was tinged with regret. He had lost his prime position in this realm. But then he felt something else that he couldn't quite pin down.

Pride. He felt proud of Mark Howard for what the young man had accomplished and grown into.

"You may be right," Smith announced. "We cannot afford to ignore the possibility. Mark, let's divide our attentions. I'll concentrate on our current mission in Colombia. I want you putting all your efforts into working the security breach. Figure it out. Who did it. What tipped them off. How much has CURE been exposed. That's vital. You know the consequences if we're exposed."

"Of course."

"And figure out how to keep it from happening again."

"I will."

THE CALL HAROLD SMITH had been waiting for finally came. The red telephone clanged and Smith answered with "Hello, Mr. President."

"Smith, what's going on in South America?"

That caught the CURE director off guard. "Nothing of interest."

"What? Are you lying or just totally oblivious? There's been a big DEA screw-up and some sort of drug-smuggler war and the missile blast on a village and what all. Are you telling me none of this is on your radar, Smith?"

"I'm quite aware of these events. However, they're occurring off the coast of Central America."

"Central, South, it's all south of the border."

"The phrase 'south of the border' typically refers to Mexico, which is part of North America."

"You've got that one wrong, Smith. North America is the United States. And Canada, too, I guess."

"Sir, the North American continental landmass includes Mexico, as well."

"Yeah, right. Forget that and tell me why this guy is taking us on."

Smith wasn't in the habit of debriefing the President on security situations that did not, as far as the President knew, involve CURE. "We know his target is not the U.S., but the Fortoul cartel. He calls himself the Hurricane, and he claims to have stolen a valuable shipment of cocaine with the intent of extorting a ransom from the cartel."

"Lone operator, that what you're saying? Taking on an honest-to-God drug family? He's a maniac."

"We agree he is likely mentally unstable, but it's premature to assume he's taking suicidal risks. He's devastated every attempted assault upon his person."

"I guess so," the President said. "How?"

"That's not entirely clear."

"Uh-huh. Is it a little bit clear?"

"It is partially clear."

"Right. So give me the partially clear version."

Smith couldn't lie to his President, so he said, "He appears to be creating atmospheric displacement using crude particle entanglement field emitters."

"Whoa, Smith, what are you trying to do to me? Give me the nonscientist explanation. Something a normal person can understand."

"Compare the effect to a microburst," Smith said.

"A what?"

"A meteorological phenomenon."

"Nope. Give it another shot."

"It makes twisters," Smith said finally.

"Tornadoes?"

"Yes. Small ones, but more powerful than any natural tornado. It blows away attackers and their ordnance."

"You mean bullets? Missiles? Are you telling me this freak used a big fan to deflect a missile?"

"That's our best guess. A 300-mile-per-hour wind could easily deflect an air-launched explosive."

"Got any proof?"

"No, sir."

"Yeah. Okay. Right. Are you doing anything about it?"

"Our field agents are trailing him now."

"Okay. Keep me posted."

The President hung up.

Smith lowered the receiver into the cradle of the old red phone, replaying the conversation in his head. It had gone better than expected. The President had not asked Smith if he'd had anything to do with the air strike and had not come out and requested that CURE obtain Harry Kilgore's technology. Smith had told the truth, without showing too many of his cards. CURE could still act as Smith thought best without being in direct opposition to the President.

Not that he would hesitate to take action that was counter to the President's wishes if it was clearly in the best interests of the United States—but it was always good policy to avoid rubbing him the wrong way. After all, he held the power of life and death over CURE. As such, he held the power of life and death over Harold W. Smith.

Absently, Smith's hand fell to the hem of his suit jacket lapel, and he rubbed the small, coffin-shaped lumps sewn into the lining.

If the time came for CURE to cease operations, then CURE would have to vanish completely. There would be no incriminating evidence left, and that included the vast warehouse of memory inside the brain of Harold W. Smith.

If the order came, Smith would take the necessary steps. Order the Folcroft Four to self destruct. They would purge their vast data storage drive, then activate a power surge through specially designed cables. Every internal memory storage and processing system would be electrocuted with enough voltage to fry the circuits and melt the metal housing. Then, as a final safeguard, the entire computer enclosure would be destroyed using phosphorus-based incendiary devices.

Nothing would be left of the Folcroft Four except ash and slag.

As the computers burned, Smith's doomsday protocol would next call for the erasure of the human components of CURE, and this was where Smith would have to be extremely careful. Because, despite their pledge of loyalty to CURE, Smith wasn't totally convinced that Mark Howard and Sarah Slate would go willingly to their deaths.

More specifically, Smith doubted that Mark would allow Sarah to die. Mark himself would take his own coffin-shaped pill, but he would first get Sarah to safety. Safety meant away from Harold W. Smith.

Smith knew this. He understood why Mark would protocol Sarah. Smith also knew he had to prevent Mark from doing it. Sarah knew about CURE, and she had joined willingly, if only to be with Mark Howard. She even had her own coffin-shaped pill.

As a part of the CURE dissolution protocol, revised to account for Sarah Slate, Smith intended to find and kill Mark Howard first. If conditions were optimal, he would simply bring Mark into the office alone and dispatch him with a bullet to the brain. It would be quick and painless.

After all, he was extremely fond of Mark Howard, and he didn't want the man to suffer.

With Mark Howard out of the way, he would track down Sarah Slate. He would arrange to meet her outside the office, of course, and would dispatch her in a similar manner. Then he would take the coffin-shaped pill himself.

One major uncertainty to this plan was the presence of the Masters of Sinanju. Chiun was especially fond of Sarah Slate for reasons Smith failed to understand. The old Master would never allow Smith to assassinate her. Remo was even worse. He would do his best to make sure Smith killed no one, not even himself.

If the order came to dismantle CURE, Smith sincerely hoped it would come at a time when Remo and Chiun were far away from Folcroft; it would make the entire process so much easier.

"Well?" Mark Howard asked. Smith had been pondering his phone call in silence.

"It went fine. He asked none of the right questions, so I was obligated to give him none of the leading answers," Smith explained.

Smith had been calmly defiant of presidents in the past, but he was not a man to abuse his powers. He had been granted a level of extreme authority because he was believed to be incorruptible. Not only was he intensely patriotic, but he was also lacking in the imaginative skills required to be a power monger.

Other men would have been insulted at the psychological assessments performed while he was with the Central Intelligence Agency. The reports on Harold W. Smith called him a man of extraordinary intelligence and extreme banality. Back in those days the mental health fields had not yet developed concepts like "artistic intelligence," so they used less scientific terms.

"He's smarter than all of us put together, but he's so dumb he couldn't find a butterfly in a hundred ink blots," explained one of the psychologists who was debriefed on Harold W. Smith. The man doing the debriefing was a young United States President. Why the President was interested in a profile of that sourpuss Smith was beyond his understanding.

"What do you mean, butterflies in ink blots?"

The CIA psychologist showed the President a Rorschach sample. "Yes, I'm aware of them. They all look like butterflies to me."

"Exactly, Mr. President," the psychologist had said. "That's they idea. They're just ink, but they look like something, if you use your imagination. But Smith, he doesn't see anything. He's got no imagination. None."

"I see." The President seemed pleased. "And this makes a person inherently trustworthy why?"

"Practically dictates it. A man like this can think about being duplicitous, but he can't imagine or dream of being duplicitous. He's so practical and unable to imagine intangible goals, he's unable to comprehend the attraction of those kinds of dreams. I promise you, a man like Smith never wanted to be a baseball star or a singing sensation. He simply couldn't see it. Same reason he never got far up the ladder at the Agency. He didn't even see the practicality of trying to rise above the level where he was most competent."

The President couldn't possibly understand what he was talking about. Right? But the young President from the East Coast was pleased, as if the psychologist's explanation was somehow reassuring.

"There are some in my field who think creativity dwells completely on one side of the brain, on the left. And logic dominates the right side of the brain. If that were true, our man Smith would constantly be tipping over to the right." The psychologist chuckled. The President stared at him, then realized it was a joke.

"Ha." He laughed politely. "Ha-ha."

The psychologist left the appointment, and he never learned what it was all about. He guessed the young President was going to offer Smith some sort of a position in his administration.

But it didn't happen. Smith retired from the CIA and, the last that the psychologist heard, had got himself made director of a private hospital in Rye, New York. Just as well for Smith—the President who had made the inquiry was assassinated shortly afterward. An administrative post would have been short-lived.

Twenty-some years later, the psychologist was long retired and he happened to hear through the grapevine that sour old Smith was still serving as the director of that sanitarium in Rye.

"Smith's probably driving all his poor patients into comas," the psychologist joked to an old CIA buddy.

They had a good laugh over that.

THE OVAL OFFICE FILLED UP with important agriculture people, and some undersecretary of something began orating about the need for cattle subsidies.

"Hold on a sec," the President said, and came out from behind his desk. He headed for a low set of bookshelves against a far wall. It held a long row of brown volumes in shiny new leather. The President of the United States was always equipped with an up-to-date encyclopedia. One of the dirty little secrets of the White House was that every President used them, frequently, to keep up the appearance of being well-read.

The President yanked out a volume, flipped the pages and scowled. He jammed it back in place and grabbed another volume, turning until he found the entry for Central America. Then he grabbed another volume and turned to North America.

"Mexico. Who'd have thought? I guess the old man had it right," the President announced.

"What old man?" asked the undersecretary.

13

The canvas tents stood on a patch of green that the fire had missed. The housing tents formed one small neighborhood in the new tent city, then came the large hospital tent for recuperation of the many patients passed along from triage and treatment. The triage and field emergency treatment room was still doing a brisk business in the midmorning sunlight. It was a strange contrast, the brilliant, cloudless Caribbean sky the turquoise Caribbean sea and the waving green palm trees, all standing as backdrop to the burned shacks, the decimated plank buildings and the incinerated undergrowth.

The Red Cross had arrived within hours of the catastrophe and began treating patients immediately. The problem was the burns. A field hospital could do little for burn victims.

By dawn, medical personnel moved into the tents and were operating on those who could benefit from it.

Finally, when those patients were dealt with, they turned to the hopeless cases—the patients who would almost certainly die but who deserved some token effort to save their lives.

Now the medical staff began the routine of its first day as a field hospital. They changed dressings and carted out the patients who hadn't survived the night. They started making breakfast. Those who could stand lined up outside the mess tent, maybe just to escape the trauma of the recovery room.

Into their midst came a most unlikely figure. A man of great age and frail body—an Asian man, but what he was doing on the east coast of Honduras was anyone's guess.

He strolled among the gawking survivors and found a spot at the edge of the stony shore. He watched the sea as if he expected someone to come out of it. And that was all he did, for more than an hour.

More than once patients and staffers approached him and asked him if he needed help. He ignored them. Completely. And eventually they walked away.

Then, to the onlookers' amazement, something *did* come out of the ocean. It was a younger man. And not an Asian, and not dressed in brilliant Asian robes. He was in Chinos and a beige T-shirt.

When they first spotted the newcomer he was coming out of the surf, approaching the old Asian man, and he seemed to have swum in from the sea. There was nowhere else he could have come from. There was no boat to be seen. His clothes weren't soaking wet, which was odd. In fact, there was a shimmer of steam coming from his clothing. There were spreading spots across his chest muscles where the fabric already looked dry.

Some of the patients held their hand up to the sun. It was hot, yes, but not that hot. The sun couldn't dry clothing that fast. They knew, because they had lived here forever.

The riddle of the two strangers was a welcome distraction from the suffering.

The young one conversed with the old Asian, got little better response than anyone else had from the old man and then he approached one of the Red Cross site leaders. She was a middle-aged woman with severe silver hair pulled back in a ponytail, and she didn't know what to make of this stranger.

"Can I help you?" she asked in Spanish.

"Uh, speak English?" the stranger asked.

"Sure," she answered with a gentle smile. "I'm from Ohio."

"Jersey. I'm lost. Can I use your phone for a collect call?"

MARK HOWARD WAS ASSESSING the damage. He knew there was nothing to be gained from this, and there was nothing more he or CURE could do. Still, he felt compelled to review the reports coming in from the infamous brothel village of Del Carmon.

As he was viewing another casualty roster, Remo called.

Smith barely glanced up from whatever he was

doing on his own desk, and he opened the connection on the speakerphone. It was now their habit to conference call when Remo reported in.

Remo was not pleased.

"It's an effing mess, Smitty," Remo snapped.

Smith raised his head from the glass surface of his desk, and the bright displays mounted beneath the glass went blank.

"I hear people in the background, Remo," Smith said. "Where are you?"

"Where do you think? Del Carmon."

"Where in Del Carmon, precisely?"

"Where precisely? Let me tell you all about where precisely," Remo said. "There's about a hundred poor Hondurans around me as I speak to you. Some have sheets over their faces, and some of them don't. Some are bleeding. In fact, a lot are bleeding, or mangled or seared all over. I see a guy over there with a big wad of bright red bandages where his arm should be. There's lots of folks with crusty stuff on their outsides where skin used to be. There's lots of people trying to help them. But let's face it, they're just a bunch of dirt-poor Third World types. Not too important to anybody."

"I see," Smith said. "You are at the Red Cross hospital. "

"Only phone in town."

"You investigated the wreckage of the submarine?"

"Yeah. I investigated. It's just about exactly where

you thought it would be. You really nailed it." Remo's tongue was acid. "Good job, Smitty."

"What's the sub's condition?"

"The condition is sunk. Now, let me tell you some more about the condition of people from Del Carmon. Here's a kid who ought to be out playing soccer. Only he can't, 'cause he's dead. Here's another kid who should be out playing soccer. He can't, not because he's dead, but because he's only got one leg. It looks like the leg was there up until very recently, and it looks like it didn't come off without a fight."

"I get the idea, Remo," Smith said. "I'm fully aware that you blame me for the human toll. Believe me when I say that I'm not unaffected by it."

"Wow, way to unburden your soul," Remo said. "You pulled the trigger on those innocent people and that's all you have to say for yourself?"

"What do you want from me, Remo, my resignation? I've given you my apology and you know the explanation. Now there is a job to do and that starts with you giving me a better idea as to the condition of the sub."

Remo roamed his eyes around the village, then looked out to sea, where the ocean sparkled brilliantly and nearly washed out the peaceful, still figure of the Master of Sinanju Emeritus. Chiun was regarding the open water, meditating. What was he thinking about?

"The sub's a write-off, Smitty," Remo said. "It's trashed. Blown to bits."

"Not salvageable," Smith clarified.

"Very not salvageable. Neither is the crew. It looks like a few of them were still inside when it went down. Parts of them are still trapped in the debris. The Hurricane hit them hard. I guess he's the one I should be blaming, huh?"

"Christophe Fortoul called in a few favors," Smith said. "He had a Colombian naval vessel intercept the Kilgore catamaran. The Colombian vessel radioed that it was under attack, then it vanished."

"The Colombians are setting up a blockade. They've mobilized every armed ship in their Atlantic fleet. It's not an insubstantial naval force. It is difficult to imagine even Harry Kilgore getting past it."

"Chiun and I are on our way to Colombia, I hope?" Remo asked. "Just in case?"

"Yes. Just in case."

14

Harry Kilgore knew that this was going to be a hell of a demonstration of his engineering genius. If he got through this mess—and he knew he would—there'd be little doubt that he *was* the Hurricane. The world would finally come to understand that he was a force of nature that no human power could stand against. They'd all know they had made a big mistake when they discounted Harry Kilgore.

Harry had a portable television bolted in the cockpit and it was getting feeds from the satellites, his little dish struggling to stay locked on to the signals. Harry stalled until the image of the Colombian naval blockade showed up on the global news networks, then moved in on the fleet in his little catamaran.

"You in the catamaran, you will cut your engines." It was a loudspeaker from the small approach cutter.

Kilgore didn't respond. The Colombians had been radioing him for hours, and he had ignored them. He considered answering with some taunts and racial slurs, but decided he would look more powerful by simply ignoring the whole lot of them. They were beneath contempt. He would deliver the ultimate insult and pretend they weren't even there.

More of the vessels closed ranks around him. Kilgore was sweating. Truth be told, it was tough to even pretend to ignore a flotilla of armed vessels closing in on your secondhand pleasure boat. They took up positions around him and paced him. They were an escort. Kilgore liked having a military escort.

But they were escorting him to their leader. On the dramatic news video shot from far-off news helicopters, Kilgore looked like their prisoner already. He turned up the television volume. He could see the image of his own little craft surrounded by a flying V of Colombian naval vessels. Sure enough, the announcer mentioned that the renegade catamaran was now a "prisoner."

Kilgore didn't like the sound of that. He wasn't a prisoner. He wasn't in a position of weakness and he never would be, not in this lifetime. He was the embodiment of power over man, and he was going to illustrate the point graphically.

A sleek, modern-looking destroyer waited broadside to him and directly in his path. It was going to play chicken with him. That was just fine. Kilgore never turned from his course.

"Stop now, or you will be fired," the radio barked.

"I guess English isn't your first language," Kilgore muttered, and he increased his speed.

"You will force us to gun you," the radio insisted.

Kilgore ignored it.

"He's clearly not thinking clearly," said the news anchor with rising excitement.

"This is your last warning," the Colombian naval vessel said.

Kilgore was itching to talk back, but it thrilled him to picture the growing agitation rising from his refusal to acknowledge them. It was a way of taunting them, yes, of getting their ire up. Get them madder and madder until they exploded—and then watch the sheer fury and panic at what happened next.

The attack came, but not from the destroyer. It was a small gunboat that sliced swiftly away from the escort and closed in on Harry Kilgore.

Kilgore's attention was drawn by the image on the screen—it was him! A bouncy, jittery image from an extreme long-range camera, but they were getting a live shot of him from one of the hovering helicopters. Kilgore exerted all his self-control to not even glance at the approaching gunboat.

The gunboat cut through the water and slowed to run parallel to the Kilgore catamaran, then unleashed a barrage of machine gun rounds. They were big bullets, too, and the gunners were probably trying to disable Harry's two engines.

But this was never known, because the bullets never reached the twin hulls. There was a cracking of continuous airbursts between Kilgore and the gunboat. The sea became a maelstrom in that contained vicinity, and when the gunfire halted, the airbursts stopped. The ocean was left with a monstrous crater, unnatural and somehow as ugly as a corpse. The water rushed into the crater and thrashed about, while torrents of rain descended for a full minute in that tiny vicinity. It was like watching a miniature thunderstorm.

When it was over, the gunboat tried again with small missiles.

"Ho-hum. Little rockets make me numb," Kilgore said to himself. Another automatic burst from the air cannons, and the thunder cracked a hundred feet above the surface. The train of flaring rockets exploded in midair with yellow flashes of light, like uninspired fireworks. This time, the ocean barely rippled.

The gunboat crew didn't wait long for their next, and final, attempt. They upended steel boxes on the deck and a pair of finned projectiles slid into the water, where they came to life with sudden brightness.

"More of the same," Kilgore said. He waited with one finger on the emergency reaction switch—but he never needed it. The proximity sensors detected the torpedoes and responded with an instant series of bursts.

More air-cannon blasts occurred, and this time they were right on the surface of the ocean and quite near to the gunboat. The torpedoes detonated abruptly. Rollicking waves tilted the gunboat from side to side.

"You bore me. You go away now," Kilgore said to himself, and began firing manually. One blast after another tore the surface of the ocean apart—one hundred yards away from the gunboat. Seventy-five yards. Fifty yards. The gunboat turned away and increased its speed, heading back to the flotilla. It moved fast. Kilgore compensated for their retreat and placed his next blast right where it should have been—twenty-five yards off the back end of the gunboat. No more, no less.

The next blast was right on top of the gunboat as it reached the flotilla. The airburst struck with just as much force as the bursts that had come near to the catamaran. Distance wasn't much of a factor for the Kilgore Air Cannon. It crushed the gunboat's center and burst apart the fore and aft sections, which bubbled below the sea in seconds. The scarlet remains that floated on the surface were too crushed to be called bodies. Nearby Colombian naval boats tossed in a violent wash.

"Not bad," Kilgore said. Then he watched the replay on the news. "Not bad at all. But I can do better."

The navy destroyer started moving, put on speed and turned away from the catamaran. Kilgore saw he was on TV again and he put on a grimace. He couldn't help it. He was enjoying this too much—the big Colombian ship was running away from Harry Kilgore.

"If I didn't know better, I would say the Colombians are turning tail," a news anchor reported. Kilgore sure hoped this was being broadcast live around the world.

The destroyer put on speed. Despite its size, it was quick. Kilgore was at top speed and he couldn't catch up. The destroyer lengthened the buffer zone between the vessels.

"Now what?" the news anchor asked. "Are they escorting him all the way to Colombia?"

"Good question," Kilgore responded.

The news said, "Wait, more navy vessels arriving. All Colombian. United States ships are reported en route, but the U.S. has said it will not participate unless formally requested by the government of Colombia. We think the Colombians will target the little boat with a coordinated assault when all their forces are in place."

"Big fat yawn," Kilgore said, but the truth was, he was thrilled to death.

THERE WERE A COUPLE of dozen ships pacing Harry Kilgore's little power catamaran when the coordinated assault began.

Colombia possessed about as much technological expertise and defense equipment that could be expected of a bicoastal, Third World nation, which was saying little. Still, it should have been enough to obliterate a pleasure boat constructed almost entirely of plastic.

But it wasn't enough.

Kilgore let the automatic systems take care of the machine gun rounds and the antiaircraft projectiles as the battery of ships closed in to port, and he kept an eye on the response time and accuracy. His primary systems were good enough to deflect almost everything they could throw at him, and his redundant shielding systems got the rest. Not one round penetrated his wall of air-cannon fire.

With all systems go, he felt at his leisure to try his hand at a new defensive technique. As soon as the big rockets started flying, he grabbed the joystick and turned to the laser-based motion-mapping display. It showed the airbursts as billowing clouds of pink particles, and the rockets as tiny tubes traveling above them. The trick was to get the airburst underneath the rocket just so. This allowed the rockets to bounce off the top of the airburst, sending them high over the top of his catamaran, and then the rockets just kept on going until they fell among the boats on the opposite side of the flotilla. The rockets stopped firing.

Next came floating explosives, which never came anywhere near the catamaran. Low-power airbursts at the surface of the water steered the floating explosives around Kilgore and again sent them into the midst of the Colombian vessels at the rear of the blockade. The navy ships veered around them, then sent chaser boats to detonate them before they were lost in the open sea.

The Colombians already seemed to have run out of ideas. Harry Kilgore waited for some new and ingenious form of attack, but it never came. The Colombians seemed resigned to simply escorting Kilgore to shore, probably in hopes of passing him off to some ground-based military force.

Kilgore didn't want his media spectacle to end with a whimper. He wanted it to end with a bang. His GPS showed they were passing into the Golfo del Darién and he had only forty-five minutes before reaching the Colombian shipping port of Turbo.

He thought he'd better get a move on.

KILGORE STARTED OFF with a couple of extreme-range blasts on the outside of the flotilla ships, too weak at that distance to do much damage to a military boat. But the Colombians didn't know that. They saw the big explosion on the surface of the ocean and were drenched by the sudden saltwater rain squall and assumed that violence was closing in on them.

The boats retreated from the blasts, actually coming closer to Kilgore. It wouldn't take long for them to undo that mistake, so Harry acted fast. He fired truly destructive blasts from all sides of his ship, and his target was now the waters just inside the flotilla. The blasts formed deep craters in the sea surface and put thousands of gallons of water into the air. Hulls collapsed and rudders sheered off. Many of the smaller ships became helpless in the water.

The navy went on the offensive again, simply because it didn't know what else to do. The hail of rounds burst upon the little power catamaran from every able-bodied vessel.

Kilgore's barrage deflected the rounds and bounced the rockets up and over, and with the ships bunched together he was able to get some hits. The Colombian ships were taking their own friendly fire. A cutter exploded when a rocket slammed through its deck and exploded inside its hull. As it went down in flaming pieces, more ships were being battered by the bursts of air cannons. Kilgore was getting better at this. Battering a boat along the outside hull wasn't very effective on most of the ships. Their skins were too thick. The trick was to blast open the deck from above, again and again, until the ship's hull was separated from its ribs and rivets. Once that happened, the boat took on water and went down quickly.

Soon enough, the ships that remained afloat were smoking, flaming wrecks of metal. In a matter of minutes there were no more viable sea craft, and Kilgore began playing the death dealer.

He targeted a small gunship that was beginning to fall behind. He triggered tandem blasts five yards above the water, and the gunboat was crushed on either side like a grasshopper being squeezed between a thumb and forefinger. The compressed mass of metal that was left over upended itself and sliced into the depths of the ocean. More ships followed after it as Kilgore became better at aiming his device. He crushed the bridge of one navy ship after another, leaving only disabled burning hulks on the surface. He let them be. Their billowing columns of smoke were excellent visual drama for the networks.

Only one boat had so far escaped unscathed. Kilgore

had not forgotten it, but merely saved it for the finale. Now was the time. The survivor was the new Colombian destroyer, and Kilgore had no doubt it was the pride of the Colombian navy, and probably the most expensive single piece of equipment in the entire Colombian military.

But as he was finishing off the small craft, the destroyer began putting distance between itself and the power catamaran. It was faster than Harry. It would be out of range in a hurry.

Kilgore aimed his air cannon at the waterline at the rear of the destroyer and blasted away at full power. The water channeled out of the surface of the ocean, hundreds of feet into the sky. The pressure waves in the water pounded the armor on the drive fans. The constant blasts removed the ocean and exposed the propeller cage, and Harry let the air cannons keep firing one on top of the other until the water was a mist that shrouded the destroyer's bare aft end.

The air cannons ground to a halt.

Kilgore was startled by the silence. First he thought a finger had slipped from the trigger controls, then saw his charger system was in the red. The emitter chargers were too hot. They had shut down as a safety measure.

Kilgore was surprised. His design specs had allowed for the possibility of overheating, of course, and he had installed the overheat protection, but he never expected to need it.

He checked the trigger monitor. It showed a count

of 1,099 airbursts delivered since he intercepted the Colombians' blockade.

That was a lot.

But 1,099 airbursts had been just the right amount. The Colombian blockade was decimated—including the big, shiny destroyer. As the water mist settled back into the ocean, a gaping mouth showed in the raw metal ruin of the destroyer's aft end. Water was flooding into the ship.

Had he even tested the overheat recovery time? He didn't believe so. He watched the controls, hoping to see a rapid fall in the temperature. The gauge didn't cooperate.

The radio was making noise. It had been making noise all along, but now the tone was different.

There were no further demands for his cease-fire. Now it was the sound of the Colombian navy surrendering to him.

Kilgore took some of the strain off the little power catamaran engine, allowing himself to drift alongside the destroyer.

The crew had its hands in the air.

"Please respond," the radio begged in struggling English.

Kilgore simply observed them as he circled, until he was in front of the destroyer and he turned away as if to abandon them there. That was surely what they hoped for.

But then, as he began pulling away, Kilgore's temperature was reduced enough for one last barrage. The single, powerful blast came into being just alongside the tall deckhouse, smashing it off the deck. The three-story building toppled from the ship and slammed into the ocean. Then a series of small blasts swept the deck clean of surrendering sailors. Their bodies splashed into the waters of the Golfo del Darién.

The next air-cannon burst hit a sensitive spot. Something inside the destroyer detonated with a bang, and a hole opened at the water level. When the water poured in, steam billowed from the open deck at the top. The destroyer listed then submerged itself over the next ten minutes.

Again, Harry Kilgore's face was on the network news, emotionless. He had just wiped out the better half of the Colombian navy and his attitude suggested it was not that big a deal. It was exactly the impression he wanted to give.

He had made his point.

15

It came as quite a surprise to Thomas Shep to realize he was the most powerful man in the government of the United States of America.

It was ironic that a bureaucrat whose sole function was to police the checks and balances of the intelligence system could become, because of loopholes in the checks and balances, the mastermind of all government intelligence. Through the judicious use of intelligence, he could affect any other aspect of government. And there was nothing beyond the reach of the U.S. government.

"Guess I'm king," Shep said, laughing at his own reflection in the little mirror he kept in his desk. The mirror reflected a pasty-faced cherub of a man with pink skin and a scraggly comb-over. His skin was blotchy. His nose displayed a road map of broken capillaries. What he noticed when he looked in the mirror, however, was the reflection of the room behind him.

"A king ought to get a better office," Shep announced.

The problem with his current situation was that he was omnipotent but he had to keep quiet about it. He could go on consolidating his hold on the world as long as nobody knew he was doing it. If they ever got wind of him, they'd just fire him and be done with it.

He dreamed of going public. That wacko who took on the Colombians with the windstorm guns, he had it made. Going out and giving the big blow-off to anybody who got in his way.

Of course, it was all for show. The guy with the blowguns was all bark and very little bite. He'd get his own pretty soon. Just a matter of time.

Meanwhile, there was much to be learned from the people who were trying to stop the Hurricane.

Shep had used his accidentally broad security clearance to create his own official authorization to have even greater security clearance. This was one of those loophole areas where there should have been a system of checks and balances—but there wasn't. Shep's authorization gave him the power to authorize any kind of surveillance. He tapped into intelligence feeds from around the world and through the federal government, and he had been laboriously backtracking the authorization for all activities in relation to the Hurricane.

The level of autonomy that they had—whoever it was who was chasing the Hurricane—matched Shep's. Shep refused to allow anyone else to have what he had. Otherwise, there was no point in his having it.

He was going to find out who it was and find out

what they were up to and who they reported to and what their sphere of operations was. Once he knew all about them, he'd know if he could place them under his control. If he could, great. If not, he'd sabotage their whole agency, one way or another, and get rid of them entirely.

"Preston Huich," Shep said to his dingy Pentagon office. "There's a name for you."

He was looking at one of those funny orders, issued overnight during the few hours that Shep had gone home for a shower and a change of clothes.

The individual on record as having issued the order was Homeland Security Special Projects Commander Preston Huich.

Preston Huich did have a personnel file of sorts, and it was so well constructed that it survived Shep's initial inspection. Only when he started background checks to verify the personnel files did he stumble upon the truth. Huich had nothing *except* a personnel file. No registered status with the DOHS. No military clearance. No driver's license in any of the eastern states or in D.C. His home address in Arlington was a plumbing-supply store.

"They're starting to get sloppy," Shep announced aloud. He was alone in his office, as always. He didn't have an assistant. He couldn't even get access to a secretarial pool. "Preston, you're not covering you're tracks as well as you should."

IT WAS LUNCHTIME when the nonexistent DOHS official issued more orders. Shep heard the alert beep and dropped his corned-beef sandwich. Preston Huich had just issued an order for U.S. peacekeeping forces in Colombia, working side-by-side with the Colombian army, to evacuate civilians from the projected path of the blowgun boy, the Hurricane, but to refrain from engaging the Hurricane at all costs.

"How come?" Shep asked aloud. "Answer—so they can send in their own people to handle the situation."

What would be really cool, Shep decided, would be to find out who those people were. If they were CIA agents or military intelligence, dispatched by a secret agency to do dirty work, then Shep could issue his own, higher-level orders to those same agents, requiring they report all their activities to him.

But that didn't pan out. There were seventy-eight federal agents inside Colombia without the authorization of the Colombian government. Fifty-one of those agents were there to spy on other U.S. federal agents. A few of them were there to investigate reports of illegal U.S. agents inside Colombia. They all checked out as perfectly legitimate intelligence operatives and they had been there since before the current crisis.

The agents the supersecret agency was deploying had to actually be employed by the agency, meaning they might not officially exist—just as the agency itself did not officially exist.

The only way he was going to get a line on the field agents was by tracking them in the field. Presumably, the agents would be on the heels of the Hurricane in Colombia.

Thomas Shep went looking for an enforcement arm.

They'd have to know how to work in Latin America. They had to be experienced special-operations professionals. Since they would be working with him, he'd prefer not to take personnel already working for the CIA or military intelligence. It wouldn't be prudent.

Better that it be a small, multipurpose paramilitary outfit, with the skills and training needed for operating in a variety of situations. They had to be ruthless and fearless, but mostly they had to be available.

Thomas Shep scanned the assignments databases from every branch of the military. There were SEAL and Ranger teams all over the world at any given time, but, damn, those guys needed a lot of support. Shep could order up whatever military support was needed, but that would create conspicuous activities that might raise questions. Cover-up would be a headache.

There were other outfits that were trained to be placed into dangerous field assignments with little or no support, but they were tightly controlled. Acquiring their services would invite notice at the top level.

He'd been hard at work for an hour and hadn't found what he wanted, and it was frustrating.

"Oh. Well, here we go," he announced to no one. He scanned the relevant assignment details. Yes. These guys were doing busywork in Louisiana. They took the heat for some major screw-ups a while back, and they were paying the price with an unpleasant, trivial assignment.

Shep could conscript these guys and no one in the federal government would bat an eye.

He began making the arrangements.

16

The docks at Turbo were deserted. The people cleared out in advance of his arrival, and Harry Kilgore was almost disappointed. As he cut the engines and drifted to the shore, he felt a waft of disillusionment. Maybe he'd had enough. He had proved to the world he was as unstoppable as a true hurricane.

What was the point of going on? Would it be a better use of his time to get back to the U.S.? He had a long stateside to-do list.

But Kilgore hadn't yet fulfilled his mission. It was carefully mapped out. He'd gone to the Bahamas to set the stage for the mission, which was to illustrate that the Hurricane could not be cheated or tricked or outsmarted. He would allow no entity on this Earth to resist or thwart him. No matter how powerful they were, no matter how feared by normal society, the Hurricane was *more* powerful. Even an entity as ruthless and evil as the infamous Fortoul cocaine cartel was helpless against him.

The Colombian drug cartel was a perfect foil.

Christophe Fortoul had survived assassination, governmental interference and an international arrest warrant. Fortoul was known worldwide. To enter the man's own realm and take him down would stamp Harry Kilgore indelibly and permanently with prestige such as no other man had achieved in the modern age.

This prestige was all-important to Harry Kilgore. It would be the start of global payback.

Kilgore's scheme had depended on the cartel refusing to pay ransom for the stolen cocaine. Kilgore knew before this started that he would be chasing Fortoul to his very home in Colombia. This bold, extraordinary act that would help make Kilgore's reputation.

But there were lots of cartel kingpins, all of them known killers. Kilgore could have targeted any of them. What placed Fortoul at the top of the short list was his hobby. Christophe Fortoul was a collector of fine gemstones. His collection of only the rarest, highest-quality stones was as famous as he was, and it was known to be worth upward of a hundred million bucks.

Harry Kilgore thought gemstones were cool. What was more, cash was big and bulky. Gems of a comparable value were compact and lightweight.

As he drifted in the silent waters toward the docks of the city of Turbo, Kilgore knew he could take or leave the gems, but he couldn't fail in his mission to cement his reputation as a man who could *not* be betrayed.

So, into Colombia he would go. His ocean voyage

ended here, in the port town of Turbo, and here he would find suitable transport to the interior.

Kilgore saw a sign of life and realized the wharf was not completely abandoned. A man hurried to hide himself behind a brick wall, but Kilgore spotted the assault rifle. Why would there be a man with an assault rifle when everybody else had clearly evacuated?

Kilgore directed his catamaran to the man with the rifle. He found himself in a section of the wharf posted with Keep Out signs in Spanish, English and a few other languages. The skull on the sign reinforced the message.

The signs looked new, and this part of the dock was well-maintained. Kilgore pulled into a wharf with a long ramp leading to a dry dock. It was obviously used to repair the more expensive vessels that sailed Colombian waters.

Kilgore didn't care whom the big boat belonged to. What he cared about was the value of the boat, and the value of the guards. Hopefully that would translate into expensive ground-based transportation, as well.

He was looking up the ramp at the stern of a beautiful white hull. Stylized turquoise swirls that represented waves were outlined and half-painted. When she was done, she'd be gorgeous.

"Be a shame for her to get all banged up," Kilgore announced. His voice carried far amid the silent, empty docks.

Kilgore fired an aft air cannon. It burst against the

hull of the yacht. All of a sudden, she wasn't beautiful anymore. He blasted her rails. He directed a blast over the top deck. Teak planks flew out and bounced on the floor of the dry dock.

"I assume this boat belongs to a very important man who will be very angry when his boat is ruined," Kilgore shouted. "Especially when he finds out that none of the men he assigned to protect his boat did anything to stop me."

The man with the assault rifle showed himself and opened fire on Harry Kilgore. He wasn't alone. Kilgore let them pepper the defensive airbursts until he had located all of the men in their hiding places.

As they were firing, Kilgore was playing with the Deer-Destruct-R range finder. He'd bought it in Wisconsin at the Outdoorsman's Mega-Mart, and the salesmen swore up and down it would work on any prey. Not just deer. The output data was pretty basic, but Kilgore got it to feed into his autofire systems.

"If this doesn't work," Kilgore said, "there's a Mega-Mart sales associate in Madison who goes on my death list."

The sales associate would never know Harry Kilgore's merciless vengeance, because the Deer-Destruct-R range finder worked reasonably well. The air cannons delivered their bursts on top of each of the gunners. The gunfire stopped. There was only the squish and drip of the remains.

He found their vehicles nearby. A lone sentry was

guarding the cars, and he tried to figure out what he was looking at. Kilgore's out-and-about suit had many little gadgets hanging from it on hooks, linked together with power cables. Kilgore was also carrying a megaphone, but when he pressed the power button the only sound that came out was a rude *poot*.

The guard was squashed as if stepped on by a giant, invisible boot. It crushed his bones and liquid squirted out in all directions.

Kilgore was quite pleased at how swiftly he was able to improve his design. The first operational air cannon had weighed down the rear end of a station wagon and had been too powerful, really. Kilgore had dialed down the volume of gas to be entangled to ten percent of the maximum, and still it blew Professor Laft into the wall hard enough to make him stick to it.

Now Kilgore knew how to miniaturize the entangler and his emitter design made them easier to control. He squashed the car guard from about the same distance as Professor Laft, just as effectively, and he did it with an emitter he could hold in his hand.

He *was* a genius.

There were three vehicles, and they were just what Harry had hoped for. New, powerful, fully equipped SUVs. He chose the Hummer. Lots of cargo space. Low mileage. Fewest flecks of gore on the paint. The keys were in the ignition. Harry drove it down the dock ramp and filled the rear end with equipment from the catamaran.

Then he parked the SUV in a workshop adjoining the covered dry dock and secured the doors with alarms from a very cool scientific surplus store he found in Rochester, Minnesota. The alarm was made for old ladies, who put them on all their windows and doors so they would know if a bad man was breaking into their condominium. Kilgore had replaced the beeper with a shotgun emitter. It could mortally crush a human being at a range of six feet or less.

Kilgore needed to work in safety.

He mounted a quartet of air cannons atop his new vehicle, and that was just for starters. He covered the windows with protective shields. He mounted video and audio pickups, antennas and transmitters.

There was a ruckus outside that lasted just a moment.

Kilgore started making trips to the catamaran. The boat had remained unmolested during his absence—although there were the corpses of Colombian army commandos on the wharf and a few more drifting in the murky waters. The boat's autodefense systems remained operational. Kilgore turned them off by remote control each time he hauled a load of supplies from the catamaran. Finally he stripped off the emitters themselves. He unclamped them from the boat, clamped them onto the vehicle. The SUV roof was forested with horn-shaped devices.

He pulled out of the workshop as another gaggle of paramilitaries moved, guns blazing. Kilgore wanted to do a full systems evaluation anyway, so he test-fired each emitter in sequence. The paramilitaries were annihilated by the time he was finished.

He sent a big blast into the catamaran. He'd learned to like the big boat. He'd miss it, but he sure couldn't take it with him.

Kilgore felt the eyes of the people of Turbo on him as he drove through their city. It was disturbing at first to be watched by all those eyes from all those buildings and from all those hidden shadows. But then Harry began to think it as a sort of ticker tape parade, without the ticker tape or the applause. A gravely serious ticker tape parade. What mattered was that all those people were looking at him. They were all in awe of him. It took a special kind of power to shut down a city—and that felt good.

But then it went back to being unnerving, hearing only the sound of his engine and the snap of rocks under his tires. He craved a fight. Where was the army that was supposed to protect the people? Would they let him traverse their city without resistance?

His concerns were answered when he reached the Cacarica River, which sliced the city in two. Kilgore found the city police, or army, or whoever they were, waiting for him on the far side of an old concrete bridge. On the other end of the bridge were armored cars, tanks and sandbagged bunkers. There were police cars and a fire truck that had lost more red paint than it kept. The equipment was arranged into a half-circle around the only way out of town, on the far side the bridge. The message was clear. If the Hurricane wanted out of the city of Turbo, he would have to go through them.

Which was fine with Harry. He drove onto the old bridge, listening to the whine of his wheels on the steel grates set into the surface, and headed into the fight without hesitation.

But then he paused and hit the brakes, realizing he had put himself into a precarious position. What if there were explosives already staged up and under the bridge, ready to go off as he crossed?

The men in the defensive force on the far side of the bridge appeared subdued. Not ready for battle, but waiting for something to happen.

Ah. The military never really expected to engage him, because they fully intended for him to be at the bottom of the river ravine.

Kilgore stopped the car, got out and walked around the front.

The forces on the far side of the bridge seemed to shift as one, nervously.

Harry adjusted one of the air cannons to point it far out in front of the vehicle, then he sat back in the driver's seat and engaged the weapon. The military men were visibly startled by the first blast of the already legendary thunderclap.

It wasn't a big airburst, and it didn't detonate any explosion. The bridge trembled, then was silent.

Harry was wondering what it was all about when he noticed daylight peek through an opening in the bridge surface. More holes appeared, as the air cannon blasted the surface ahead like a noise minesweeper. The bridge surface progressively disintegrated. Harry observed the entire bridge surface crumble like a cookie and sprinkle the muddy river at the bottom of the ravine.

"Aha!" Harry announced.

The Colombians had acted with greater-than-expected intelligence. They had set their structural engineers to work on the bridge long before Kilgore got there. The integrity of the bridge was hammered away, leaving only a thin shell that disintegrate beneath him. All that was required to make the trap work was the weight of Harry's vehicle.

"Smart," Harry said. "Good thinking. Not good enough, though. Can't outsmart me."

That's what he said aloud, but silently he was wondering how close he had actually come to driving over the booby trap and ending his Hurricane career right then and there.

Not close. He hadn't screwed up. He was too smart and too careful to screw up. If anything, he had just proved how sharp a tack he really was.

Harry rummaged behind the seat for a tool pack and stepped out of the car again, this time with a tape measure.

The bridge's welded steel support beams had survived the man-made collapse. Harry measured their diameter, the space between them, then examined the front end of his Hummer critically. He stretched the metal tape in front of the Hummer, measuring the wheelbase.

The Colombian defenders were watching him. The day was eerie, dominated by the rumble of their equipment but not a single human voice. He could feel their eyes watching him curiously. He didn't dignify them with so much as a look—just clambered back into the high seat of the SUV and shoved it into gear, then adjusted the wheel until the body panels on the passenger side came into contact with the concrete barrier. The metallic body supports screeched. The plastic panels sounded as if they were being chewed up. Harry kept the car precisely on this course and drove into the place where the concrete surface no longer existed. The front end dropped and bounced, and then Kilgore was driving on the steel support girders.

His hands locked on the wheel. He couldn't afford even a minute deviation. A few inches to the left and his wheels would ride off the supports. His Hummer would bottom out on the supports, and he'd be in a hell of a fix. Worse, the vehicle might manage to slip through the gap in the supports and he'd fall with it to his death.

But that wasn't going to happen. All he had to do was drive straight. He could do that. He did do that. The car pulled onto the solid concrete bridge surface on the far side, and then Harry Kilgore had conquered another barrier. There was nothing else in his way except for the Colombian military, police force and fire department.

They were of no consequence, as he was about to make abundantly clear.

He grabbed the microphone from the case on the passenger seat and announced, "I just got this car."

The nervous Colombians hadn't known what was coming next, but that sure wasn't it. The translation spread like wildfire through the ranks and there was a collective look of bewilderment.

"I'm extremely displeased. I haven't had this car for more than half an hour, and it's really the nicest car I've ever owned, and you guys made me go and ruin it."

There was silence. Kilgore let the Colombians think about what to do next.

"People have been treating me like crap for twenty-nine years. The other kids in school. The teachers in school. The other grad students at the university. And especially the professors at the university. My bosses, every boss I ever had. They all treated me like crap. I never had a good job. I never had any money. So I've never had a good car. Until today. I get this beautiful Hummer with the most perfect paint job I ever saw, and I drive it a few miles and now it's ruined."

Kilgore spotted the commander of the gathered forces, who stood up in his jeep with a megaphone held to his mouth. He was wearing sunglasses and had a huge swoop of dark bangs hanging over his face like an awning.

He spoke through the public-address horn. "Get out of joor car. Joor under arrest. "

"I wasn't done talking," Kilgore said. "You can just shut up."

"No, joo shut up," the commander answered.

"No, you shut up," Kilgore insisted, and he backed up his command with a highly precise blast from the air cannon. It was his finest sniper emitter, designed to pinpoint a small, distant target. The sales associate at the Outdoorsman's Mega-Mart had showed it to him.

"I ain't even going to try to give you the sales pitch on this baby," the sales associate said. "It's too damned expensive. Look at the price tag. I don't expect you to buy the thing, my friend, but if you're a *real* hunter and you want the best range finder there is, this is it. You want to hunt deer? You could be on one rim of the Grand Canyon and tag a deer on the other rim. Yeah, it is that good."

The price tag was outrageous, but Harry's latest armored-car job had made him a millionaire for the first time in his life. So he bought the range finder. It was now mounted on the dashboard with suction cups. Kilgore focused on the loudmouthed commander who was his target and let the little computer find the distance. The readings triggered the emitter, which *poot*ed softly and delivered an airburst only a yard in diameter, but centered exactly six inches from the commander's skull.

His head and shoulders were inside the burst zone, and those parts were crushed by a wall of 400-mile-per-hour turbulence. The other occupants were smashed into their seats as if by a giant hammer. The jeep was pushed down until its tires burst, and then the body panels deformed against the old highway as the jeep's doors bulged open and glass flew.

The commander's crushed remains were propelled into the windshield frame hard enough to force the flesh and bone to wrap around the edge. The mangled head came off the body as if his neck had been beaten apart with a table leg.

"Good shot," Kilgore announced to himself.

The shot was so precise, in fact, that the commander's personal guard, standing at the front corners of the jeep, escaped serious injury. They realized how lucky they were when they jumped up and took in the sight of the ruined vehicle.

The machine gunners started firing without orders. The tank commanders popped into their holes, slammed their hatches and commenced the attack. Foot soldiers unleashed an undisciplined barrage from behind their sandbags.

Kilgore let his automatic systems take care of the incoming fire, which was exceptionally easy for them to handle since it all came from the front. No attack from the rear this time. The Colombians had learned something from the debacle at sea.

Still, they failed to truly believe that their weapons weren't going to penetrate his protective force field. They were wasting ammunition. The streaks of brown and the brilliant tracers would seek out the Hummer, then seem to change their mind and head elsewhere. The low-mass rounds from the rifles bounced off like marbles. Even the heaviest, most powerful rockets were wobbling off course like spitballs. They thudded into the river or cracked on the bridge. A few even struck buildings across the ravine and opened up fiery holes.

Harry laughed, his adrenaline skyrocketing and his nerves jingling. Even with his air cannon shielding him, it was an unsettling thing to be on the receiving end of so much military aggression. Still, he wasn't afraid, really. Just angry—and he enjoyed anger. Right now, he was getting angry all over again about something that happened a long time ago to his very first car.

Harry bought his first car when he was seventeen. It was a true beater, a 1974 three-speed Ford Maverick with rusted-out body panels and a hole where the back-seat floor should have been, but he was proud of himself for making enough money to afford it. He waxed the paint—what there was of it—by hand, and he thought it didn't look all that bad.

But within twenty-four hours, somebody had taken a key to the paint and scratched the word *loser* on the driver's door in huge letters.

His beautiful car was ruined, and Kilgore knew who did it, because the kid bragged about it in class for weeks. The kid even taunted Harry to his face. He dared Harry to do anything about it.

Harry was too afraid to stand up to the kid. "You really are a loser!" the kid announced.

Kilgore had looked up the kid just a couple of weeks ago. It had been one of his planned stops on his long drive from Portland to Miami. The kid, now in his thirties, was Henry Founder. Call him Hank. At first he couldn't even remember who Harry Kilgore was. Harry reminded him about the 1974 Ford Maverick.

"If I did that I'm sorry," Hank insisted, trying to free his foot. Kilgore had ingeniously blasted Hank at the moment he was into his very car, which was sitting on the driveway of his house. The door was crushed on Hank's ankle, and then Harry strolled up to explain the reason for his visit.

"Even that doesn't even the score," Harry explained to Hank, referring to the wounded leg. "My pain and suffering and the value of my old car, plus interest on all of that. You'd be amazed how much you owe me, Hank."

Harry blasted the house. It was convenient that Hank lived out in the middle of nowhere in Utah, and his wife had already left for work. Hank had been about to head off to his office job when Harry caught up to him.

"My house," Hank gasped.

"Not anymore. Now it's your pile of trash. I think it's only fitting that I ruin your car, too, since you ruined mine." Harry had still been using the station wagon emitter back then, and he adjusted it with the hand crank while Hank sobbed.

"Let me go, Harry."

"No, thanks, Hank."

"Please!"

"Who's the loser now, Hank?"

Hank blubbered. Harry fired. Hank's Toyota caved in and flipped across the front yard, taking out a decorative tree in the process. They were going to have to use tweezers to separate the pieces of Hank from the pieces of dogwood.

Oh, man, that was sweet.

But it still didn't settle the score. Nothing could make right what Hank had made wrong. Kilgore had been cheated out of the pride and pleasure of his first car—just as he was cheated out of every other normal good thing that other people took for granted.

Yeah, his life had sucked—until recently—and revenge was sweet, and right now there were a bunch of Colombian Hank Founders out there just asking for a sweet plate of Kilgore revenge.

"Scratching the Hurricane's car is a crime punishable by death," he announced into his speaker. The barrage was weakening. The Colombians realized they were doing no damage.

Kilgore pulled forward and commenced firing. He blasted far ahead, in the paths of the retreating foot soldiers. They stopped. The blast reversed into them and they were sent flying. The ones who were still alive tried to get to their feet, but invisible cracks of thunder crushed them to the ground like giant flyswatters.

The mobile units were fleeing, and Kilgore hit them high and low. He triggered a blast of air inside the tank gears and watched the tread belt unravel. He burst a big round alongside the fire truck as it raced away. The truck reared up on half its wheels, then flopped on its side. A small series of bursts were placed at the windows, obliterating the interior and whoever was inside. The other jeeps and troop trucks were simply crushed. The sandbags were demolished, along with any human being who hid behind them.

The tank remained sealed. Kilgore was stymied momentarily. He couldn't let the tank crew escape unpunished simply because they had good armor. He blasted the outside of the tank, denting the shell and pushing it around, but they were just dents. The inside would still be intact. As he blasted it again and again he realized he was pushing it toward the river, and that made it clear how to finish off the tank. He sent more bursts under the front end, shoving it to the lip of the ravine.

The hatch clanged open. "We surrender!" shouted the soldiers as they clambered out, their hands squeezing their ringing heads.

"Whatever," Kilgore replied, and he delivered a blast to the top of the tank that sent the tank crew flopping end over end into the ravine.

Then, as a final touch, he sent the tank in on top of them.

In the quiet that followed, Harry could actually hear the mournful hot breeze.

HARRY ENGAGED THE TRACTION control when his wheel spun in the pond of blood, and he felt the accusing eyes of the city on him again as he moved back into the narrow streets. It wasn't like a parade anymore. They weren't even in awe of him. Harry could feel only the hatred of the people of Turbo.

That was nothing knew. Kilgore had always been an object of disdain to the kids at high school. He was disdained by the stupid students in his engineering classes as an undergrad. He had been despised by his professors while working toward his doctorate—how they hated him for succeeding in doing what they could never do.

Harry had always been forced to take a certain stance in the face of this disdain: simply stand there and let the hatred pour down on him or fight back. But he had never had the strength of character to fight back.

Not until now. Now he was a new person, and he never had to put up with that disdain again.

He sure didn't have to take that kind of attitude from a bunch of Latin American ghetto dwellers.

He shot into the apartment buildings, and he imagined the silent hatred of the people transforming to sudden horror when their homes exploded around them. He struck the cars alongside the streets until they burst into flame. He targeted the front support pillars of a concrete walk-up flat until it crumbled and the building trembled visibly.

Harry hit the gas and drove fast as the walk-up collapsed into the street. Cartwheeling bricks chased Harry Kilgore up the street and made him whoop.

That showed 'em. He was Harry the Hurricane and now they understood all about it.

And to be sure the message was hammered home, he kept bursting buildings all the way out of town.

17

They stepped off the relief-aid supply ship at the dock in Turbo, and Remo decided that one messed-up dry dock wasn't nearly as bad as he had expected. Still, the people working the wharf had the hollow-eyed look of citizens who'd just endured an air raid.

A car was waiting for them, courtesy of Harold W. Smith.

"You sure this is the right town?" Remo asked the aid worker who handed him the keys.

"I'm sure."

"Because this doesn't seem so bad, really. Just some property damage."

The aid worker wanted to get back to his duties, whatever they were. He sneered at Remo and jerked a thumb over his shoulder. "Why don't you head into town that way and see if there's enough destruction to satisfy your exacting standards."

Remo slid behind the wheel, and Chiun was already in his seat with a sort of expressionless look that Remo knew well. On any other human being, it would have been a look of serenity. On Chiun it meant irritation and impatience.

"You would be even more ticked off if we ended up driving around the wrong town," Remo said.

"The Emperor would not send us to the wrong town."

"We'll know soon enough."

They drove through the somber crowds in the streets of Turbo, following the main highway to a bridge over the river that split the city. Across the bridge was a ruin of still smoking vehicles.

Remo steered the compact Japanese car over the surviving bridge supports, and when he was halfway over he noticed an upside down tank at the bottom of the ravine, with the sluggish river water rising behind it and flowing over the corners.

"We shall join them in the river if you do not watch the road more carefully," Chiun said.

Remo steered around the cleanup crews working the remains of the battle, and found himself on a street lined on either side with devastated buildings, burning apartments, crushed cars. The ruin stretched ahead of them for as far as they could see. Amid the rubble of dismantled bricks and snapped lumber, Remo spotted flashes of gray-white flesh. A body was being extracted from a pile of cinder blocks by a feverish rescue crew. Remo pulled around them and could hear one of them calling excitedly for a medic.

They thought they had a survivor on their hands. Remo regarded the body carefully.

"They're wrong," he announced.

Chiun said nothing.

Remo could read a human body like he could read Korean: expertly. He could spot the changes in blood flow in a human finger as it squeezed the trigger of a gun—and he could distinguish the unique pallor of flesh under which the blood had ceased to circulate. He knew the cast of skin that had been devoid of blood for minutes or an hour or a day.

The body of the man that had just been pulled from the rubble was in the first category. The blood had stopped minutes ago. The man had survived the attack of Harry Kilgore and had survived being trapped in the rubble for hours—only to die just as the rescuers reached him.

Remo could see ten, twenty more destroyed buildings up ahead.

"Guess he went this way."

THE DESTRUCTION CONTINUED to the very edge of the city. "This Hurricane is really mad about something," Remo said. "I thought I had a clue about this guy, but I don't get this."

"One of you can be likened to Master In Yeom the Younger," Chiun said. "The other likens to the warlord encountered by Master In Yeom."

Chiun looked at Remo expectantly.

"Well?" Chiun asked.

"What?"

"Will you not tell me that you recall In Yeom from your studies, but cannot quite remember what it was he accomplished as Master of Sinanju?"

"Matter of fact, I do remember Masters In Yeom. A couple of them. In Yeom Senior and In Yeom Junior."

Chiun lowered his forehead over his eyes. "No Sinanju Masters were called Junior and Senior."

"Something like that, though. In Yeom the Elder and In Yeom the Younger."

"You are correct. Thus far."

"Homebodies, right? Worked for Koreans and the Chinese and In Yeom Junior never even left the peninsula if he could help it. I think he's not highly regarded in the scrolls."

"In Yeom the Younger was known to be skilled, but his career is undistinguished," Chiun admitted. "He lingered too close to the village, even when there were few opportunities for employment."

"Hated to travel, huh?"

"He allowed himself to be too enamored with the woman who bore his children," Chiun said. "He was known to have bypassed urgent, high-paying employment for the sake of remaining close to his offspring."

"A family man?"

"A mediocre performer."

"I envy the guy."

"But I pray you shall never emulate him. He made just enough to maintain the fortunes of Sinanju."

"Hold on," Remo said, looking into the sky for tidbits of Sinanju history. "I remember that In Yeom Senior made a mint. So In Yeom Junior inherited a load of cold, hard gold. Right?"

"What of it?"

"So In Yeom Junior managed to hold on to all that wealth during his time as Master and you're giving him grief? What more do you want?"

"In Yeom the Younger could have done better. He might have increased the riches of Sinanju to greater levels than his father. Instead, he was complacent, and that equates to failure."

"You say failure. I say he had his priorities in the right place."

"And I say this is not his story," Chiun said, exasperated. "What know you of In Yeom the Elder, besides his celebrated income levels?"

Remo struggled to come up with relevant details. The problem was, there had been a lot of Sinanju Masters whose history was recorded during the past five millennia. Remo had studied the scrolls until his eyes bugged out, and he could name them all, in order of their stewardship. But naming them was not good enough. Chiun was perpetually asking for details. No matter how good he got, Remo knew he'd never be able to store as much historical data as Chiun. Remo wasn't exactly the scholarly type.

Remo snapped his fingers. "Spent a year in Africa. The kingdoms across the north were jostling for good land because the forests were turning into desert. In

Yeom the Elder saw it as a place he could make some real money and he was right. That's where he earned his big fortune."

"An example In Yeom the Younger would have done well to follow," Chiun said.

"But this is not In Yeom the Younger's story," Remo reminded him.

"Yes. In Yeom the Elder found many opportunities in Africa, where the shrinking of the forested lands spelled doom for the many kingdoms that had thrived there for centuries. The people were driven out of their territories, and so they made to take the lands of their neighbors by force. And then those lands became un-livable, as well. There were centuries of perpetual war-fare, and this meant great opportunity for an assassin."

"Sounds real nice."

"Hush. In one such land was a king named Jun B!k and his son, Jun D!k." Chiun's tongue clucked to replace the vowels that should have been in the middle of the names.

Remo said, "I see."

"You wish to titter."

"I don't."

"Jun B!k was a noble king, with a great wealth of gold, which he wore on his person. These kingdoms had little use for stone palaces, but they made much of their adornment. Jun B!k's ancestral lands were reclaimed by the sands, but he had taken new lands by force, and was a powerful king. But he had a devious son in Jun D!k."

"You can never trust those sons."

"Jun B!k told Jun D!k as a boy that he would be king. Why should he not, when Jun D!k was clearly his heir? Jun D!k grew up to become an extremely tenacious man, who always obtained whatever he put his purpose to. It is said he slew the women who spurned his advances— even the daughters of his father's generals. Eventually, he was of age and took his place as a prince in the court. This did not satisfy him. He was impatient to be king."

"I saw that coming."

"He began assuming powers, only to have his father strip them away again. Jun D!k claimed power was his birthright—and even demanded of his father to know when he would die, so Jun D!k could have the throne that was rightly his. Jun B!k began to suspect his son would even do him harm in order to take the throne."

"What? That would never happen. Would it?"

Chiun ignored him. "Jun B!k was on guard, and soon enough caught his son in the act of putting poison in the family's food. The boy would have murdered not just his father, but his mother, his father's other wives, many of his younger brothers and sisters, all so that he could take the throne before his due time. Jun B!k stood Jun D!k before the court in chains and proclaimed the son was no longer his heir and did not have any claim to the throne. Jun B!k banished his son, and named another son his heir."

"Did he stay banished?" Remo asked. "The bad sons never stay banished."

"He did not stay banished," Chiun confirmed. "Jun D!k gathered brigands and criminals and waged war on his own father. Twice his father captured him and elicited his promise to remain forever outside the kingdom. Each time, Jun D!k failed to keep his promise."

"Rotten sons never keep their promises. You have to wonder why the dads keep trusting them."

"Finally, Jun D!k contacted Master In Yeom. He wished to hire him on contingency."

"Huh. In Yeom knew better, I hope."

"Of course."

"What kind of a contingency?" Remo asked.

"It does not matter."

"I'm interested."

"He wished to pay Master In Yeom a small retainer," Chiun explained, making it clear he was exercising great patience. "Then, after In Yeom assassinated King Jun B!k and Jun D!k became king, he would pay In Yeom in gold from the treasury. Jun D!k did not take well to Master In Yeom's unwillingness to bargain for his services, and even accused the old Master of being a fraud. Jun D!k realized a moment later that three of his highest-ranking soldiers had been beheaded, silently and in a matter of a few heartbeats. Jun B!k was convinced then that In Yeom was no fraud."

"I should hope so."

"Jun D!k performed his most duplicitous deed then. He returned to his father's court, claiming to have seen the error of his ways and eager to take his place again among the family. He claimed he wanted no position of power. He fooled his gullible father, who allowed him to take up residence with the family. Within days Jun D!k had fled again—taking many of the gold ornaments of the king. He melted the adornments into bars, lest In Yeom be reluctant to accept stolen goods, and thus purchased the services of a Sinanju Master. In Yeom accepted the gold and assassinated Jun B!k. After all, we judge not. Sinanju is simply the tool of gold-rich kings, and it is not our place to weigh what is perceived as right by some, and what is perceived as wrong by others."

"Speak for yourself," Remo growled.

"Jun D!k stormed in with his ragtag army and put himself on the throne. The court and the people rose up against him, slew his companions and drove him out, all this coming to pass even before his father's funeral feast was done. Jun D!k summoned In Yeom and demanded that In Yeom keep his side of the bargain."

"Uh-oh," Remo commented.

"Yes. In Yeom, quite reservedly, explained to Jun D!k that he had kept his part of the bargain. 'And yet, I do not sit on the throne!' Jun D!k replied, speaking with the elegance of a snarling hyena.

"To which In Yeom answered, 'Our agreement was that I assassinate your father, the king. This deed was carried out perfectly. My part of the bargain is fulfilled.'

"To which Jun D!k said, 'The purpose was not fulfilled, for I do not sit on the throne.'

"To which In Yeom said, 'If that was your wish, then that is the bargain we might have reached. I would have gladly assassinated all the warlords and princes and other men of power in your father's kingdom, and the price for each head would have gone down as the count rose. But this is not the bargain we agreed to. Moreover, I will no longer take your assignments, Jun D!k, for you are no longer a powerful, deposed prince, but merely an inept schemer, with no hopes any longer of becoming king. The Masters of Sinanju do not take assignments from rabble."

"I say again, uh-oh," Remo said.

"Yes. You see what comes next. Jun D!k was enraged."

"I'll bet."

"He called In Yeom coward, traitor, thief, and set his last surviving soldiers, twenty men or more, upon the Sinanju Master."

"Poor In Yeom!" Remo said regretfully. Chiun gaped at him. "Kidding. I'm certain In Yeom wiped them out, no problem."

"He did, but he left Jun D!k alive and disfigured, so that he might become infamous throughout the fading north African kingdoms and enhance the renown of the Sinanju Masters. This practice was most effective, and never again did In Yeom face accusations of deceit, or any other disrespect."

"I see."

"There is more."

"I'm listening."

"Jun D!k, as I said, was a tenacious man. This tenacity did not fade with his disfigurement. Even he knew that he would never sit on his father's throne, so he transferred his energies to the waging of war on In Yeom."

"Sure. He blamed In Yeom for ruining everything."

"True," Chiun said. "How did you know this?"

"Those kind of people always find somebody else to blame for whatever goes wrong with their own lives."

"Yes. This sums up Jun D!k precisely."

"So," Remo concluded. "In Yeom lives in fear for the rest of his life, always looking over his shoulder in case June-Dork shows up to kick his ass."

When Remo glanced over, Chiun appeared seriously distressed.

"Kidding!" Remo said. "Just a little fun to cut the gloom."

Chiun shook his head and plodded on. "Jun D!k did indeed pursue In Yeom, even out of Africa and across the ocean, to India, and eventually all the way home to Sinanju. Many a time Jun D!k caught up to In Yeom, and each of his attacks made him a mockery in the eyes of the people. In Yeom was quite pleased with the impression this produced among all the local kingdoms, so time and again he spared Jun D!k, although mercy would have demanded otherwise.

"Jun D!k fell far behind on their travels and spent time imprisoned and enslaved, but was driven by his passion to escape each time. He came at last, as I said, to Sinanju, some thirty years after In Yeom. He tracked In Yeom as the old Master walked through the village, and the African prince was so driven by his obsession that he seemed to have forgotten all he had learned about the skills of the Masters, for of course In Yeom smelled Jun D!k's putrid stench and heard the thuds of his clumsy feet.

"In Yeom at last showed Jun D!k compassion. He turned on the trail, leading Jun D!k into the thorns, where the pathetic creature became ensnarled. The rains eased his thirst, but he starved to death some weeks later."

"Quite merciful on In Yeom's part," Remo said.

"Yes."

"But not really a reassuring story, Chiun. I don't see me as In Yeom, that's for sure. If I were to guess, I'd say that I'm supposed to be the African dingbat, June-Dork, right? Are you trying to tell me I'm going to keep biting at the heals of this blowhard Kilgore until I die of old age?"

Chiun pursed his mouth. "The lesson of this story careened over your head—this is astonishing to me, as your head is so huge, it is unlikely anything could miss colliding with it."

"Thanks for adding insult to insult. What's the moral of the story, then?"

"What you should hearken to is the nature of the man Jun D!k. He is like the one with the mighty billows. He is filled with obsession and this shall be his undoing. He was an effective robber of currency transporting trucks. Did not the Prince Regent tell us he made millions of dollars with this enterprise? But now he has left all that behind to strive fanatically on the one purpose of getting his due from the drug merchant."

Remo considered that. "I do get it, Chiun."

Chiun narrowed his eyes, unwilling to take Remo at his word.

"This guy's a brainiac and geek and he's been pushed around all his life. Boo-hoo. He got sand kicked in his face, you know, probably been ridiculed and taken advantage of. Now he's a Charles Atlas success story and he's got big muscles and he can kick anybody's ass on the beach."

Chiun shook his head. "You speak nonsense. Sandy beaches have nothing to do with the story of In Yeom and the tenacious Jun D!k."

"Sure, it does. Kilgore's always had to take whatever crap's been flung at him. Now he's not going to take it anymore. He's not going to let anybody get away with it, not ever again."

"Yes."

"He's obsessed with righting the wrongs against him, no matter what lengths he needs to go to make it happen, like June-Dork."

"Yes. Like Jun D!k."

"So we need to attract some of that single-mindedness away from Fortoul," Remo added. "If we get Kilgore really mad, really determined, we might make him do something really stupid."

18

Gherhard's Grunts had a reputation, once upon a time. They were one of the paramilitary outfits sent into the caverns of Afghanistan to try to flush out Osama. Gherhard's Grunts never found Osama, but they found plenty of trouble in the form of maddened Taliban and other maniacal disciples of the anti-American cause. The Grunts came, they saw, they kicked a lot of al Qaeda ass. They soon had the reputation of being the baddest sons of a bitches in Afghanistan.

They were sent to Iraq and given the toughest, deadliest missions. They always succeeded in those missions, and they always left a trail of bodies in their wake. They were talented, they were fearless, they got the job done.

They were also the most foul-mouthed, unpleasant bunch of soldiers ever to come out of Special Forces training, which meant they weren't ideal for use as a public-relations tool.

Gherhard himself was interviewed just one time for television. He ended up using the F-word so many times the interview couldn't be aired. Even bleeped, it was obvious that Gherhard was describing his military mission in the crudest sexual terms.

To make matters worse, Gherhard was rumored to have engaged in intimate relations with the British reporter who conducted the interview, only to drive the woman out of their hotel, sobbing, in the middle of the night.

"She was butt ugly," Gherhard was known to have said. "I couldn't lie to the poor bitch."

Sadly for Gherhard, the unattractive BBC reporter was his last-ever taste of female delights. The Grunts were ambushed—in Topeka, of all places. Actually, a few hundred feet under Topeka. Gherhard's gnawed bones were collected weeks later.

Only two Grunts came out of the Paradise Caverns alive. Grunts Yeepod and Lay attributed their survival to their sense of loyalty. They had stayed with Gherhard after he sustained wounds, even when their attackers ordered them to march ahead. They were just steps away when the captors set upon the wounded Gherhard. It was a cannibalistic feeding frenzy.

Not the first cannibals Yeepod and Lay had run into. Shit, what do you think the al Qaeda were living on while they hid in the mountain caves for months at a time? Yeepod and Lay weren't so shocked by the feeding they didn't know when to make a run for it. They bolted back up the main cavern, shimmied into a side crack in the limestone and stayed there for days.

When they came out, they learned that they were the only survivors of the subterranean grunt maneuvers.

BUT THERE WERE TWO OTHER Grunts who hadn't even gone on the Topeka mission. Konk and Shredder had been in a hospital in Frankfurt for months recovering from recent wounds. Some idiot SEAL stepped on a land mine during a joint mission in Tikrit, and Konk and Shredder were nailed by a load of sharpnel. They were enduring therapy to regain the use of their damaged limbs. When they heard that their fellow Grunts were all but wiped out in battle without them, they closed down a wing of the military hospital with a profane demonstration of mourning.

There was a reunion months later. Just the four of them, sullen and bitter. They had a few beers in a bar near Fort Bragg and toasted their dead buddies.

"The fucking Grunts."

"The fucking Grunts!"

They had been stifling their emotions but now they felt ready to let some of the sorrow come pouring out. A table full of Marines asked them to keep the swearing down, and that was all it took to open the floodgates. The brawl resulted in three broken tables and seven broken Marines.

But was it the last gasp for the Grunts? There was nothing left for them to do. Four men didn't make an effective paramilitary unit. Joining the ranks of another unit seemed like a sacrilege. Then an opportunity opened up in Louisiana and they grudgingly took it.

GHERHARD'S GRUNTS Elite Special Forces Training Facility was the best idea to come out of the United States military in years. It solved a host of problems—and it spurred recruitment.

It was the only civilian Special Forces training facility in the United States that was actually operated by the Special Forces.

The facility was built on an old army base in Louisiana. That meant the military could avoid trying to market the property, which would mean going public about high levels of pollutants that had been collecting in the soil since the base had opened in 1941.

The facility gave the military great publicity, since it attracted high-profile clients.

Even better, it raked in the dough.

It was the brainchild of a Marine colonel who was a recruitment director, but who disliked sullying the Marine ranks with professional boxers and heavy-metal rock stars. It seemed every year there was another world-famous tough guy who wanted to join the Marines to prove just how tough he was.

The problem was, these celebrities required special treatment, because there would always be reporters and girls trying to get in to see them while they were in basic training.

The boxers and rock stars were never as tough as they thought. They always ended up with a discharge from basic training. They just couldn't hack it, plain and simple. But they couldn't admit *that* to their fans, could they? So invariably there were charges that the Marines forced the star out by giving him a training regimen that was way more rigorous that the regimen of other, non-famous Marine recruits. This meant a lot of bad publicity for the Marines, no matter how untrue it was. It also required a response and recruitment marketing efforts to combat the bad publicity. It was a lose-lose situation for the Marines.

The wars in Afghanistan and Iraq also created more public interest in the Special Forces. Recruiters were flooded with applications for the Rangers and the SEALs. The Rangers and the SEALs didn't add to their ranks that way. First you had to be in the military, and show some aptitude, before you could even be asked to apply for Special Forces training. Of course, that didn't stop recruiters from accepting thousands of enrollees with vague assurances of Special Forces opportunities.

That created its own backlash.

Then came the Sunday-morning infomercial for a fitness academy in Napa Valley offering Special Forces–style fitness-training retreats. A week of training with "genuine ex–Special Forces commandoes" cost you $4,899. The Marine colonel saw the light.

He developed the Elite Special Forces Training Facility concept. Get *real* Special Forces training with *genuine, working* Special Forces commandoes. They didn't offer "retreats"—they offered boot camps. "You're not going to learn Special Forces skills in

Napa," said the straight-talking infomercials, which were mailed on DVD to every celebrity in Southern California. "You wanna learn paramilitary tactics, you come to a military base. You wanna learn how to drink wine, you go to Napa Valley if you want."

The cost for a week? Twenty thousand dollars. "That's about how much the U.S. government pays to train a Navy SEAL for a week," the grunt on the infomercial said. "Yeah, you can pay less if you want. But you won't learn a fucking thing. So what good is it?"

The phones rang off the hook. America's toughest celebrities vied for enrollment. When the first session started, there wasn't an empty bunk.

Gherhard's leftover Grunts put them through their training—two professional wrestlers, a British hard rock singer, the playboy son of a California senator and several businessmen looking for thrills.

"They're all fucking losers," reported CO Lay to the Marine colonel, whose reputation had a stake in the camp's success.

"Fail one of them," the colonel said.

"Why? Sir."

"It'll be good for business."

"Making a guy who paid us twenty grand look bad is gonna help get more business? How the fu—how do you figure, sir?"

"Trust me."

Rap superstar Ominuss Bulj flunked Special Forces training and the news spread like wildfire. He was supposed to be the toughest music maker in the East Coast hip-hop scene.

Yeepod was interviewed wearing his signature grin. "This ain't a spa. It's military training. We're not giving out free diplomas. If you don't qualify as a Special Forces paramilitary commando, you just don't qualify, and I don't care if you're a rapping loudmouth or not."

Ominuss Bulj claimed he was set up to fail, but the other celebrities from his class were not supportive.

"That Bulj bloke's so muscle-bound he can't even tie his own shoes," said Oswald Shrieker of Birmingham, England's retro metal band Shriek. "You shoulda seen 'im in a wet suit. He almost drowned the afternoon we learned our underwater rescue skills. Course, I came through with flyin' colors."

The Marine colonel was right. Failing the rap star cemented the credibility of the Elite Special Forces Training Facility. If Ominuss Bulj couldn't hack it, it had to be really tough—because everybody knew what a hard-ass Bulj was.

This was real training, and not everybody could handle the intensity.

If anybody could do it, they wouldn't be called *Special* Forces, would they?

"WE'RE A BUNCH a fucking whores," Yeepod griped over a beer. The four Grunts made a habit of gathering in their private rooms in the evening. "We've been doing this for months and there ain't been even one guy who's come here that I couldn't kick his ass in my sleep."

"Whatever," Lay said. "They go away happy."

"Even fucking Bulj was happy." Konk laughed. Ominuss Bulj, the only attendee ever to fail, had actually paid another twenty grand for a second week of Special Forces training, determined to salvage his reputation. He passed, and now he had only praise for the facility.

"Well, I ain't happy," Shredder complained into his bottle of Bud.

"Yeah," said Yeepod.

"Yeah."

"Yeah."

Then came the phone call and Lay got Yeepod off the obstacle course. "Phone call. They want to talk to all four of us Grunts. Yeep, it's the fucking Pentagon."

The four leftover Grunts gathered in their slovenly office and were addressed on the speakerphone by an intelligence officer named Shep.

"I need you boys," Shep said.

"We ain't a fucking unit no more," Yeepod said. "We're, like, fucking gym teachers."

"But you're still the best that there ever was."

"You got that right," Konk said. "But there's only four of us left. Sir."

"That's exactly right for a tough, low-profile foreign insertion force. You want the job or not? I'm not going to order you to take it—this is too important. I need dedicated soldiers. What I need are the fucking Grunts. Is that you, gentlemen?"

When it sunk in, the Grunts couldn't believe their luck. "It sure the fuck is," Yeepod said. "Sir."

19

When Remo glanced over a few minutes later, he was surprised to see Chiun fiddling with a plastic box of electronics. The screen came to life and tiny sounds came from the speakers.

"Since when do you carry a laptop?"

"Hush."

Chiun watched the screen intently. From the sounds and dialogue, it seemed to be some sort of bad reality show about cheating housewives.

Remo didn't care for reality television shows, even though he had almost starred in one himself. He had never known Chiun to be interested in reality TV, either.

The sound from the speakers was dominated by the voiceover of a man who described the heinous infidel-ities of the women he was apparently videotaping at a distance.

"Now the little tramp's going into the convenience store," the narrator said. "Probably needs more con-doms or liquor. Look at her. Look how she talks to the jerk behind the counter. Surprised she's not going in the back room with him. Here she comes. Getting in her car. Betcha five bucks her next stop is the motel on the highway. Sure enough. There she goes. And there's the guy. Look at them go. Surprised they don't gag on each other's tongues."

Remo was bursting with curiosity. "Chiun, what is that?"

"Quiet!"

"In they go. Room 12 at the Sleep-Easy Motor Inn. In they go. Door gets locked. Drapes get pulled. See you in exactly fifty-five minutes, folks."

Chiun's thumb worked the little buttons on the device. The buttons tilted this way and that as Chiun flipped through the channels.

"Okay, now tell me what you're watching," Remo insisted.

"Vlog," Chiun said.

"Huh?"

Chiun folded the device and displayed the lid. Remo read the logo.

"iVlogger? What happened to your iBlogger?"

"This is the next step in the technology," Chiun said. "It shows vlogs instead of simply blogs."

"I never quite understood what blogs were," Remo admitted. "Seemed to me they could be anything that people write on the Information Superhighway."

"That is essentially true," Chiun said. "However, no one refers to the Internet as the Information Super- highway any longer."

"Since when?"

"It ceased being used about the same time as 'Y2K,'" Chiun said.

"And when was that?"

"Fah." Chiun was scanning programs at an unbelievable speed.

"Wow. How many channels you got on that thing?" Remo asked.

"Tens of thousands. But they are not channels. They are vlog sites."

"Where you read blogs?"

"Where you view vlogs. Vlogs are video blogs. Any person may put a vlog on a vlog site and I can view it on this device. The iVlogger includes a service to find all the vlogs on all the computers in all the world and present the most interesting via the invisible information that bounces from space satellites."

"Are we talking homemade dirty movies?"

Chiun pursed his lips. "There is much filth. I do not watch any of it, of course. The service knows my tastes and keeps the filth from ever reaching my iVlogger. The vlogs I watch are records of human drama. The vlog I watched a moment ago was the recording of a private investigator who specializes in exposing unfaithful spouses."

"He's got a real enthusiasm for his work."

"Which is why his is a highly popular vlogger," Chiun explained. "Especially when he exposes the unfaithful woman. People around the world tune in to see real human conflict and emotion happen on the screen."

Remo nodded. "They're soap operas."

"Not soap operas. They are reality. There is an intensity to them that cannot be found in any scripted drama."

"I see," Remo said. For years, Chiun had been a soap opera fanatic. "As long as they're not soap operas."

Chiun turned to face him. "You do not like soap operas?"

"You know I hate them."

"Perhaps you should have said something sooner."

"If I told you once I must have told you a thousand times that I hate soap operas."

"Perhaps that is it—you said this thing so many times it became unheard, like the knocking of annoying pipes," Chiun mused. "Maybe you imagined telling me so."

"Trust me. I told you over and over."

"But you followed the stories," Chiun said.

"Never. Some of it sank in because I couldn't escape 'em. Even when I was on the far side of the house I could still hear them—damn these bionic ears!"

"You enjoyed them from a distance, then," Chiun concluded. "Like the great pianist whose wife becomes a competent composer as a result of a lifetime of listening to her husband's practice."

"I liken it more to husband who gets lung cancer from the secondhand smoke of his wife's cigarettes. The Spanish ones were the very worst."

Chiun sniffed. "This I can understand. They were less mired in sleaze and debauchery than the American stories became. This would be less intriguing to any standard white."

"Well, I don't know about that."

"Also, because of your mind's inability to store languages, you would understand little of the drama that unfolds."

"I understood that it was pretty much the same crapola, whether they were speaking Spanish or English or Finnish. The real difference with a south-of-the-border soap was more halter tops and a bigger glycerin budget. Boobs and bawling. Bawling and boobs."

"If you bothered to learn to speak the language, you would know that the stories are sophisticated. The drama is more sincere."

"But you don't watch them so much anymore."

"Not true." Chiun touched a button on the iVlogger, and the screen changed to a list of Spanish titles. With another touch, the screen filled with three rotating images. Three women of various ages, each with a face streaming with glistening tears. All wore halter tops or sleeveless dresses to show off their bare arms and highlight their bosoms.

"¡Excito Totalamente VII!" the screen proclaimed.

"Now I may watch them at my leisure from a disk," Chiun announced. "I have entire seasons with me always for easy viewing."

"Whenever you want?"

"Exactly."

"What if you get interrupted halfway through?"

"I would be vexed. And yet, I could pause the program for as long as I wish and return to it later."

"That's gonna save a lot of lives," Remo said, thinking of all the hapless delivery people and hotel bellboys who had met a premature demise because they happened to knock on Chiun's door at the wrong moment.

"You speak nonsense," Chiun replied. He turned back to his vlog scanning and settled on a video featuring a sobbing woman. Remo drove and couldn't help overhearing.

"It's not your baby!"

"What are you saying, Barbara?" a man demanded.

"Stan, do you remember the semen test? I told you your results were fine but they weren't. I wanted to spare you the humiliation."

"What?"

"So I slept with someone else. I wasn't going to tell you—I did it for you!"

"I can't believe it," said a shocked-sounding Stan. "Who, Barbara? Who did you do it with?"

"It doesn't matter, Stan."

"Tell me who!"

"Ray! It's Ray's child!"

Remo took his eyes off the road long enough to glimpse the screen. The image was static and grainy. The man and woman didn't look like actors.

"Please tell me this isn't real."

"Hush. Of course it is real."

"But it is a soap opera. It's *just like* a soap opera."

"And yet it is true life. This makes it something more."

"Ray?" Stan was barely able to say the name. "My very own brother?"

"Oh, come on," Remo interjected.

"Hush."

"It's a farce."

"It is true life."

"No way. Even if it was real, which it isn't, nobody would let themselves be filmed while they were going through something like that."

"People will take video of themselves doing anything, Remo. The Internet has become the great emotional release valve of the world."

"Okay, but then they wouldn't put it on the air or on the satellite. At some point they'd want to keep it private. It's human nature."

"You are mistaken. Accept this reality in silence."

Remo stewed as Stan and Barbara discussed the situation. Stan was aghast. Barbara insisted she did it all out of love for him.

"You've always had eyes for Ray," Stan said accusingly. "Don't tell me you didn't enjoy it."

Pregnant pause.

"Well? Did you like it or not."

"She loved it," Remo said.

"It was the best ever," Barbara sobbed.

"I knew it." A door slammed.

Chiun's screen dimmed.

"You'll have to tune in tomorrow to see how it all turns out," Remo said.

"Because it is reality, one can never know when the drama will pick up again. Maybe never. Human beings don't always resolve their conflicts in a single simple discussion. Sometimes they don't ever resolve them. We may never know what becomes of Stan and Barbara—but I suspect there are more challenges ahead for them. Barbara, you see, is being pursued by Raymond, brother of Stan. She is tempted by his charms. Those who frequent the discussion groups for this vlog series speculate that she will find herself in his bed again soon."

"So, she's been making videos of her whole affair? And Stan and Ray went along with it, but Stan doesn't know what's been happening?"

"Exactly."

"I bet."

"Meaning?"

"Meaning, they're putting you on. You and everybody else who watches it. It's just some story they made up—which makes it nothing except somebody's home-made soap opera."

Chiun regarded him for a moment, then said, "None of them has the sophistication to act out such a story. They would announce their lies in every word. Many would not see it, but I would see it."

"You have a point," Remo admitted. Chiun knew when people were lying. He could see it in the minute flicker of their eyes, in the changes in their respiration and in the variations in their pulse. Watching someone on a television screen, with the image reduced to faded dots, made it much more difficult to see these reactions—but not impossible. Remo realized that if Chiun had repeatedly watched the show, or vlog or whatever it was, he would have seen through the fakery. "Okay, Little Father. I guess if you believe, then I believe it. I don't quite get it. But I believe it."

"What is most important," Chiun said, "is that you be silent about it."

"Fine."

"Good."

Remo drove on through Colombia and said not a word.

Chiun flipped through the channels, noting with displeasure the flashes of snow that interrupted his viewing. The device was quite expensive, as was the service that charged a fee each month to permit the transmissions. For such an exorbitant sum, the device should work perfectly, even in Colombia. Were there not many satellites staged above this nation, even now, to monitor the movements of the drug merchants? Could those satellites not be made to send vlog signals as well as any other?

Chiun realized he was bothered still by Remo's accusations. Could it be true that the drama of Barbara and Stan and Stan's brother Ray was a falsehood contrived for the vlog sites? In truth, the video quality was poor, and the iVlogger was an imperfect viewing device. Perhaps, through a combination of acting expertise on the part of Barbara and Stan and the poor quality of the vlog, they were fooling everyone and even fooling him, Chiun, Master Emeritus of Sinanju.

In truth, there were vlog episodes that were scripted, but Chiun normally saw through the fakery in an instant and simply passed them by.

He would repeat the Stan-and-Barbara vlog later and view again some of the older episodes, involving Barbara's attempts to keep Ray at arm's length after she allowed him to plant his seed in her womb. If there was any sign of fakery, he would see it.

"Here we are, Little Father," Remo announced, pulling the car onto the shoulder of the road. "I think."

"This is the place Emperor Smith told us of," Chiun agreed, getting out of the car.

They were in the rising foothills, and a huge billboard welcomed them to the Colombia Central Expressway. The highway ascended the hills ahead, while a dirt path left the road nearby.

"Should I bring these?" Remo asked, dangling the car keys.

"No," Chiun said. "We walk from here."

"To where?" Remo asked.

"To a place that is ahead of the Hurricane. The road

winds through the hills. We may scale the mountains on our own feet and intercept him."

"Gotcha," Remo said. "And then?"

"What?" Chiun asked.

"Right. And then what?"

"By then, the Reigning Master of Sinanju will have conjured a plan to disable the Hurricane."

"I see. I guess I better fire up the ol' brain box. Hope I can think and walk at the same time."

"We all hope this."

20

The road descended from a mountaintop plateau, then rose again to a narrow pass between a pair of higher peaks.

Once, the Helenes Pass almost brought the construction of this highway to a halt. The initial plans for the road had called for the highway to simply scale the pass—until a fresh set of surveyors corrected the height of the pass on the engineering plans. It was then realized that the ascent to the top of the pass would have been dangerously steep. The cost to blast the pass down to a reasonable height was too expensive.

"Let's think outside the box, people," said the Colombian president when faced with the crisis. "I want a fresh approach."

The nervous engineering staff tried to explain to the president of Colombia that there were few options. "Engineering is about numbers and terrain. Numbers don't lie and terrain doesn't change on its own."

"What's your point?" the president asked the engineer.

"That there is little room for creative thinking in the realm of engineering."

"Course there is," the president said impatiently. "Easy to see why you're an engineer. No imagination. So why can't we just plant a bunch of big bombs and flatten the whole mountain?"

The chief engineer looked uncomfortable. "That's what we intend to do," he said. "That's what would be so expensive."

"Not if the military did it," the president barked. "He pushed a button on his 1970s-style phone intercom and ordered his military advisers be brought in.

"I want to bomb this mountain," the president said without introduction, tapping a finger sharply on a surveyor's photo of the Helenes Pass peaks.

"We don't have the firepower."

"Why not?" the president demanded.

The minister of defense said apologetically, "Our weapons are designed to kill people. They're soft. They blow up easy. Ground doesn't."

The president was displeased. "What about a bunker-buster."

"We don't have bunker-busters," the defense minister said.

"We could buy a few. Dig some holes in the mountain. Send in the bombs. Watch the whole landmass fall apart."

"Too expensive," the defense minister announced.

"Wouldn't work. Not the right kind of explosive-charge," the engineer added.

"Why am I the only one coming up with ideas here?" the president said.

There was a tense silence. The chief engineer's assistant's intern, who was sitting at the back of the room, became agitated. The skinny, smelly young man was skootching around in his seat and trying not to look at anyone else in the room.

"Go relieve yourself, for God's sake!" the engineer's assistant said under his breath.

"I think," the young man said, "I think."

"You think what?" the engineer demanded.

"I think I know how to get the pass excavated. At no cost."

"Go relieve yourself," the engineer's assistant repeated, and pointed for the door.

"Wait a moment," said the president of Colombia. "I want to hear what he has to say. Young man, what is your idea?"

The engineer's assistant's intern told them his idea.

The engineer rolled his eyes. The engineer's assistant pointed at the door. "Go relieve yourself."

"No. Wait," said the president of Colombia. "It's a good idea. I think it will work."

The engineer looked sullen. His assistant was in shock.

"There's a man who thinks like a real engineer!" the Colombian president said happily. "Let's go with it."

THE HELENES PASS, the Colombians announced, would be left intact. The new national highway would scale the incline, making it one of the steepest road grades in the world.

Colombians were outraged and pointed out that only high-performance vehicles would even be capable of cresting the pass.

"This can't be helped," the president lamented. "We are a poor Third World nation and we don't have the finances to undertake the work of opening the pass. Besides, there are many vehicles in Colombia that will have no problem making use of the Helenes Pass Overlook."

The uproar was immediate. The antigovernment factions pointed out that there *were* many high-performance vehicles in Colombia and they belonged almost exclusively to the drug industry.

"Colombia is building a superhighway exclusively for use by the drug cartels!" announced one government critic.

The outrage spread outside of Colombia. Soon the U.S. Drug Enforcement Administration took up the cause.

"We're going to give the cartels a productivity boost," the DEA told a congressional committee.

"We? We're not doing anything," protested a junior congressman from Utah.

"What we are doing is ignoring the problem," said the DEA liaison.

"Why is it our problem?" the congressman demanded.

"It's directly linked to the flow of drugs to the United States, Congressman," the DEA official explained. "It will cost U.S. taxpayers less overall to address the issue now than it will to fight the more productive drug cartels."

"The issue can't be that simple."

The DEA official nodded. "You're right. Here's our overall-impact study of cartel productivity over the next five years. In scenario A, the Helenes Pass proceeds according to plan, giving the cartels a level of transportation freedom they've never enjoyed before. They'll be able to move goods, weapons and people across Colombia with greater freedom, and the drug flow into the United States will experience a thirteen percent increase in narcotics imports as a result."

"Because of a hill?" demanded the fresh congressman from Utah. "That's lunacy!"

"Okay, Congressman, that's enough," said the committee chairman.

Three days later, the U.S. agreed to fund the leveling of Helenes Pass.

THE HELENES PASS was a narrow, two-lane highway cutting through a V-shape blasted out of the rocky mountain ridge. Remo and Chiun emerged from their hilltop hike to find themselves high above the road on the east rim. The great Colombian highway was deserted for now.

"I just thought of how we'll nab Harry Kilgore,"

Remo announced. "When he drives through, we toss rocks."

"I see," Chiun said.

"That's the plan, take it or leave it. Since you haven't suggested anything better, it's what I'm going with."

A sound caught Remo's attention. He recognized the gentle flap of parafoils. There were four heavily encumbered soldiers descending rapidly on the far side of the mountain they had just come from.

"The Americans are coming," Remo said.

"They always are." Chiun glanced at the figures that disappeared behind the rock. "It is astounding that any intelligent general would dispatch his warriors to battle encumbered with so much matériel they become helpless and clumsy."

"We better see what this is all about," Remo said.

They crossed the mountaintop to the landing place, where the soldiers were stowing their skydiving gear in the undergrowth and making a quick reconnaissance of the area. Three of them faced different directions with their large rifles, on guard against an attack. Remo and Chiun watched from the rocks close by, but the soldiers never saw them.

The one in the middle set up a tripod with a small folding communications dish. "We're on the ground. Beginning reconnoiter."

The four of them hiked to the road overlook where they fell onto their elbows, examining the empty highway with their field glasses.

"I don't see their car," confirmed a sandy-haired soldier, who had an air of command.

Remo frowned. "Who is this *they* that they keep talking about?"

Chiun shook his head, his interest piqued. "I know not."

"You think they're looking for us?"

"Let us question them."

Remo shook his head. "Wait. I think I hear Harry."

They listened to the approaching car until the sound became distinctive enough to be recognizable.

"Somebody else coming," said one of the soldiers on the crest. "It's Subject Blowhard."

Another soldier announced, "No sign of Subject Mao or Subject Buck."

"Buck?" Remo said.

"Mao?" Chiun seethed. "He labels me a Chinese!"

"We'll deal with them later," Remo said. "Come on. Let's get our meet-and-greet ready for Subject Blowhard."

21

The Helenes Pass was now the pride of the Colombian national highway system, and the famous road sign proclaimed in large Spanish words that it was Built with Pride by the People of Colombia. Kilgore deciphered it with his Spanish-English traveler's dictionary. In English, in type too small to be seen by passing cars, was another legend. Kilgore parked by the sign and read the legend, which explained that the earthmoving services were provided by a firm in Flagstaff, paving services came from a Provo, Utah, firm, consulting came from a New York partnership and further consulting services came from a company in Los Angeles. In even smaller type was the explanation, Financed by a grant from the United States of America, but it was almost unreadable under a streak of black spray paint.

Kilgore sat in the car wearing the grin of a man who was enjoying himself. The pass was now just a gentle slope from where he sat. The space between the mountains had been blasted out, and now the highway ran between two steep, jagged walls of stone. A few boulders were sitting on the shoulder of the road where they had fallen.

The sign on the side of the road was yellow and had an urgent message for all drivers. Kilgore didn't need to translate it to know it was warning him to watch for falling rocks.

"Hate to be under a falling rock," he commented to himself, then he lowered the window on the Hummer and turned off the engine. The loud rumble died away and left Kilgore in a blissful silence.

The mountaintop breeze was light, and there wasn't another car on the road. The wide grassy hillside next to the road seemed to soften the daytime sounds. There was nothing but the gentle hush of the breeze.

He couldn't hear any sounds from the pass ahead.

"Looks safe," he told himself. "Still, you never know. Could be an ambush. Oh, well, it's not like I've got another option."

He whistled "Raindrops Keep Falling on My Head" and restarted the Hummer.

Then he drove into the Helenes Pass.

"THIS PLAN WILL NOT WORK," Chiun declared. He stood on the top of a rock, behind a ridge that hid him from oncoming traffic. He'd climbed up on the rock to see what came down the road, and decided at once that the vehicle could only be the SUV used by Harry Kilgore.

Kilgore paused at the roadside, then drove on. He would enter the trap.

Chiun waited with his hands in the sleeves of his robe, gazing at the empty rock face on the opposite side of the highway.

"It might work," said a disembodied voice. It was Remo Williams, who was stationed on the top of the rock on the other side of the pass, hidden behind a rock column, but the strange acoustics of this high, still place carried his voice across the chasm at almost undiminished volume.

"I see little chance for it to work."

"So are you not even going to try?" Remo asked.

"I shall not try. I shall do, and what I do will be executed with absolute precision. You will not have cause for complaint."

"Good. Here he comes."

"Although not having cause has never stopped you from complaining."

"Just send down the danged rocks!"

Chiun sighed and stomped his sandal on an invisible fracture in the cliff side, and the rock wall fell away underneath his feet. It was a two-ton slab of granite. Chiun wasn't on the falling rock slide. He stepped off neatly and moved on to the next unstable rock fracture. Although it might have clung to the mountain wall for another century if left undisturbed, Chiun knew just where to deliver the series of sandal stomps to create a perfect vibration, which undermined the structural integrity like the release of the latch on the back end of a dump truck. Another massive slab surrendered to gravity and tumbled down—until it stopped in the invisible air and crumbled into a thousand fragments.

The thunder was cracking in the Helenes Pass.

KILGORE REACHED the middle of the pass. The sunny day turned suddenly dark. The sky was falling. The alarms blared. The emergency response systems sprang to life. Kilgore took his foot off the gas and drifted.

The interior came to life with the *poot! poot!* of the air cannons, and then the world above changed to a maelstrom of cracking thunder. Kilgore's face was frozen in a grin, but he wasn't perfectly settled. Inside he felt the twinge of doubt. The air cannon had never been tested in this sort of a scenario. It wasn't deflecting the rocks so much as supporting them and carrying them away from Kilgore. Were they powerful enough to do this?

THE OLD KOREAN HAD EXPECTED as much. Kilgore was blocking his ridiculous car with his cracking thunder. It served as a barrier above him, catching the stones. Chiun loosened boulders with his stamping feet until the air filled with a collapsing landslide, and none of it reached Kilgore. It jostled over the barrier until it toppled onto the shoulder of the road, or it flew around the pass crazily and even came soaring out again. Chiun's thin, frail-looking arms swatted at an occasional rock that hurtled back at him on an impact trajectory. These rocks were transformed into gravel. Like Harry Kilgore in the pass below, they flew in every direction but never hit his person. Not so much as a granule of sand touched Master Chiun.

Reaching the end of the blast-rock cliff over the pass, Chiun found a shelf of rock many feet below, then an outcrop of stone. Chiun saw little value in the deed, but still he determined to give Remo's plan his full effort. He stepped off the cliff, fell twice his own height and touched lightly on the loose rock of the blast shelf. He knelt, touching his hands to the swell of stone. It protruded far above the pass like a goiter. It was extrastrong, well anchored. No wonder the blast crews saw fit to ignore it. But Chiun tapped his fingers until he had the measure of the protrusion. It would fall, with the proper application of vibration, and it would create a missile large enough that it just might turn around Remo's ill-advised rock-throwing scheme. A glance told Chiun that the Kilgore car would be beneath this place soon, but Chiun would have just enough time to make it work.

Chiun pounded the rock with his foot, pounded again, pounded rapidly, making the rock vibrate, and he glided across the mound to another tiny fault and slapped the surface with his foot, making a vibration discordant to the first, and he felt the minitemblors meet deep in the muscle of the rock.

The stone goiter rattled like fluttering parchment prayers dangling on twine in a frigid breeze.

The stone lurched, and Chiun felt it give way beneath him. His fingers grasped the rock wall above him, and one sandaled foot found purchase on a ledge the width of a finger. It was a comfortable perch from which to see the results of his action. He doubted it would have an effect on Kilgore, but if it did work, Chiun would be more than happy to accept the credit for making Remo's plan actually succeed.

"Nice work, Little Father."

Remo appeared on the opposite cliff top and together they observed the progress of the great mass of stone. It came down on Kilgore. Chiun thought of a jumbo jet with its wings fallen off and coming to earth on a grass hut. It was odd to think that the grass hut stood any chance of survival.

KILGORE CRAWLED OUT of his seat until his front half was on the dashboard, looking up at what he had created—a bubble of turbulence so powerful that rocks crashed against it and spread out, forming a flow like water over a clear plastic dome. It was almost—beautiful.

His breath caught when the ceiling of bouncing earth above him opened up, penetrated by a spear of stone. Like the tip of an iceberg it came through the surface of the air-cannon blasts, and like an iceberg Kilgore knew it was the great, unseen mass of the larger body of the rock that gave it momentum and forced it through the blast. All this he came to realize in the heartbeat it took for the rock to reach the hood.

The Hummer's front end was pushed down and the hood buckled.

Then the smaller defensive air cannons got to work on the intruder, wrapping it in a swell of airbursts. The rocky tip scraped deep into the collapsing metal hood, which screeched in protest. Kilgore was fascinated to see the rapid erosion of the stone mass under the blasts. The tip of rock was dragged off the hood and the Hummer bounced up, and the hovering stone bobbed in midair, then was lifted up again. The high-level air cannons were concentrating their pounding blasts on the unseen body, and forcing it skyward as its weight was reduced. Then the balance shifted, the air cannons extracted the rock like a sliver extracted by tweezers, and they twisted it overhead, decimating it and driving it away until it exceeded their range and fell heavily to the road shoulder.

REMO STEPPED OFF the cliff side and came to rest atop a bulge in the stone much like the one Chiun had loosed, but this was in the shape of a solid shaft of extrahard stone that seemed to have been driven into the softer cliff rock at some ancient time. Remo felt for the weakness in the stone, but the shaft was deeply imbedded. There might be no way to free it, not in time.

Remo got to his knees, tapped the rock cliff with his knuckles and listened to the faint vibrations of the solid stone. He heard the fractures in the stone cry out from the vibration, but the fractions were minute.

Remo began tapping and pounding the face of the cliff, creating vibrations in the rock that met with one another at the fracture points, turning the small cracks into bigger cracks, turning the bigger cracks into gravel-filled wounds, until the separation of the stone shaft and the rock wall grew halfway to the ground. Remo could sense the movement of Kilgore's Hummer, and knew it moved too fast. It was going to get out of the pass too soon for Remo's plan to work.

There was nothing he wanted to do more than walk up to that stinking car and tear it apart with his bare hands. It was maddening that he couldn't do it. He heard the rock cracking and separating inside the cliff, but Kilgore was almost through the pass.

Kilgore came to a halt with a slight squeak of his brakes, and the sound of his thunder bursts increased in intensity. What was he firing at? There were no more landslides, but there was Chiun standing in the middle of the road

"Chiun," Remo called, "what are you doing?"

"Cutting you slack," Chiun announced. "Hurry, please."

Remo worked his way down the imbedded shaft and heard a crack of thunder that sounded as if it had to have been right on top of Chiun. Remo didn't look. A force like that could crush a human skull—even the skull of a Sinanju Master. Remo didn't have time to look. He would not look.

He looked.

Chiun was still standing there, as if the thunder blast had not even happened.

HARRY KILGORE'S HEART leaped into his throat and for the first time since he had started this project he knew real fear.

The air cannon had failed him. He heard the *poot* followed by the crack of the particle entanglement displacement, but the old man in the brilliant robe was still standing there.

Kilgore triggered again. His aim was dead on. The crack came and the airburst cracked right on top of the old Asian man.

The old Asian vanished and reappeared, back in place. Okay. Kilgore understood now. The old fart was a quick one.

"You wanna play dodge ball, old man?" Kilgore snapped. He lobbed another big blast at the fragile-looking head.

CHIUN HAD THE MEASURE of the Kilgore cannon now, and when he heard the rude little telltale emission of sound from the car and when he felt the sudden diminution of air pressure around him, he knew a blast was upon him. It was but an instant from the delivery of those signals to the percussion of the blast, but Chiun could accomplish much in the passage of time that most people called an instant. He could sidestep a bullet in that much time, and he could just as easily sidestep the long-distance boom of Harry Kilgore.

He slipped away from the boom zone, felt the blast flower behind him and slipped back into place while the pressure dissipated.

"I'm not going to play your oldman games," Harry Kilgore said to himself, but Chiun heard his words.

"You have failed again, like so many times before," Chiun announced in a mocking singsong. Just as he had the measure of the Kilgore booms, so too did he have the measure of Kilgore. He knew how to keep the man in the pass between the mountains until Remo accomplished his deed.

Kilgore answered Chiun with filthy profanity.

"Failure after failure, that is the story of Harry Kilgore," Chiun chanted. "All who know of you also know you are prone to loss at every attempt."

Kilgore sneered. "Is that old man saying I'm a loser?"

"Yes, Harry Kilgore the Magnificent Loser," Chiun taunted.

More filth spewed from Kilgore's mouth. He snapped off a shot. Chiun heard the *poot*, felt the pressure drop and slipped away as the blast came. Then he was right back where he'd been, unharmed and not even ruffled.

"Look up the word *loser* in a dictionary and one is sure to find a picture of Harry Kilgore," Chiun added.

"You wanna be roadkill, old man?" Kilgore fired and Chiun vanished, then came up away from the blast point. Kilgore spun the SUV and fired. Chiun dodged the blast and showed up a few paces away.

Chiun raised his hand, created an L shape with his finger and thumb and pressed it to his forehead.

The profanity streamed out of the vehicle like water surging out from a ruptured dike. Kilgore grabbed his controls and Chiun heard twin *poots,* then felt a large-scale drop in pressure all around him. Kilgore was using bigger guns now. Chiun ducked, slipped, moved away, spidered across the rock-strewn surface in search of the limit of the low-pressure area signifying the edge of the blast zone. His time ran out just as he felt his scrabbling hands enter a zone of normal pressure, and he slipped into the zone after his hands—but he slipped too late. The boom came and the blast of air felt as powerful as a fiery explosion from any bomb. It burst around the small, withered limbs of the old Master.

Chiun wafted into the force of the blast, allowing the energy to dissipate as his body flowed with it, and then he stepped to the ground again, his robes settling around him. Kilgore was scanning for him, but this time Chiun had moved farther than before. The Hurricane was eager to see that he had finally struck Chiun a decisive blow.

Chiun tucked his hands in his sleeves. Kilgore's eyes alighted on him and he voiced his displeasure.

"I'm tired of dawdling with losers," Chiun announced in his lilting voice, which carried into the vehicle. "I leave you to play with yourself."

Chiun drifted away more slowly and Kilgore spun the wheel to race after him—and then the whole mountain collapsed on top of the Hurricane.

REMO POUNDED THE ROCK carefully. Extracting a shaft of dense, hard rock from the column of slightly softer rock was something you had to do just right. You couldn't hurry. Remo tried to make his moves more rapid, but a lot depended on the movement of the fracture through the rock. Chiun was stalling Kilgore and pulling some surprising tricks, but how long would Kilgore wait around?

It was long enough. Chiun moved like a phantom from the pass as the shaft of rock abruptly parted company from its cocoon in the Helenes mountains, and it came out so perfectly that for a moment it remained upright, walking into the pass on its crumbling base.

"Fall!" Remo ordered.

The pillar reached a point of equilibrium. The base was heavy and wide. Remo stepped off the mountain, touched the ground and bounced skyward again, grasping the perpendicular rock and feeling its movement. It was finally beginning to topple.

"That's the wrong way!"

The monolith wasn't listening.

"Do I have to do everything?" Remo slipped to the road and delivered a swift kick into the crumbling base, then swept the fragments of rock out with his hands. The erroneous tilting stopped, and the rock settled on the cushion of gravel that was helping to keep it erect. Remo recalled the old bar trick, where you bet somebody you could stand an egg up on its pointy end. All it took was a little salt sprinkled on the bar top. Settle the egg upright in the mound of salt and it would stand there and you could collect your free beer.

"That's not what I was going for," Remo complained to the rock, then he pounded and kicked at the base, sweeping out the gravel. It was like blowing the salt out from under the egg.

The egg would fall sooner or later.

The monolith lost its balance and came down. Remo felt the cool shade as it moved over him, heard the waft of wind, but mostly he felt the pressure waves in the air and in the earth that told him something big and *heavy* was coming right down on top of him.

It had all taken just a few seconds, but that might have been long enough for Kilgore to get by.

Where was Kilgore?

HARRY COULDN'T BELIEVE what he was seeing now. The young one had wrestled a chunk of the mountain right onto the road and now he was standing under it, breaking off pieces of stone with his hands and his feet, and then the stone began coming down. The young one didn't even try to run. He just stood there, like a lumberjack committing suicide by bringing a sequoia down right where he stood.

Forget that guy—Kilgore dragged the car into reverse and stomped on the gas. The monolith was coming down on him. The air cannons wouldn't stop something that big; they could only accomplish so much.

The monolith crunched hard on the road. The pavement bucked around it. The car bounced so hard on its springs that the front end was airborne and the boom seemed to echo in the hills for long seconds.

Kilgore idled to a stop. The young one wasn't dead. He emerged on top of the fallen monolith, and with a rainbow of color, the old Asian man spirited atop the stone giant, too. They regarded Kilgore and looked smug.

Kilgore snuffled. Then he guffawed.

"You call me a loser?" he shouted. "Morons! Check this out."

CHIUN CRINKLED his brow.

"Why does he call you a moron?"

"He said '*morons*,' with an *s* for more than one. I don't know why."

Kilgore rolled down the window and leaned out. "Were you trying to smash me and just plain missed, or were you trying to trap me and just plain don't know what you're doing?"

"An honest question," Chiun observed. "Which one was it?"

"Well, both, actually," Remo said. "I mean, I thought I'd try to get him under the rock when I knocked it over, but it wasn't my real plan. The plan is just to keep him from getting through. And it's a good plan."

Kilgore couldn't hear them. "Whatever it was it's a screwup. Who's the loser now, Grandpa Chink?"

Kilgore drove to the monolith, rolled up the windows

and began firing into the Masters of Sinanju. Remo and Chiun moved away, but Kilgore didn't follow them. He stayed where he was, and the pass echoed with the cacophony of his blasting cannons.

"He's not serious," Remo said. "He's gonna try to blow his way through that rock?"

"And why not? Wind shapes rock."

"Over thousands or millions of years," Remo said. "Not in an afternoon."

"It will not require an entire afternoon," Chiun observed. The blasts of the cannons were pummeling the monolith like rubber hammers, turning the surface to powder and flinging the powder away.

"It's impossible. Right?"

"A single man without tools freeing the heart of the mountain is impossible to many," Chiun replied. "When it comes to the destructive powers of science, no deed is beyond belief."

Kilgore pretended to be bored. He rummaged in the seat behind him and pulled a sandwich and a soda out of a cooler. By the time the sandwich was gone, the monolith had eroded by eighteen inches.

"Son of a bitch," Remo said. "He's gonna do it. And we're standing here like a couple of dopes with our thumbs up our butts."

"Do not include me in your deranged scenarios. What would you have us do? We've exhausted the possibilities of this particular place."

"You wanna give up?"

22

"Base," Konk reported, "are you fucking seeing this?"

"I'm seeing it," Shep responded, sounding out of breath.

"Who are these fuckers?" Konk demanded under his breath.

"Grunt One," Shep radioed, "my image quality is poor. Can you give me a better shot of those two operatives?"

"Give it a sec, Base. The dust is clearing except at the activity point. Yeep, try for a close up."

THE LAST THING Remo needed at this point was to be in the secret-mission movies made by the American hard-man squad.

"I never give up," Chiun was saying. "I do wish to move on to new opportunities."

"Quit CURE?" Remo said. "Okay, but I'm not working for the Persians."

Chiun stepped off the far side of the monolith. "You know perfectly well what I mean. Other opportunities to overcome Harry Kilgore's insidious machinations. This road goes down the mountain, and there will be many poor villages for him to pass through on his way to the drug lord."

Remo took one last look at Kilgore. He glared at the commandos on the overlook. A lot of help those guys had been. He waited until their little movie cameras were getting a focus on his face, then he turned and stepped off the monolith. He hurried to catch up with Chiun.

"DAMN. I ALMOST GOT a shot of that guy," Yeepod complained.

"He was looking right at us," Konk said.

"We're camouflaged. And we're a halffucking klick from where he was standing."

"I swear he saw us," Konk said.

"Base," Yeepod radioed, "subjects Mao and Buck left the vicinity before I got pictures. I can tell you this much—they match the description you gave us from the Hondurans. Old Chinese guy in a girlie robe and younger white guy with big wrists."

"That's not good enough, Grunts," Shep said.

"You got video of those guys in action. They're fucking unreal."

"The video's shit, Grunts. There's not enough detail to see what's even going on half the time. You can do better than that."

"Understood, Base. We're on the move," Yeepod said, and snapped off the radio. "What a fuck."

THE THUNDER GREW QUIETER as Remo and Chiun descended the mountain. It was a relief. It made it easier to think without all the racket. Still, Remo's brain wasn't delivering any fresh ideas.

"This is stupid," he announced to the towering mountains. "He's just a guy in a silly-looking car. There has *got* to be a way to stop him."

"There is," Chiun said. "If only you would think of it."

"By the way, Little Father, you were talking some excellent trash back there in the pass."

"I don't consider this an achievement to be proud of. It is against my nature to be derisive. If you had dawdled less on the mountain, it would have been unnecessary."

"What about the loser thing. Where'd you ever learn it?" Remo demonstrated the L gesture on the forehead.

"I saw it performed in a vlog and determined that it was understood to signify the word *loser,* which is quite incendiary to Kilgore. He reacted to this gesture with much passion."

"Yeah, you really pissed him off. I thought there was gonna be steam blowing out his ears he was so mad. Who would have thought you knew how to make somebody hopping mad?"

"No one," Chiun admitted. "Certainly not I."

"Yeah."

"I guess you were right, Chiun. It was a stupid plan. But it almost worked, huh?"

"Huh? Yes, the plan left much to be desired, but it was almost made to work."

Remo turned on Chiun. "Thanks to you."

"Yes."

"As stupid as my idea was, you were almost able to turn it into something worth doing. Almost. But not quite. Well, don't do me any favors next time, huh?"

"Huh."

"So my ideas are a stupid. At least I have ideas. You're not coming up with anything. If it were up to you, what would we be doing? Chasing this blowhard cross-country without even trying to stop him?"

"Exactly," Chiun said.

Remo said, "Really?"

"Of course. The man has a goal. We know he is like the African prince Jun D!k, compelled to go to all lengths to right all wrongs against him. Let him travel to the home of the cocaine kingpin with whom he is obsessed, and allow them to have their way with one another. Then we shall be on hand to take our stance against him."

"Tagging along after an enemy is not like you, Chiun.

"More like me than wasting my limited energies on foolish trickery. The Colombian drug mongers are not known to be gentle."

"It's also not like you to let somebody else soften up your targets before taking them on yourself."

"And yet, the man is unlike most, is he not?"

"Yeah."

"There is a lesson I have learned in my years as an assassin for the lunatic Shadow Emperor, Smith."

"What?" Remo said. "You learned something? You mean, you didn't already know it all when you came to CURE?"

"I knew virtually all. Still, no man knows everything. Even a Master of Sinanju cannot understand all the lessons the universe has to teach. Hearken to Wang, the greatest of our forebears. It was he who discovered the Sun Source that is the art of Sinanju. It was he who slew the rebellious assassins of Sinanju and instituted the tradition of one Reigning Master, which has continued to this day."

"I've heard of Wang," Remo reminded Chiun.

"Even Master Wang did not have all secrets revealed to him."

"Okay. I get it. I won't think less of you if you admit there are still lessons to be learned."

Chiun looked at him coldly. "I did not say there are lessons I need to learn now. I said there were lessons left for me to learn at one time. Decades ago, when I first came to the shores of this mad nation to teach an ungrateful new student."

"Fine. Yes. So what was the lesson?"

Chiun withdrew a hand and held up a finger. "It is this—there is always a new kind of enemy. The old ways of Sinanju always serve, but employing them in the customary ways is not always the answer. Time and again we have seen the enemy who perverts the natural laws for his own benefit."

"I think I see. You and I have met more than our share of geeks and freaks."

"I said nothing about geeks and freaks."

"Geeks are techno geeks. The ones who come up with some new ugly twist in the lab and then we have to clean up after them. Freaks are all the rest of them."

"Perhaps this will be the moral of the story of Master Chiun," Chiun said. "Promise me you will refrain from using the words *freaks* and *geeks,* should you ever see fit to record my history."

Remo inhaled. There was a faint twinge of smoke in the clean mountain air, and soon they could see a small village along the roadside, miles below them. A haze of cook fires covered the village. The higher elevations were temperate but they were rapidly descending back into tropical climates, and the homes were mostly wood plank and thatch. The only brick structure was a tiny outpost with a few gas pumps on the roadside.

"Think he'll stop for a fill-up?" Remo asked. "We could put sand in the gas."

"He has many plastic containers in the back of his vehicle," Chiun pointed out. "I think he has much fuel in reserve."

"It was a stupid idea anyway."

"Yes."

Remo sighed, then he said, "Have you got a magnifying glass?"

"I have no need for one. My eyes see perfectly, although I am growing older by the moment and I would not be surprised if they fail before your fruitless fretting is ended. Why, Remo, do you ask for a magnifying glass?"

"I thought maybe we could burn the gas tanks from a distance. You can't stop light with a big wind."

"True."

"Wait. I've got it."

"A big wind?"

"The answer."

Chiun narrowed his eyes. "What answer?"

"I know how to put a stop to him. We burn him. We burn the land all around him."

"He will blow out the fire like a candle flame."

"Maybe. Maybe not. Not if we put him inside a big, big fire. Surround him with it. Light the road on fire. Raise the heat until it cooks him or sucks out the oxygen and smothers him or something. It'll work, Chiun. It's worth a try."

"It is a cheap trick," Chiun said. "Why not shoot him with a gun?"

"Why not throw rocks at him? We can't pull Sinanju moves on him until we can get close enough to him. Until then, we gotta improvise. Fight gadget with gadget. I'm going for it."

Chiun was looking ahead, not answering.

"With or without you," Remo added.

"With or without the Colombians?" Chiun asked. He drew air through his nostrils.

Remo followed his example. There was a tiny extra twang in the air now. Diesel fuel. Machinery. A hint of gunpowder. It was miles away, beyond the village.

Chiun silently asked the question.

"I know an army when I smell one," Remo said. "Maybe they'll take care of the Kilgore situation for us."

"You don't believe that."

"No," Remo said. "I believe he's gonna kick their asssess all the way to Machu Picchu."

23

They were around here somewhere. Those weird special agents couldn't have gone too far, right? Kilgore knew they were superfast runners—on the surface of the water, anyway. No reason to think they couldn't go as fast as a car on land. But he knew they'd be sticking close to him, trying to trip him up.

Whatever they were, they weren't too much for Harry Kilgore to handle. He'd proved that in the mountain. They'd put freaking Stonehenge in his way, and it had only slowed him for a half hour or so.

Really, it was only making the trip all the more interesting. He was getting to try new things and test his capabilities. Every battle gave him data for adjusting the configuration of the emitters, so you could say that every run-in with the old Asian and his younger sidekick was an exercise field optimization.

"Thanks, boys!" he said, but he had to admit he wasn't as chipper as he sounded. The truth was, the strange agents could still have some surprises up their sleeves.

"Naw. They gave it all they had back at the pass," he reasoned. "The young one was about to burst a blood vessel. He gave it his best shot and I got through it fine."

Harry stayed on the alert. They'd try again—they'd try something.

He expected it in the squalid little village along the side of the great highway. They were poor farmers in rickety wood homes with thatched roofs. They had a tiny gas station, with an outhouse-sized building and one pump, and it couldn't have seen a lot business from the nearly nonexistent highway traffic. The operator of the fuel station roused himself hopefully as Kilgore approached, then settled back in his plastic lawn chair to resume napping as the car went past without slowing.

If the strange agents were in town, they didn't show themselves.

Harry Kilgore didn't see the gas station attendant jump to his feet and run into the building after he drove by.

"HE IS ON HIS WAY to you," the attendant reported. "He shall be at the straightaway in ten minutes."

"Good." Colombian General Juanes Rea punched off the phone and issued his orders. His tanks were positioned alongside the road, and more firepower was dotted among the rocks. They were set up at a place where the rolling road emerged from the last of the mountains and became dead flat and arrow straight. The straight-

way went down the middle of a widening corridor between the hills. The house-size rocks lay scattered
around the edges, but the road itself was out in the
open, without cover.

The perfect place for an ambush.

General Juanes Rea monitored the battleground
from far above, in a mobile command center parked on
a rise a mile from the opening into the straightaway. It
was a perfect, high-altitude position from which to
monitor the activities and direct the battle—and far
enough to avoid getting caught in the Hurricane winds.

The dusty Hummer rolled out of the rocks and sped
onto the straightaway. The Hurricane had to have seen
the tanks up ahead, but he never slowed.

"Block his retreat," General Rea ordered into his
handheld radio. He watched through his binoculars.
The tanks flanking the entrance now rolled into the
road, came side by side and reversed into the narrow
passage in the rocks. The way was blocked. The Hurricane wasn't going to escape back the way he had
come, that was for sure.

In fact, the Hurricane showed no inclination to turn
back. He was driving merrily along at undiminished
speed, as the long line of tanks tracked him from ahead.

"Here he comes. Ready the demolition charges."

General Rea watched the vehicle drive across the
dull black X painted on the highway surface,

"Detonate now."

The detonation blasted the road to rubble in two

places. More explosions threw up dirt in a half-circle on either side of the pavement. The Hummer slowed to a halt.

"Excellent," Rea announced to his command crew. They were mostly window dressing. Rea's command needed no assistance.

"He's retreating!" announced a call from the field.

The vehicle did a three-point turn and headed back the way it had come. There was another trench where the highway used to be.

The vehicle rolled off the pavement onto the flat earth and came to the freshly excavated trenches that circled it. The earthen craters were deeper and wider than those in the road.

"Trapped!" Rea exclaimed. "Now pound him!"

The tanks commenced firing.

KILGORE FULLY EXPECTED the Colombians to start pounding him with everything in the arsenal. That's exactly what happened. The automatic defense systems came obediently to life, creating their invisible force fields of particle entanglement over Kilgore and his car. Rockets and gun rounds scattered to the winds before they could touch him. Kilgore's car was an oasis amid the chaos of war, albeit a noisy oasis.

The worst thing was the noise, and for the life of him he couldn't come up with any idea for silencing the air cannons. Their very nature made suppressing the noise impossible. Add to that the racket from the exploding rounds, on top of being under a nerve-rattling rock slide not long ago. Was it any wonder he had a headache? He popped ibuprofen and downed them with a root beer.

"Being the Hurricane isn't all fun and games," he lamented, and he set to work on putting the noise behind him.

CHIUN SAT CROSS-LEGGED on the sun-baked slab of stone, facing west.

"The Colombians aren't thinking outside the box," Remo said. "They have him boxed in, but they don't know what to do with him."

"What do boxes have to do with it?" Chiun asked.

"They're lobbing everything they've got. None of it's getting through to him. His blow horns don't ever seem to fail."

"Why should they?"

"They're machines. Machines never work like that. They break down or misfire or whatever. I guess that's why he's got a zillion of them going at once, huh?"

"Does your 'huh' demand an answer."

"It was a rhetorical 'huh.' Anyway, he'll be free in a minute. He's excavating a ramp."

"WHAT'S HE DOING?" General Rea demanded. "Report!"

One of his field spotters came on the radio. "He's using Hurricane powers to shake up the ground. The trench is caving in."

Rea understood the implications. The earth was collapsing on either side of the detonation crater. The rocky soil and the asphalt became rubble and sloped down to the bottom of the crater. The Hurricane car drove down the slope, where a sheer, three-yard drop-off had once been.

"Bomb the trench!" Rea ordered.

"We've got no more explosives inside the trench," an assistant explained. "They all exploded. In the explosion."

"Bomb the road in front of him. Bomb the way out."

The tank gunners pointed their guns at the gentle slope, but the Hurricane was already driving easily up the incline. The rockets that bombarded him were deflected. He drove onto the pavement at the top of the incline.

"Target the road ahead of him! Destroy all of it!"

The Colombian military responded. Their barrage ripped up the highway for a half-mile stretch.

The Hurricane had no choice but to drive onto the grass and jounce over the ground until he was beyond the ruined road. Quite to Kilgore's agitation, the jostling spilled his root beer.

"SCHMUCKS."

"They failed to kill Kilgore, I assume," Chiun said without turning away from the afternoon sun.

"They barely managed to inconvenience Kilgore. It's ridiculous. All he has is a car that makes noise, noise and more noise and blows hot air.

"Why ridiculous?"

"It just doesn't make sense. He's driving a novelty car, not a superweapon. But the freaking Colombian army can't touch it. Come on, Chiun. It's up to us after all."

"It never was not up to us," Chiun said as they moved like ghosts over the boulders of an ancient rock slide and closed in on a crew of long-range Colombian gunners stationed on the rim of rocky hills surrounding the straightaway. "You don't think the Colombians ever had a chance of disabling him?"

"I guess I was hoping they'd pull some kind of rabbit out a hat," Remo said. "He's just a guy in a freaking car. Seems like somebody ought to be able to bring him to a halt."

"Someone will. We will. But nincompoops such as this?" He grabbed a Colombian soldier by the collar. "Never."

"Okay, Little Father," Remo said. "Don't snap the poor guy's neck. See if he has keys."

The alarmed Colombian was twice the old Korean's weight, but Chiun flipped him upside down and shook him by the ankles until his teeth clacked. A suede wallet tumbled out. A pocketknife. Some coins.

Reinforcements arrived. Three Colombians covered Remo and Chiun with their ancient AK-47s and said something in Spanish that Remo didn't bother trying to interpret.

"Mind if I borrow your car?" Remo indicated the nearby jeep.

The Colombians said something that required the emphasis of a warning shot into the ground at Remo's feet.

"I don't speak Colombian, but I'll assume that's was a 'Sure thing, neighbor.'" Remo moved in on the three gunners, who fired straight at him. No more warning shots. Remo stepped around the flying bullets and extracted their guns. The soldiers saw their weapons become deformed in the hands of the English-speaking, dark-haired stranger.

"There. You. Go." With each word Remo placed a circular band of metal in each pair of hands. "Use them for ring toss. It'll give you something to do while you wait for a ride. Now, keys?"

"Keys?" the tallest soldier repeated.

"Yes," Remo said impatiently, removing the bayonet from the fist of a stocky soldier who was trying to drive it into his liver. The bayonet spun away into the mountains, never to be seen again, while Remo's switch on the spine froze the attacker in position like a wax museum display.

"No keys," said the tall soldier.

"Yes keys," Remo insisted gently, touching the frozen solider on the wrist and making him scream like a soul entering eternal damnation.

"No keys!" the tall soldier repeated desperately. "Stick! Stick!"

Remo touched the stocky soldier's wrist nerve. The screaming stopped.

"Stick?" Remo asked.

"*Sí.* Yes. Stick," the tall soldier said.

"Stick. *¡Sí!*" the second soldier, with his terrified eyes bulging.

"Stick," gasped the stocky frozen soldier.

Remo shrugged and held out his hand. "Stick?"

The jeep roared to life. They all turned to see Chiun sitting in the passenger seat, looking into the distance as if daydreaming.

REMO SLID BEHIND THE WHEEL and found a twig jammed in the ignition key slot.

"You would have discussed the topic of keys and sticks all afternoon, had I not taken the jeep by the stick," Chiun said.

"Yeah. Thanks." Remo depressed the metal gas lever—the actual pedal was missing—and steered the jeep down the hillside, making his way to the highway. When he emerged on the straightaway the military was miles behind them picking its way through the rubble of its own making. Nobody took the initiative to give chase.

A cloud of bluish smoke from their tailpipe polluted the road in their wake. Loose components rattled under the hood, and something was rubbing against the tire, creating a whine that rose and fell with their speed.

"What a noisy affair," Chiun complained. "Every aspect of it is an assault to the ears."

THE COLOMBIAN OUTFIT trudged down the back slope of the overlook, where they were brought to a halt by four more Americans. It was almost a relief that they were normal looking. Their clothes were military camouflage. Their weapons were honest-to-goodness guns.

"We're all friends here," Yeep announced. "All we want is your vehicle."

The glum bunch of Colombians looked at one another. One of them snorted and translated. Another one shook his head and chuckled.

"What's so fucking funny?" Lay demanded. He was in full operational mode, which meant gritted teeth and more gritted teeth.

The Colombians pointed up the way they had come. "You are the Grunts? The other Americans who took our car said you were coming."

Yeepod's jaw dropped. "We're made!"

Gherhard's Grunts went instinctively into a back-to-back formation. Their four evil-looking weapons jabbed at the four cardinal points of the compass, and they slowly rotated. Their footwork was impeccable.

The Colombians applauded politely.

"We need transport," Lay said.

"But the other Americans went away," the English-speaker explained. "In our jeep."

"Give us something else," Yeepod snapped.

"Plenty are available for stealing down below."

"Too risky!" Konk said.

"You're Americans. We are not enemies," the soldier explained. "I think we can lend a car to the United States of America."

"For the record, amigo, we never said we were American," Yeepod snapped.

The Colombians watched the four soldiers vanish into the rocks. The commander pulled out his walkie-talkie and rattled it until he got static. Then he pressed the send button and spoke in Spanish. "There is a U.S. Special Forces team in the vicinity."

"Really?" asked his contact. "How come we haven't spotted them?"

"They just got here. They need transport. They're trying to stay invisible."

"Aren't they always?"

THE RADIOMAN JOGGED UP to the nearest officer he could find.

"Americans? This is just what I need!"

"Special Forces. They're trying to stay unseen. They want a car."

"Good. Fine. Maybe they can do something about the Hurricane." He ordered the oldest rattletrap jeep to be parked at the base of the rocks in a hurry.

"Now, everybody within the sound of my voice," the officer shouted, "look busy in this direction for the next five minutes."

The medics grumbled, but they dragged their patients around so they could face away from the rocks.

The officer went back to berating his men. They faced away from the rocks and he stood behind them, yelling at the back of their heads.

There was a grinding of gears and a powerful bang. An engine whined and stalled. The starter spun and struggled, caught, lost it, struggled. The engine turned over again. Bang! went the backfire. There was profanity murmured in English—vivid, creative profanity. Finally the engine struggled to life again and the sound faded in the distance.

"Can we turn around yet?" asked a soldier in the ranks.

"Wait," the captain advised. There was a faraway bang, beyond the rocks. "All right. They're gone."

The soldiers fell out and returned to their cleanup. The officer received the report from his gun crew about another vehicle taken by the Americans.

"What are they up to?" the officer asked. "Why not cooperate with us instead of lurking over here and sneaking over there?"

"They are Americans." The gunner shrugged. "Who knows?"

THE PRESIDENT of the Republic of Colombia took the reports from the field badly.

"How could this have happened?"

The minister of the armed forces described the methods used in the attack to trap the Hurricane's vehicle. "He makes the power of the wind alter the soil beneath his wheels. In this way he built a ramp to give himself a way out of the pit. We could only stand there and watch."

"What of land mines?" the president demanded.

"We tried this in Turbo. He sweeps the land in front of him."

"Poison gas."

"The tear gas is blown away."

"Electrocution."

"His tires are rubber, just like any car."

"What about some sort of electrical static thing to zap him from a distance?"

The minister of defense tapped his chin dimple thoughtfully and repeated, "Electrical static thing."

THE ELECTRODES CAME from above on heavy-lift helicopters. The generator came with them. The massive cables were connected with bolts, and the apparatus was fired up as the Hurricane's car rolled toward them.

"I say again, this won't work," said the engineer from the electrical-power-generating station. Pieces of the floor of the generating station were still attached to the bottom of the electrodes—that's how much of a hurry the operation was in.

"Why not?" demanded the military officer in charge of the operation.

"He's got all kinds of electrical activity coming off of those microbursts. He's probably some sort of an electrical engineer. Who knows what he could do with a loose static charge."

"What's the worst he can do? Blow over an electrode with a big wind? I don't think so."

"I can think of worse things."

"We're doing it. Deal with it."

The Hurricane's car came closer. He could surely see the great electrical devices sitting on the roadside, and yet he came without hesitation. He had no fear. The Hurricane assumed he wouldn't be harmed.

"This isn't going to work," the Colombian officer said.

"Of course it isn't going to work," said the engineer from the generating plant. "Have you even seen the news in the last week? Nothing stops the Hurricane. He sank half the Colombian navy and destroyed eight tanks and a fire truck. What makes you think you can stop him with a shock?"

"It's not my idea."

"It will be when it doesn't work."

"Oh, shit," the officer said.

The Hurricane drove between the giant electrical devices without slowing or speeding up. The officer gave the order to the electrical engineer, and the devices made a noise. A blue electrical discharge streaked from one of the devices, across the road to the second device, with the Hurricane right in the middle.

There came the thunder crack that deformed the bolt of electricity, bending it up until it was arcing over the Hurricane's car with plenty of cushion underneath.

But the electric arc seemed as if it was stretching too

far. The engineer yanked the power levers—too late. The arch of electricity broke apart and the ends latched on to the empty air, where they met the opposite polarity of the static electricity building in the airbursts. The electricity turned back to where it had come from, desperately seeking a path to the ground.

The engineer, the officer and the officer's crew served the purpose. They shimmied, held erect in the flashing bolts of electricity until long after they were dead.

The electrical devices reached out for one another again over the highway after Kilgore drove away. They sat there, blissfully sizzling away, until the portable generator ran out of gas.

"ONE THING WRONG with the story about In Yeom Senior," Remo said after some time. "It doesn't give us a solution to the Harry Kilgore problem."

Chiun sniffed. "Do not seek all your answers in a simple lesson of history."

"Why not?"

"Because it is not made to provide you with all the answers."

"Why'd you bring it up, then?"

Chiun stiffened his mouth. "Because there is value to the story of In Yeom and the African prince. There is insight that will aid you to understand the idiot savant Harry Kilgore."

"There is?"

"But that is insufficient, I gather. You are a white, and an American. What you want is the easy answer. You would have me quote a parable that is precisely parallel to the circumstances in which you now find yourself, so that you will know the way to solve this problem without thinking of a new and creative solution, using your wits."

"Me? Got wits?"

"A smattering," Chiun allowed. "Possibly."

"You talk like I'm in this by myself, Little Father. Do I have to come up with the solution to the Harry Kilgore problem alone, or are you going to lend a hand?"

Chiun said nothing.

"Maybe you already figured out some way to deal with Kilgore and you're not telling me, so I can figure it out on my own. Be a good learning exercise for me."

"It would. But I have not."

"So it would be nice if there was an answer to the dilemma in the story of Master In Yeom Senior."

"But there is not. What the telling offers you is insight into the character of Kilgore. How he is like the African prince who blames others for all the travails of his life, and focuses his attention on righting the balance. This Kilgore is said by Prince Howard to have lashed out first at all the learned teachers who gave him his gift of knowledge."

"They tried to steal his invention. Don't know if I can blame him for that."

"Then his classmates from his younger years. The

bullies who taunted him and the females who would not consort with him. He held his anger for them for years, however petty the insults, then went back and lashed out at them when he had the power to do so."

"That's a little extreme, I guess," Remo said. "Some people are like that. They get mad, they carry it around with them forever. He's different only because he came up with a way to get back at them."

"Yes."

"But Christophe Fortoul wasn't on Kilgore's revenge agenda."

"He is now."

"Kilgore put him there on purpose."

"He is a man who knows himself."

Remo looked at Chiun. "You're saying he set himself up to get mad at Fortoul? We know he did that."

"He is out to prove something to the world." Chiun said. "He is a man of power now, but he must show the world his power. He will prove his power by challenging a man known around the world to be powerful and brutal, and defeating this man handily. Such a figure is the distributor of drugs, who by his very position as the leader of a cartel must be ruthless, cruel, heartless and a leader of men. To insult such a man, humiliate him repeatedly, destroy his underlings and storm into his very fortress, that takes extraordinary ability. Who could do it?"

"Me," Remo said.

"Why don't you?"

"Because I don't have that same stuff to prove. I get it, Chiun. I understand what he's up to. Just seems like a lot of busywork."

"If the effort were less, the perception of the world would be less."

"I guess."

"You doubt this?"

"I don't understand it, I guess. It's just so much pomp and circumstance, just to look big and tough. Why not do good stuff instead of bad stuff? He could have become some sort of road warrior superhero guy, doing good deeds instead of bad deeds."

"Ridiculous."

"He could use the same name, Hurricane. Driving around in his blow-mobile with his super wind guns helping the innocent and blowing the bad guys."

"You speak foolishly."

"Why's it foolish to expect somebody to not turn bad?"

"Turning bad is the nature of Westerners. Bad is always more extravagant and seductive a way to turn."

"Don't kid yourself. It's the nature of everybody, from Frenchmen to Koreans. Power corrupts. Always and without fail."

Chiun, his hands neatly tucked into the sleeves of his robe, looked at his protégé. "You have power, Remo Williams, and you are not corrupt."

"Give me time."

"I am less young than you, and since childhood I

have wielded the great powers of the Sinanju Masters. I, however, have not become corrupt."

"Yeah."

"The Emperor himself—demented he may be, but not corrupt."

"Okay, I get it. Almost everybody else, though."

"Almost everyone."

"Why is that?" Remo demanded.

Chiun didn't answer that.

"Okay. So. Let's go back to In Yeom Senior."

Chiun looked at Remo. "For what purpose?"

"Still looking for the answer to the Kilgore dilemma. That's why we're tripping through Colombia. Remember?"

"Of course I remember. Why must you fail to remember that the story of In Yeom contained no solution to what we now face? You must come up with this solution on your own."

"Exactly what I'm doing, isn't it?" Remo asked. "I know that In Yeom never had to take care of Prince June-Donk like I have to take care of Kilgore, but what would In Yeom have done if Prince June-Donk was like Kilgore? If I can come up with that answer, and it applies to my situation, then I'll have thought up my own solution. Right?"

Chiun cocked his head. "Yes. Although it is a convoluted way of searching oneself for an answer."

"No matter if it works. And it's not like we don't have time."

Chiun made a face as if he agreed in principle.

"So what would In Yeom have done?"

"You ask rhetorically?"

"Yeah." Remo bit his lower lip. He looked over Chiun's pale pate at the descending landscape to the left. He looked up the mountain to the right. He asked again. "What would In Yeom have done?"

Chiun said nothing. Remo peered back over his shoulder for a moment, at the road behind them. He craned his neck to see the road ahead.

"Aw nuts."

"Do not eat them."

"I meant to say, aw crap."

"My edict holds."

"What I mean is, shucks I can't think of an answer. How about you, Little Father? You got anything?"

"Perhaps. But this is a lesson you must learn on your own."

"Understood," Remo said.

24

Kilgore turned off the highway at Uribe and found himself in farm country.

The crops hugged the dirt road, and the air was filled with the fresh smell of the short trees and the taller, shade-producing jungle trees. The aroma from the short trees wasn't anything like coffee, but it was coffee. Even in this part of the world, they didn't plant coca in plain view of the well-traveled roads.

The orchards were empty, with not a field hand in site. Not a single soul was around when he drove through a small farming village. In fact, the only human beings Harry Kilgore had seen in the past hour was the pair of strange agents. They had apparently helped themselves to a Colombian military jeep, and their plume of acrid blue smoke was sticking on Kilgore's back end.

That was fine with Kilgore. At least he knew precisely where they were.

At the next small, empty village, he was flagged down by a man wearing nothing but a tight European-style bikini swimsuit and holding up a plastic bag filled with American dollars. Kilgore stopped and rolled down the window.

"Good afternoon, Mr. Hurricane, sir. Thanks to you for stopping." The man eyed the roof of Kilgore's car, where a rotating emitter mount made tiny motor noises. The trumpetlike emitter opening was locked on his unclothed person. "As you can plainly see, I am unarmed."

"Obviously. What do you want?" Kilgore asked.

"The government of Colombia would like to offer you a generous fee in return for your agreement to leave the country at once."

Kilgore snorted. "How much?"

"One million dollars, U.S."

"You gotta be kidding. You know how much Fortoul owes me?"

"No."

Kilgore had to think about it himself. "I guess I should know this, huh? He was up to four million. Then he pulled another double-cross when he came at me with his yacht. That automatically doubled the price. So we're up to eight million."

"The government of Colombia can't raise that kind of money," the man said.

"You know what's funny? It's not about the money. Laugh if you want, but it's true. With these babies I could have raised eight million dollars without ever leaving the West Coast of the United States." He patted the dashboard emitter controls. "This is about teaching the world a lesson. Nobody ever takes advantage of the Hurricane. If you try to take advantage of the Hurricane, you pay the price. I'll hunt you down. I'll follow you into hell if I have to. I'll kill anybody who gets in my way. But make no mistake, when I'm done, I'll get what's mine. You tell the Colombian government that there's only one way you're gonna get rid of the Hurricane. I want Christophe Fortoul to personally hand me eight million dollars' worth of gemstones—and apologize for the inconvenience."

"It is impossible," said the man in the swimsuit.

"Not at all. In fact, I estimate I'll be at Fortoul's place in two or three hours. Then we'll settle this."

"He won't just hand you his valuable gems. His collection is his pride and joy, and it is one of the national treasures of Colombia!"

"He'll cough them up if he wants to stay in business, and if he wants to stay in the land of the living."

Kilgore rolled up the window and drove away.

The man in the swimsuit looked despondent and went to retrieve the cell phone he had hidden under the bushes. He was scrounging for it, with his Lycra-clad butt thrust out behind him, when another car pulled to a noisy stop. It was a Colombian military jeep that was reported stolen from the battle earlier this afternoon. The driver was a dark-haired man in a T-shirt. The second man was immensely old and shriveled.

The Colombian was so surprised he forgot his state

until the driver looked him over, nearly naked and holding a clear plastic sack of cash.

"What exactly were you trying to try to bribe him with?" the driver asked, and the Colombian government official turned beet-red, all over.

THEY KEPT KILGORE in their sights. The roads became bumpier and the villages less developed. Where there were no fields or villagers, the land reverted to jungle.

Remo stopped the car suddenly. The land was descending again, and they could see the road ahead make a hairpin turn. The road would pass beneath them.

Remo and Chiun slipped into the dense growth and spirited through the woods with all the ruckus of phantom jaguars.

"Crap. I forgot the stick," Remo complained. "Somebody could drive off in our jeep."

"Good riddance. I would prefer to return home on foot."

They crossed the road. Kilgore was ahead of them, but there were three more passes below them. And they emerged from the undergrowth the next time before he was even in sight. On the next pass there was a little thatched-hut collection of hamlets. Remo and Chiun raced down the dirt road and found themselves surrounded on both sides by shrubs with red-brown bark. It was Colombia's most notable crop.

"I advise against this scheme," Chiun said.

"It's the only scheme I've got. You gonna help or not? I don't exactly have time to stand around discussing it."

"I shall assist."

"You take the front."

Chiun vanished into the fields of coca, which grew under the camouflage spread of jungle trees. Remo remained close to the road until he heard the approach of Kilgore's car, then he pulled back in the fields far enough to be unseen by Kilgore.

The vehicle drove by.

Remo grabbed a pair of fallen branches and rubbed them together at blinding speed. In seconds, the branches were alive with fire.

He flung the branches into the sky to signal Chiun. The blazing branches fell into the fields and flared to life among the shrubs. Remo ripped a pair of limbs of a dead tree and used friction to kindle more killing flame, then he marched into the road, giving birth to fire all around him.

He hurried up the road when the familiar sound of the air cannons boomed across the crops, and then Remo saw a vast conflagration up ahead.

Chiun had outdone himself. The field was transformed in acres of fire. Chiun was nowhere to be seen, but Kilgore's vehicle was attacking the flames. The air cannon pounded at the wall of fiery vegetation and blasted it away. The plants turned to confetti. The fire was snuffed out instantaneously by the forceful winds.

Kilgore careened off the road. He wasn't watching where he was going.

Remo watched through the haze. Kilgore was untouched by the flame, yet surrounded by smoke and racing to and fro. The air cannon were perfect fire extinguishers, in their way. Where Harry Kilgore blasted, the flames vanished. The fire would never reach Kilgore.

But the air cannon's residual wind gusts breathed new life into the fire outside the blast zone, raising higher and higher walls of flame.

Remo heard the whine of the straining vehicle. Kilgore was reversing fast, then racing forward. He was searching for a way out. Could it be that Hurricane Harry was finally losing his cool?

Remo sucked in his breath, opened his arms and ran into the blazing vegetation, harvesting a bale of flaming bushes. He jogged through the fire, watching Kilgore, trying to judge where the man would go next. The object here was to keep him confused. Remo twisted his body like a Scottish caber thrower and sent the big bundle of burning matter into the path where Kilgore had just been.

Kilgore came to a copse of jungle trees and stopped cold. He could get through them, given time, but he didn't have minutes to spare. He spun into reverse, twisted the wheel and found himself back in the conflagration.

He was confused. Where was the path he had just

cleared? Which way had he come from and which way
had he originally been going?

Remo could see the sweat on the Hurricane's face,
the roll of the eyes, the openmouthed coughing.

It was working.

Kilgore hit the gas and barreled forward, blasting a
black streak out of the coca fire. He hit the brakes when
he came to a rock and looked into the rearview mirror
just in time to see a new load of flaming coca tumbling
out of the sky across the path he had just traveled.

Remo was gratified to see the mass of flaming
shrubs come out of the fire to cover Kilgore's tracks. It
was Chiun, keeping pace with Kilgore just as closely
as Remo was, although Remo couldn't see the old Master through the flame walls.

Kilgore was trying to find them in the flames. He
would know by now that he was facing the enemies
from the Helenes Pass. But he seemed to have lost his
focus, and he sat there with his airbursts cracking all
around him while the smoke swirled inside the SUV
and poisoned him.

Kilgore was having a coughing fit, and his face was
bright red from the heat. He was in distress. Remo felt
calm. His blood flow shifted to dissipate the excess
heat, and Remo's flesh rippled in tiny waves to channel the heat off his skin. He exhaled slowly, releasing
carbon dioxide in a trickle. He wouldn't inhale, as the
smoke itself would be poison, even without the unknown toxicity of the burning coca.

Remo revealed himself. Kilgore witnessed the ghostlike appearance of a man who seemed to melt into existence from the very flames. Kilgore coughed spasmodically and shouted in rage, then hit the gas. Remo moved at a measured pace. He didn't want Kilgore to lose him.

Kilgore swerved, chased after Remo, sending out probing airbursts. Remo was leading Kilgore to a dead end inside another growth of jungle trees. All he had to do was keep the Hurricane inside the zone of poison air for a few more seconds.

But Kilgore seemed to snap out of his temper tantrum, hitting the brakes and jerking the wheel into a sharp turn away from Remo. Harry had guessed the plot.

He did what he should have done at the very beginning of the fire; drive straight through the flames until he reached the end of them. Remo pursued him on foot, but when Kilgore emerged from the field fire, there wasn't anything more Remo could do to stop him.

He cursed himself while his enemy sat in his car not a hundred feet away, breathing in the clean cool air and hacking the bad stuff out of his lungs. The cracking thunder encased him, blowing away the vegetation and scouring the tiny tendrils and roots that clung to the dirt.

Remo felt a silent presence at his side.

"It almost worked, Little Father."

"Yes, my son."

"I don't think I can standing listening to that damned racket for another minute."

Kilgore was still coughing violently when he hit the gas again to escape the new pollution cloud he was creating by vaporizing the raw soil around the car. His face was bright red and streaked with sweat and his eyes were red with irritation. He blinked hard to keep them open.

Kilgore pulled another sharp U-turn and headed back into the flames. The coca plants didn't have the density of a forest and the fires were running out of fuel already.

But Kilgore wasn't making his escape.

"What's he up to?" Remo asked.

Chiun hardened his steely eyes but provided no answer.

"I have a bad feeling," Remo said.

Kilgore made some sort of change to his controls, and the endless racket of the air cannons changed their timbre. Kilgore drove into a low-lying copse of burning shrubs, and the air cannon pushed the flames forward without snuffing them out.

"He's moving the fire," Remo said. "Come on!"

Remo rushed into the path of Kilgore's car and threw himself bodily into the flaring mass of vegetation, opening his arms and legs and immersing himself in the bale of plants. He closed on the burning weeds and flames as his momentum carried him out again. He opened his limbs, flung the burning vegetation to the side. His hands traveled down over his body, whisking away the burning ash that still clung to him, and he was just in time to see Chiun entering the zone in front of Kilgore's fire plow, but then the air cannon triggered their response. The air convulsed, and the mind-numbing sound of the cannons erupted in a circle around the moving ball of vegetation.

Chiun felt the eruption materializing almost exactly on top of him. Remo knew the old Master would be forced to retreat from the coming wallop.

Chiun didn't retreat. Chiun sought refuge from the blast by speeding into the nearest blast-free zone—the sphere of flame itself.

"Chiun!" Remo called just as the old Master disappeared inside the twisting, filthy ball of rolling fire.

Remo moving into the tremendous blast noise, not thinking about what he would do when he got there. All he could think about was the vision of the tiny old man sinking into the mass of orange fire like a beautiful bird slipping into the turbulent waters of a lake.

Remo thrust himself into the wall of the blast and felt the sheer power thrust against him. The wind was like jet exhaust. He was fighting the current of a raging supernatural river. He was piercing the shell, but the very dust in the air was tearing at his flesh. His eyes wouldn't open. He couldn't see where he even was in relation to the burning ball that engulfed his father.

Until his hand emerged suddenly from the blast wall into a searing heat and Remo felt another human hand land in his. At that moment his eyes came open just long enough to see though the gray sheer of the blast.

Kilgore was amazed by what he saw. Remo had overcome the force of the Kilgore Air Cannon.

But not for long. Kilgore stabbed at the controls inside the vehicle. Remo locked his hand on the hand he was holding, and then the miserable noise of the blast turned into the sound of a raging, exploding, world-ending explosion. The blast rose in intensity. Remo was crushed from all sides, but he screamed into the wall of noise and withdrew through the storm until the force took hold of him and expelled him like a pebble being ejected by a tectonic eruption. Remo was airborne, tumbling in the air, holding tight on the hand in his hand, and experiencing the searing heat that wouldn't go away. He hadn't just extracted Chiun from the blast. Chiun had brought a ball of flaming debris with him.

Then a friendly tree ended their flight.

25

Remo didn't have much energy left, but he came up with some anyway. He twisted his body when a knobby branch inserted itself like a battering ram in his spine. He tumbled through the leaves and vines, wondering how much farther the ground could actually be. When it loomed up at him like a speeding bus coming on a pedestrian in the crosswalk, he moved through the impact automatically. His body knew how to disperse the energy. Remo was only thinking about getting his bearings and assessing the damage. He found himself standing on his own two feet, but the world was spinning and where was Chiun?

Something colorful descended from the tree, trailing smoke, and hit the ground out of sight. Remo heard the sound when it touched the earth.

The sound was wrong. Any sound was wrong. A healthy, hale Chiun could jump from the highest tree in the forest and land in perfect silence. Remo careened around the tree, almost losing his balance.

And there was Chiun.

"Little Father."

"My son." Chiun was facedown in the grasses, and he wasn't moving.

"Are you okay?"

"I am not."

"Can you stand up?"

Chiun only took a deep breath.

In Sinanju, the breath was everything. The breath was life and strength. After battle with a worthy foe, the entrance of the breath into the body, when channeled into all the limbs and organs, sent back to the mind a signature of the health of every part of the body.

This was little-used in battle, in truth. A Master of Sinanju rarely met a foe so skilled in fighting that he could wound the Master, and even when he did, he was usually wounded in a specific place, in a specific way, and there was no need to perform a full-body medical checkup.

Chiun exhaled, and then levitated off the ground like an acrobat and stood before Remo.

"I am fine."

Remo relaxed, and the world tilted out from under him. Chiun snatched him by the arm and steadied him.

"I'm fine, too," Remo insisted. "I just feel like I've been on one too many carnival rides. And it ain't over yet."

HARRY KILGORE TURNED UP the blasts in all directions. The emitters were getting hot. But he was in danger, and he had a job to do.

The most important thing was taking care of business, and that meant taking care of the strange agents with the weird abilities. They had annoyed Kilgore. They pestered him. And they committed the ultimate sin: they had scared Harry Kilgore.

Not once but twice he thought they had him beat. Surrounding him with burning fields, confusing him, he had almost succumbed to the smoke. If he had passed out, he would have been defeated.

Then he used his brain and got free. Kilgore created his fire plow and began moving it. The young one almost snuffed it out. The old one tried to finish the job but became trapped in the ball of fire. Then the impossible happened.

The young one penetrated the blast and rescued the old one.

Kilgore thought he was done for. If they could get through his air cannon, then he was as good as helpless and it was all over.

But Kilgore realized that the young one was struggling mightily to penetrate the blast, and the blast was a low-volume, controlled shield. A slight adjustment to increase to a higher power would solve the problem.

It was amusing watching the strange agents go flying away like spit watermelon seeds. Kilgore didn't even mind that they had extracted his fireball with them.

He just turned around and grabbed himself another fireball, and drove into the village.

The villagers retreated and the little village became a hell of dancing flames.

REMO AND CHIUN RAN at a steady pace. The run was restorative. They needed to recover their equilibrium. Remo fought to hold on to his self-control—he wanted to tear off after Kilgore with every ounce of remaining energy.

Chiun was seemingly calm, but there was a subtle tension in his very breath, and he kept snatching at the fabric of his robe to examine the singed places.

They walked toward a column of rising black smoke, and emerged from the trees to find the village burning from end to end. The terrified Colombian farmers gathered beyond it, watching miserably as their lives disintegrated.

The thunder noise preceded the appearance of the Kilgore car from beyond the flames. He was circling the village, admiring his handiwork.

He spotted the ragged-looking Masters of Sinanju and waved excitedly. There was a blare of feedback from the public-address speaker tucked among the emitters on the vehicle, and then Harry Kilgore addressed them directly for the first time.

"See what you made me do?"

Then Harry Kilgore raised one hand, made an L with his thumb and forefinger and pressed it against his forehead.

"Guess we knew who the real losers are, huh?" he announced.

His hyenalike laughter became a screech of feedback, and the whole noisy contraption drove off through the smoldering fields.

IN THE LITTLE POLICE outpost, the officer's gun trembled, but he pointed it at the strangers.

"Think again. You no come in here," the officer said bravely in broken English.

"I yes come in there."

"I shoot you first."

Remo nodded seriously. "You're overexcited."

"Say again, please?"

"You've been hearing all kind of reports on the news about awful things happening out in the countryside. You've seen the Hurricane on the TV maybe. You know he's coming your way. You don't know what to do about it. You're under a lot of stress."

The Colombian officer squinted. *"No comprendo."*

"You must believe me, Barney."

"Rodrigo."

"I'm not the Hurricane."

"Proof this."

"He's sure not the Hurricane," Remo added, nodding at Chiun.

Chiun was ignoring the conversation. He was too busy glaring at the scorched embroidery on his sleeve.

"If either of us was the Hurricane, we would have just come and blown you to hell anyway, right?" Remo added. "You think the Hurricane would be so polite?"

The officer examined them. They were ash smeared. They were disheveled. They were entirely out of place in the central cocaine-producing agricultural outposts of Colombia.

"Barney," Remo said sincerely, "you have the only phone in thirty miles. Right? I am gonna use your phone. See? Nothing you can do about it. So just go with the flow."

"Take once step more and jer brains will blow."

Chiun rolled his eyes at Remo. Remo felt the same way. He just didn't have any more nice in him.

He closed in on the officer. The officer saw him coming, but it was too quick to even pull the trigger. Then the gun was gone, and the officer was clinging to the arms of his ancient swivel chair as it spun across the room. It hit the wall and lurched to a stop.

"That's nothing," Remo told him as he worked the phone. "Don't ask for more." He managed to get an operator who spoke enough English to connect him with another operator somewhere in the United States.

"*Korean Gourmet Magazine,* San Francisco," he asked the American directory assistance operator. The number rang and was answered by a distinctly non-Korean young woman.

"Hey. It's me," Remo said. "Is it really you?"

"Depends on who you think I really am," said the woman. "This is *Korean Gourmet Magazine.* "

"Are you Sarah Slate?"

"I'm Rainbough Jerweski."

"Do me a favor. Breathe in and out."

"Pardon me?"

"Deep breath. Release it. Humor me."

"Sir, I'm hanging up now."

"Fine," Remo said, and followed it up with the most insulting four-letter word he knew.

The woman gasped.

"Remo!" Chiun snapped.

"I knew it!" Remo said. "No computer breathes that good. It is you, Sarah. I know it is."

"Hello?" Sarah Slate asked, and yet it was a subtly different Sarah. "Remo, I didn't catch that."

Remo had been very certain of something a moment ago, but now he wasn't sure. "Just chatting with the voice identification droid," he said lamely. "What are you doing there?"

"I work here," she said.

"Where's Smitty?"

"He's been trying to track you down all day. I don't know if you know what's going on, Remo, but there's been big trouble in your neck of the woods."

"Way ahead of you, sweetheart. We've been on-hand for every minute of it."

"That's what we assumed," said the sour intonation of Harold W. Smith as he joined Sarah Slate on the line. "We monitored the rock slide at the Helenes Pass."

"You didn't by any chance send in some paramilitary commandorks to keep an eye on us. They were at the pass."

"We made our observations from a drone spy plane," Smith explained offhandedly. "Diverted from the coca fields. Any soldiers would have been Colombians."

"They were Americans. But their equipment had all the ID removed. They knew about us."

"One moment," Smith said. "Repeat what you just said, Remo. Mark is on the line."

Remo described the commandos from the Helenes Pass. "They called us Subject Mao or Subject Buck. Kind of strange, don't you think?"

"Perhaps not, Remo," Mark Howard said. "Someone in the federal intelligence system is trying to identify CURE as we speak. We know they've been watching our activity in the military networks, so they know we're interested in Harry Kilgore."

"Junior," Remo asked testily, "are you telling me that Chiun and I are code-named Subject Mao and Subject Buck in the CURE computers?"

Behind Remo, Chiun made a noise like many angry snakes.

The stunned officer shrank into his swivel chair.

"No," Mark said. "We do not use those code names."

"They were trying to make movies of us," Remo said. "We didn't let them see our faces."

"This is of some concern," Smith said.

"I guess so."

"I've dedicated Mark to the investigation of the security threat, while I continue handling the Harry Kilgore situation."

"Anything more you can tell us about them?" Mark asked. "Physical description?"

Remo rattled off what he remembered about them. "They mostly looked like any other Special Forces guy you'd meet on the street. One was Yeep."

"Yeep?"

"They were making a movie of us and trying to see out faces and one of them said, 'Yeep, move in for a close-up,' or something like that."

"Maybe he said, 'Yep, let's move in for a close-up,'" Mark suggested.

Remo thought back. "Didn't sound like 'yep' to me. Sounded like 'Yeep.' They identified themselves on the radio as Grunts, for whatever good that does. Think that'll help?"

"Maybe," Mark said, then he announced, "Got them."

"You do?" Remo asked.

"Are you certain?" Smith asked.

"Listen to this," Mark said. There are eighteen possible Yeeps in the active-duty rosters of the armed forces. One of them is a Special Forces combat veteran named Hermann Yeepod with a hard-core special missions detail known as Gherhard's Grunts. They were all but wiped out during one of the subterranean assaults last year."

"You mean, they were albino food?" Remo asked.

"Exactly. Only four of the original Grunts are still alive, Yeepod being one of them. They're running a civilian Special Forces training camp. It's a joint effort by all the military branches to raise cash and recruits. The Grunts were authorized to take leave, together. The authorization came twenty-six hours ago."

"Okay. So what?" Remo asked.

"For now," Smith said, "let Mark deal with that part of the problem."

"Fine. I'm more worried about Kilgore anyway. Did you happen to notice that a rock slide came down on him and yet he's still on the move?"

"The rock slides looked like your work," Smith said.

"But they didn't work. Hurricane Harry just bounced the boulders off of wherever he was. Then we managed to block his path and he just melted the stone out of his way. He eroded it. No sweat."

"I see. The military intervention on the flatlands?"

"We saw it. Barely even slowed him down."

"This is what we hear. There are reports now of a fire in the undeveloped coca districts that are on Kilgore's logical route to the Fortoul estate. Did he cause those?"

"No. We caused those," Remo said.

"I see. There are reports that an entire village was burned."

"Yeah. Kilgore's payback. We almost had him. When he slithered his way out of our trap he was mad as hell. Decided on a little payback. So he took some of the fire we started and used it to burn that village."

"I see. And you couldn't stop him from setting the fire?"

Smith sounded no more accusatory than he ever sounded. Remo was thankful for that. "We were trying to relearn how to walk without falling over. He kicked our butts."

"And ruined a fine and valuable robe," Chiun piped up.

"What's that?" Smith asked.

"Nothing."

Chiun seethed.

"I mean, it'll be in my end-of-mission report."

"Are you okay?" asked Sarah. "Master Chiun, are you well?"

"He's fine."

"My old bones are wailing the story of their pain."

"An hour ago you said you were fine," Remo said. "Right now, we have an idea for you."

"Only Remo has this idea," Chiun cried out. "I have nothing to do with it."

"What is the idea?" Smith asked.

"You know anybody with a heat ray?"

"Heat ray?" Smith repeated slowly.

"A phaser or something?"

"What is a phaser?"

"Phasers are pretend, Remo," Sarah Slate piped up.

"I don't care what it is. I mean anything that shoots heat but not something that shoots matter. Kilgore can stop matter. He can't stop heat or light."

"I see," Smith said. "You're thinking we could direct a high-powered laser into the functional components of the car and cause them to fail. We've considered that."

"Yeah?"

"A laser would be immune to the air-cannon defensive systems. Kilgore considered it, too. The chrome plates covering the vehicle reflect light."

"Yeah?"

"Regardless of the spectrum," Smith added.

"Uh-huh."

"Lasers are just light, Remo. They'd bounce off the reflectors."

"Oh. Like the big winds bounce the bullets."

"Yes. But I'm curious as to why you're even bringing up the possibility."

Remo ignored the question. "You could shoot Harry himself. He doesn't have mirrors. Just fry his guts out long distance."

"Metal halide crystals are applied to the windows. They reflect the light, too, which means they reflect lasers. Light changes cause the crystals to align for greater reflectivity. But this is a most intriguing notion."

"It is?" Remo asked.

"Not one that has a chance of success. What is intriguing is the source. You, Remo. You're not usually interested in employing asymmetrical offensive vectors."

"Yeah. I'm full of surprises. But could you shoot into the car at all? What about through the roof in back?"

Smith considered it. "I don't see the purpose."

"Look, Smitty," Remo said, feeling a stir of excitement, "Kilgore's gotta be hauling fuel in the back.

We've seen plastic containers lined up. All it needs is a good quick flick of the Bic."

"He's thought of that, Remo. The car is encased in shielding. He surrounded himself with a safety housing that can't be penetrated by standard weapons. It's time to consider other options," Smith suggested.

"I'm all ears."

"But I'm afraid we have little to offer," Smith added. "The president of Colombia is considering the use of a thermal device."

Remo asked, "A thermo*nuclear* device?"

"The Colombians don't have nuclear capability. But they do have air power and incendiary explosives. They could drop bombs on top of Kilgore."

"We know what will happen to those bombs," Remo reminded him.

"But if we drop enough of them, the air will become superheated. Kilgore's car won't keep him alive if it's inside an oven. They've seen the satellite images from the village, Remo. They know the plan almost worked once."

Remo pictured the burning coca fields and the burning village.

"It might work," Remo admitted. "If he's hemmed in somewhere. But it would take a hell of a lot of fire. They'd have to act right away, right? We're getting into heavy coke country with lots of farmers."

"The president will hold off until after Kilgore arrives at the Fortoul estate."

Remo's spirits rose still higher. "Nice. I like it. Burn Kilgore, burn the cartel, take out a whole bunch of nasties in one honking bonfire."

"Well," Smith said, "no. The president will wait, as I said, until *after* Kilgore's visit to Fortoul. You have to understand, Remo. Fortoul is extremely powerful and wealthy. He's an important cog in the economic engine of Colombia. Wiping him out, along with his estate, would create chaos. The other drug bosses would rise up against him, whether they were on good terms with Fortoul or not. They would destroy the current government and create national unrest."

Remo was holding the phone too tightly. The plastic made sounds of distress.

"Smitty, are you telling me they're going to cook Kilgore's goose when he leaves the Fortoul estate?"

"That is the plan."

"And how many people live around there?"

"There are many coca-growing villages."

"Many? Lots of people?"

"Yes."

"And what's the official military estimate of civilian casualties?"

"There is no official estimate."

"Put me in the ballpark."

"Perhaps a hundred. Maybe two hundred."

"Ah," said Remo, and he hung up on Harold W. Smith.

Harold W. Smith didn't hear from Remo again for almost twenty-four hours—which was an eternity for both of them.

"HEY, BARNEY?"

"Rodrigo," said the nervous Colombian officer.

"You wanna know something, buddy? We're exactly the same, you and me."

The officer thought he understood what the crazy American was saying, but it made no sense. All he knew was that the crazy American had gone even crazier. Something about that phone call had turned off any hint of humanity in those dark eyes. His eyes, holy Mother of God, it was as if Death itself had come alive in his eyes and the officer could swear he saw a pinprick of scarlet, like fire.

"We're low-level do-gooders. Our hearts are in the right place. We do our best. Right?"

"Yes?" Rodrigo said shakily.

"But then *they* get involved. Them. Up there. The guys in charge. The murdering slimeballs of humanity. They sign off the deaths of a hundred nobodies so they can spare the other murderous scumbags who make profits go up. Doesn't matter if it's the United States or Colombia or Outer Mongolia. They're all slime bags."

"Slime bogs."

"Slime bags, Barney."

"Slime bags. Rodrigo."

"No, Remo."

The officer nodded agreeably, even when they asked to borrow his car.

26

The officer's car carried them through the little villages that peppered the jungle lands. The coca farmers were cleaning up the mess that Harry Kilgore had left behind.

"He seems to have taken a liking to arson," Chiun observed. There were patches of smoldering cottages and swatches of crops reduced to ash. The afternoon rain was still on the leaves and kept the fires from raging out of control, but the damage was bad enough.

"These people don't have anything," Remo said. "They barely survive as it is by selling cocaine to Fortoul. They can't afford this."

"There is nothing to be done for them," Chiun said.

"We can keep them from being sacrificed when the Colombian government burns Harry Kilgore."

"We can?"

"I don't know. I hope so."

"You are quite passionate about destroying this man."

"Why shouldn't I be?"

"He has not hurt you personally. His affronts were aimed at others. Others you would normally deem worthy of death."

"You're right. Fortoul and his dynasty of goons can go to hell. But Kilgore's killed lots of people whose only crime was being in their home when he came through town."

"None of these people were your people."

"I'm a Master of Sinanju. Doesn't that mean I don't have *any* people, outside of Sinanju?"

"I would allow for those who dwell in the Sun On Jo reservation. They can be considered also to be your people."

"Oh, yeah, my daughter and son and biological father. Nice of you to lump them in. You know, I can care about somebody I never met before, Chiun. Most human beings do. They see some poor Honduran family burned alive in their home, it raises some sort of a— what you call it?—*feeling*. Maybe it's because I'm a white-trash American who doesn't have a full allotment of Sinanju blood, but I get that feeling, too. Just a little. Just enough to get me all fired up."

"I see."

"You don't see. You don't know. You don't get it. You don't *care*, Chiun."

"Harry Kilgore bruised your ego, and now you seek retribution on him."

"Go to hell."

"He is a worm who bested a man. He is beneath contempt and yet he has overcome the best efforts of the most powerful assassin on this earth. You. You find this unacceptable."

"You don't know what you're talking about."

"You are so enraged that you have sought foreign means by which to vanquish this foe, rocks and torches, going so far as to suggest to Smith that he fire heat rays at the Hurricane."

"So? Nothing else will stop him."

"You can stop him."

"I can't! I haven't!"

"You will."

"How?"

"I don't know."

"Argh!"

"Exactly. You are guided by anger. Anger is not your friend."

"Sometimes it is."

"It is not now."

"Dammit, Chiun, you're not helping. You're just pissing me off even more. Shouldn't you be throwing a tantrum of your own about now? Look at your kimono—it's fried like bacon."

Chiun said nothing. Remo was watching the blank faces of the villagers who had stopped their cleanup labors to stare at the strangers rolling by.

"Why does it pain you to admit you and Harry Kilgore are not completely unalike?" Chiun asked. "Kilgore is driven by the need to avenge himself for all wrongs, even those that he imagined. Even those that he conjured. He is a madman, yes, but all men enjoy revenge. Even you, Remo."

"So what good does that do me?"

"All insights are useful."

"Thanks a lot, O wise Lama. I'll hold your words close to my heart and let them flower in my soul."

"You're being sarcastic."

"Good insight."

THEY HEARD THE SOUND echoing across the fields.

Remo Williams's body was highly tuned to prevent him from getting typical stress headaches, but the tension that he felt when he heard the noise was almost physical.

They came to the stone gates marking the entrance to the private estate of Christophe Fortoul. Kilgore had just let himself in.

"Oh, Christ." Remo swallowed hard and drove through the killing fields. Fortoul had bribed or hired or coerced a hundred local village men to stand in defense of his house. Kilgore spared them no mercy. Their crushed bodies were piled atop one another, the blood so fresh it hadn't yet begun to congeal. They still had their weapons in their hands. Pitchforks. Shovels. Metal clubs. Kilgore had to have wiped them out without so much as slowing down.

"THAT IS WHAT YOU CALL an army of defense?" asked Christophe Fortoul. He waved at the security monitor, showing the sea of bodies strewed on the road at the gates of his estate.

"What else would you have me do, Papa?" asked Carrillo, his oldest son, a trim, slick man in his late thirties. "There were no armies for hire in the area. I conscripted any live body I could find."

"They're not live now."

"Perhaps you should have planned for this," Carrillo snapped. "Again and again you underestimated this enemy and now it has practically destroyed the family."

"It has not destroyed me yet," Christophe declared. "Form another army. All my men are at your disposal. Take them and finish this once and for all at any cost. Do you understand?"

"Understood."

The spare young woman was ignoring them, biting her long, gleaming fingernails and pacing in front of the security cameras. "Don't screw it up, Carrillo," she snapped.

Carrillo gave her an unpleasant look before the doors closed behind him.

"You and you," Christophe said to his personal body-guards. "Go with Carrillo. Obey him."

"Who'll stay with us?" asked the young woman, whose skirt billowed around her knees, then clung to them momentarily, revealing gaunt, bony shins. Her silk blouse hung lifeless on her shoulders. Her deep neckline was all sagging skin and rib bones in sharp relief.

"We need no one to stay with us," Christophe said miserably.

"Papa, what if this Hurricane gets past Carrillo? He'll come to us in the house."

"This is inevitable. I have sent Carrillo to his death."

Adoncia Fortoul sank her teeth into her fingernails. The manicure had cost her two grand in Miami eight days ago, but sometimes you just had to chew.

"We have to be ready for him, sweetness," Christophe said. "We will give him what he came for."

"Papa! Not the gems?"

"The gems."

"Eight million dollars' worth?"

"As much as he asks for. Whatever the cost, it will be worth paying if it will rid me of this foe."

Christophe moved behind his desk and spun the dials of the antique-looking floor safe. When he pulled it open, he extracted several trays of black velvet. He left several more inside the safe.

Adoncia had grown up with Papa's gem collection, but she had never seen so many of them at once. She had never dreamed he even had this many. It was the only thing that could have possible dragged her attention away from the security monitors.

"Is that eight million dollars' worth?" she gasped.

"And change," her father said. He picked up the corner of the velvet material on each tray and pulled on a braided cord sewn into the lining. The velvet pulled from the tray, lifting each brilliant gem out of its fitted recess. When the cord was tightened, the velvet had become a sack to carry the gems. It took little time to make the eight million dollars' worth of rare, fine gems ready for travel. As Fortoul locked the sacks inside a small suitcase he muttered, "Oh, Lord."

The scene on the television was like the newscasts they had been watching over and over again for days. The one who called himself the Hurricane was engaged in yet another battle. Yet again the firepower was trained on him, but never managed to touch him. Once again he reached out to his attackers with invisible bursts of sound that crushed their bones with giant hammers made of empty air. It was strange seeing the action repeated on the familiar grounds of their own home. It was doubly strange to see their own men crumple beneath the Hurricane's invisible hammer.

Adoncia knew these men. Some of them had been trusted aides of her father since before she was born. Some were her uncles and her brothers. There was Carrillo himself, in his shiny new Mercedes, leaning out the window and blasting at the Hurricane. The Mercedes was flattened. Carrillo crawled out, dragging one leg. He made it into the bushes, but then the bush flew apart and the leaves fluttered all about Carrillo Fortoul, heir to the Fortoul cartel. Carrillo just sat there and screamed. It was pathetic. Adoncia was sickened by her big brother's cowardice. Then Carrillo was flattened to the ground and bones popped out through his skin.

At least he'd stopped screaming.

Adoncia was startled by the sound of the air cannons. It wasn't coming through the speakers of the security system anymore. She could hear the actual sound, rolling up the manicured grounds. Maybe a quarter mile away.

It wasn't a TV show. It was real.

"Papa, let's run," Adoncia cried, taking her father's arm in a tight embrace. "We'll take the money, go far away, go live in Barcelona. He'll never find us there. We'll have enough to be happy forever."

Her father was barely conscious, his dignity in tatters and his mind reeling from his losses. His sons were all dead now. "He'll find us wherever we go, my sweet," Christophe said. "I know when I am defeated."

"You will not surrender to him?"

"I will give him the money he wants. I should have done so from the start. Then he will go away. Then you and I will bury our dead."

"This Hurricane will not allow us to live, Papa," Adoncia pleaded. "Look at him—he's a monster! He is obsessed with having his vengeance."

"He is obsessed with showing the world who he is. It will be no mercy for him to leave me alive. He will do it because he has said all along that he will do it. Once he gets the ransom he claims is his, he will let me live. It is his way of showing the world he is powerful."

"He is a devil! I won't let him take our treasure."

"He'll take it whether we let him take it or not," Christophe said, bitterly amused.

"I will not let him, do you hear, Papa! The business is mine now! There is no more Carrillo, no more Lim, no more Dav—they're all dead. That means the business goes to me!"

Christophe looked addled. "But you want to be on television."

"I'm the only one left to take over the business."

"That's out of the question, sweet. You're a woman."

"I won't allow you to throw everything away before I get my chance."

Christophe was genuinely distressed, but he was speaking so quietly, so devoid of his usual vigor. The shock was too much for the old man; his power was drained. This was not the father Adoncia Fortoul knew. She snatched the suitcase off the desk and backed away. "I am sorry, Papa. I must not let you throw it all away."

"My sweet," Christophe said, and his voice was positively gentle. Adoncia wanted to retch. Now was the time he needed to be strong, more than any other time in his life, and he had turned into an old nursemaid.

"Keep away from me, Papa."

He just gave her a soft, revolting, angelic look, and then he reached across the desk and brought his fist into her chin.

27

The main entrance to the Fortoul estate mansion was a pair of twin doors, salvaged from a centuries-old colonial church, and they were flanked on either side by marble pillars that supported the overhanging roof. None of them lasted long. The pillars trembled for a moment as the air cannons sandblasted the bases, then they fell over, one at a time, and cracked into barrel-sized chunks. The wooden doors banged like shutters in a storm, then crashed hard enough to shatter the old wood into splinters. The wall around them collapsed in pieces, then it all came crashing down. The front of the Fortoul home was wide open.

Harry Kilgore drove inside.

The air cannon noise dropped to a low-grade racket and the speaker on top crackled. "Anybody home?"

It had to have been very dramatic to watch beautiful Colombian debutantes sweep down the wide, curving flight of white marble stairs in their cotillion gowns. An old man appeared atop the stairs, his eyes sunken, his tropical suit wrinkled. Not quite the same impression as the young debutantes, Harry thought.

"Hi. I'm Hurricane," he blared from his loudspeaker.

The man's voice was almost drowned out by the continuous low-grade rumble of the air cannon. "I am Christophe Fortoul."

"Really!" Harry exclaimed, and he stuck his head out the window of the vehicle to see with his own eyes. "*You're* Mr. F? You look like last week's leftovers. You feeling okay?"

Christophe Fortoul came down the steps slowly, with a suitcase that was small but looked as if it was weighting him down. "You will call off your campaign against me. I will give you the ransom you came for."

"You're full of surprises, Mr. F," Harry said through the speaker, which blared the words through the once elegant entrance hall. Christophe Fortoul gritted his teeth. The sound had to have been like jagged glass scraping against his nerves.

"One thing, though," Harry added. "The price went up."

"I figured as much," Fortoul said somberly.

"It doubled again."

"It is what I expected."

"Eight million dollars in gemstones. Appraised in U.S. dollars, of course. That's the current price."

"It is here." Fortoul stopped in the rubble at the bottom of the stairs.

"If you say so. Put it down."

Fortoul placed it on the floor.

"Open it."

Fortoul flipped the twin catches and opened the suitcase.

"Show me what's in the sacks."

Fortoul released the cords on one of the sacks, and it opened wide. Inside were brilliant stones in vivid colors.

"Replace it. Then you might wanna take a few steps back," Harry advised.

Fortoul put the sack in the suitcase and retreated up the steps, then Harry started up the Kilgore Autoretrieval System for the very first time. He used his joystick on the little display screen inside the vehicle, centered it on the image of the sacks and hit the Get button.

The emitters made their little noises and the air swirled in front of the vehicle in a precise, invisible tunnel of agitated air that ended with a vortex inside the suitcase. A velvet sack danced, then lifted off into the air and flew along the path of the air tunnel, into the open passenger window. The velvet sack thunked hard against the inside of the rear window of the vehicle.

Another Kilgore triumph! It worked perfectly, Harry thought. Maybe he'd need to adjust the force level a little. A bag of rocks traveling with that velocity just might knock him senseless. He vacuumed up a second sack and took care to lean away from it when it rocketed inside his car.

"Papa, stop him." The shriek came from above—a stick figure in a designer dress came down the steps.

Well, here was the Latin American debutante Harry had been imagining, but she was a disappointment.

"Who's the image of gauntliness?" Harry asked over the ruckus of the retriever.

"My daughter," Christophe said lifelessly.

"Yuck," Harry said.

"Give it back! Thief." The rest of her insults were in Spanish.

"Mr. F, you don't want her getting close to the retriever."

"Adoncia, stay back!" Christophe ordered.

"I won't let him steal our treasure." She came to the bottom of the stairs and lunged for the sacks, but the retriever gave her a vicious kick to the chest. She fell back against the hard marble stairs and groaned. Another sack flew into Kilgore's car and hit the passenger's seat with a thwack, then bounced onto the floor. Harry snatched it up and pulled it open.

They glimmered and glistened, red, green and unbelievably clear crystal. The Fortoul gems, the product of a lifetime of collecting and robbery.

Christophe Fortoul was watching him from the stairs, ignoring his suffering daughter. Harry hoisted the bag.

"I'm sure it's all there," Harry announced over the speaker.

"It is."

"Because if the appraisal comes up even a dollar short, well, you know."

"I know."

Adoncia rose painfully to a sitting position and watched horror-struck as the last little felt sack was sucked up into the invisible vacuum hose and sailed to the vehicle. The bag split open and the gems flew out, but they remained in the frantic slipstream of suction. Kilgore flung his arm over his head comically as the precious gems ricocheted around inside the car.

"Dang. I'll be fishing those out of the car seats for weeks."

Christophe Fortoul looked like a dead man.

Adoncia bared her fangs.

"Just when I think you can't make yourself look any more hideous," Harry said. "Well, tah."

"Wait a minute! Where's the coke?" Adoncia said.

"I haven't counted the payoff yet," Harry blared reasonably.

"Give us the cocaine. That's what this was all about, right? We paid you the ransom. Now give us the coke."

"Hush, Adoncia," Christophe Fortoul chided.

"I told you he was a backstabbing coward, Papa. He's filth. He never meant to give back our property. It was always just cheap extortion."

"Young lady," Harry said, "I promise you, I have every intention of returning what belongs to you, as soon as I'm sure you paid for it."

"Liar. Cheater!"

Harry Kilgore sighed into the microphone and his sigh reverberated through the ruined great hall. "Fine, okay."

"I DON'T THINK I could pick the worst one out of that bunch, Little Father." Remo scanned the scene intently, looking for—what? He didn't know. Something, anything that would give him the edge on Harry Kilgore. The man never let down his guard. The air cannons were always running, running, running. Remo couldn't get close to him. "We have to get him now."

"Yes," Chiun agreed as they hung unseen in the shadows beyond the front wall.

If they didn't get him now, the Colombians would strike Harry Kilgore outside the grounds, and another hundred villagers would die with him. Or two hundred. Maybe the villagers would die and Harry would escape unscathed again. And again.

Harry Kilgore's invisible vacuum cleaner changed its pitch. Inside the vehicle he scrounged in the rear seats and hoisted a tight brick of cocaine to the windowsill, where it shivered, then flew across the hall into the now empty suitcase, tumbled violently against the base of the stairs. White powder puffed out. Adoncia backed away hurriedly, dragging her father up the stairs with her. The next bale of cocaine slammed into the first, and more white stuff puffed in the air, and dissipated almost instantly in the turbulence of the air cannons.

"The poison?" suggested Chiun.

Remo looked straight at him. "Li Yeom's patch of thorns."

Then Remo was on the move.

28

The next bale slammed into the first two. Another puff of white dust rose and vanished, spreading out through the great hall.

Remo slipped in, giving Kilgore's car all the distance he could, and came onto the bottom step before anybody even knew he was there.

"Deep breath, everybody," he announced, then he tore into the white plastic bricks. The powder dumped out, pounds and pounds of it, entered the turbulent air and billowed into every corner of the hall.

"Stop it!" cried Adoncia. "That's not yours!"

"Mm-hmm?" Remo asked. He, for one, wasn't about to open his mouth, and he was keeping a steady dribble of carbon dioxide coming from his nostrils. He wasn't letting any of the lethal air get inside of him.

Adoncia and Christophe Fortoul came down the stairs together and they scrambled at the floor by Remo's feet, coming up with the surviving bale of cocaine. Christophe took it. Adoncia snatched it out of his arms with her claw hands and embraced it to her skeletal bosom like an infant, then she made a run for it.

Remo snaked a hand around her and took it away.

"No!" she wailed, and threw herself at the package, sinking her fingers deep into the plastic. Remo held it high, his incredibly thick wrists bulging. Adoncia dangled above the floor until the plastic opened up. A fantastic cloud of white powder burst and spread throughout the hall. Adoncia tumbled down, entered the danger zone of Kilgore's sensors and set off more rapid cannon cracks. She was tossed in the maelstrom, rose straight into the heights of the hall, dropped back down again, fell like a sack of bones against the roof of the vehicle, then another crack of thunder whisked her outside.

It was like a revelation to Remo Williams. *The skinny skank had hit Kilgore's car.* The air cannons were going nuts. The cocaine was screwing them up. Maybe it was clogging the controls. Maybe it was confusing the sensors. Remo didn't know and he didn't care. He just knew it was a gap in the defenses of the untouchable Hurricane.

"Adoncia!" cried Christophe Fortoul, then he launched himself from the steps, into the danger zone. It was a first-rate belly flop, but Christophe Fortoul bounced up, toward the ceiling, and came down against the windshield. Then the cartel kingpin sailed outside beyond the fallen columns.

This was going to hurt or make him look really stupid, Remo thought as he jumped into the storm. Or maybe both.

It was both.

29

A crushing force caught him, compressed his chest, pushed him skyward. Remo twisted out of the wind stream and came down on top of Kilgore's roof. He plunged his hands through the glass and locked his fingers around the windshield frame and then the powerful forces tried to fling him out the open front of the house. Remo held on. Making his hands into iron vises, pulling himself forward against the maelstrom. He imagined his body to be flowing and light, like the body of a bird drifting in the wind, but the wind had other ideas. It tousled him, hit him against the roof and fought him every inch of the way. Remo hooked his elbows around the windshield frame and dragged himself forward.

He was on the car. Harry Kilgore was within reach. This was his only chance. If Kilgore got away now, more lives would be lost and the blame would lie with Remo Williams. He pictured the field of slaughtered villagers down by the front gate.

He summoned the reserves of energy buried in his

gut and released them into his blood and a fragment of extra strength came into his arms. He pulled himself into the breach in the glass and fumbled blindly inside, and the steering wheel fell into his hands. He closed his fingers around it and swore to himself he would not let go.

Remo dragged his body into the opening in the glass, then everything was still. The wind vanished. The noise that never seemed to stop was suddenly just gone, and Remo collapsed against the disintegrating windshield glass. He twisted fast, dispersing the pressure of the jagged glass edges, but he still landed in a scratched, ungraceful pile across the seats.

The driver's door slammed shut.

Remo sat up.

He was alone inside Harry Kilgore's car. He hurt. He was in need of a breath, but breathing was out of the question since he was still engulfed in a thick cloud of airborne cocaine. Time to leave this nightmare behind.

THE QUIET WAS AMAZING. The front entrance drive, with its fallen stone columns and wreckage, already had the air of the aftermath of a catastrophe that was over and done.

Christophe Fortoul was slumped across the driveway, taking his final nap. Even the clouds of cocaine looked peaceful now that the noise was turned off.

But where was Harry Kilgore?

The quiet was broken by someone hacking out in the professionally manicured grounds.

"Leave me alone," Harry Kilgore said.

He wasn't talking to Remo.

Remo hurried into the garden, enjoying lungs of clean Colombian jungle air. He found Harry Kilgore on a terrace of lush, cropped lawn, dotted with circular flower beds. Kilgore was half squatting in his outfit of wires and electrodes and little horns and what all. Remo thought he looked like an orangutan just escaped from the vivisectionist lab while undergoing horrible electrical experiments.

Kilgore was coughing, shaking, with tears streamed from his bloodred eyes. He blinked in the sun, his vision burning from the cocaine, and it was clear he had breathed some of it in.

Maybe a lot of it.

"Leave me alone and get out of here." Kilgore spoke rapid-fire. "Get out get out or I'll kill you!"

Chiun was across the lawn, and he couldn't have made a more different image of a man. Small compared to Kilgore's towering height, graceful in his robe, even if it was blackened at the edges. With his hands in his sleeves, Chiun was a master of calm and self-control.

"What'd I ever do to you, old man? What's your problem, huh? Come on, out with it!" Kilgore's speech came so fast it was like a single word of many syllables.

"You singed his kimono," Remo explained. "That's what you did to him."

Kilgore turned on Remo.

"Who *are* you people?" Kilgore demanded. "What is that?"

"It's yours." Remo held the thing up.

"That's my steering wheel, you jerk!"

"Catch." Remo sent the steering wheel spinning across the terrace like a flying disk. It zeroed in on Kilgore's skull.

The noise was back, emitting from the little devices dangling from Kilgore's shoulders and arms and legs. They were up and down his back and chest and a couple of them dangled from the fly of his jeans. They filled the air around Kilgore with little air blasts—and the steering wheel bounded up over Kilgore's head, sailed high over the trees and disappeared, still on the ascent.

"I just knew you'd have some sort of wearable version of those things. It's not gonna help you, Kilgore."

"How'm I supposed to drive?"

"Harry, you don't want to get back in that car," Remo said. "It smells like somebody's been living in there for days. I guess we'll have to call you *Hurrican't* now."

"I'll kill you!"

"I'm gonna kill you first. That's a promise."

"No. I shall kill him," Chiun said.

"Why you?" Remo asked.

"He has done me a great wrong."

"Shut the hell up!" Kilgore barked, turning on Chiun, then back to Remo.

"See this garment?" Chiun held out a hand and allowed the wide sleeve to hang down. "Its value is that of a dozen Harry Kilgores. For ruining this garment, you must die."

"Go to hell, old man."

"There's lots of reasons to kill him," Remo said.

"Yes, many," Chiun agreed.

"Shut up shut up shut up!"

"But the destruction of this kimono ranks highest among them."

"No way, Little Father."

"Yes, this is the way."

"I'm out of here!" Harry Kilgore turned and walked to the edge of the terrace, and Chiun made his move.

Remo moved faster.

The air cannon on Kilgore's body went off, making small-scale thunderclaps. The air buffeted Remo before he came within three long paces of the Hurricane.

Chiun slipped to the ground at great speed, and the smooth silk glided easily on the dense grass. And his small, ancient body weighed almost nothing at all. Like a child on a backyard water slide he sailed on his chest under the worst of the cannon bursts and grasped Harry Kilgore by the ankle. The air cannon pounded Chiun back the way he came. Chiun held on, and took a hunk of jogging shoe with him. Inside the hunk of shoe was a hunk of Harry.

Harry collapsed, sobbing and cursing, grabbing at his bloody heel. He rolled from side to side.

Remo picked himself up. Chiun's precious robe was

now streaked with grass stains on top of black scorch marks, but the Master Emeritus had a tightness on his mouth that could only be great satisfaction.

"My turn," Remo said, and he dived to the ground, rolled like a log spinning down a mountain and crashed into Harry Kilgore. The air cannons blasted in all directions, but not the right directions. They were made to work best when Harry was on his feet.

Remo thrust his hand in and locked his fingers around Kilgore's throat. Harry gagged, and his bloody eyes sprung wide open. He slapped at a place on his right hip, and the air cannons were silent.

"Ah. Blessed quiet." Remo stood them both up, and his fingers dug into Kilgore's throat, clutching his Adam's apple.

"Fine. Have it your way. You kill him," Chiun complained.

Kilgore rolled his bloody eyes at the old man.

"Thanks. I think I will."

Kilgore rolled his eyes at Remo.

"Then be done with it," Chiun said.

"Quick is way too good for Harry Kilgore."

Kilgore put his hand on the hip switch. "Let go, or I'll blast you. Hard."

Remo shrugged. "I'll live. You won't."

"Please let me go!"

"No, thanks."

"Fah!" Chiun announced as his tolerance evaporated, and he reached across the lawn, reached across

a space that was five times the length of his arm, and
slapped Kilgore's hand smartly. Kilgore's hand shattered against the hip switch, which turned on. Kilgore
croaked and the air canons erupted and Remo was
tossed across the manicured lawn. He landed in a riot
of impatiens.

"Hey!" Remo tossed down the clump of matter that
had come with him from Harry Kilgore's throat. The
pink impatiens were now streaked with scarlet.

"I couldn't stand your dawdling another second."
Chiun stalked away.

Harry lay slumped over the edge of the terrace, blood
flowing from his open neck, and when he tried to
breathe it made foaming red bubbles.

"Harry!" Remo said loudly, getting the dying man's
attention. "One last thing before you go."

Remo held out his hand. He made his thumb and
forefinger into an L and held it against his forehead.
"You, Harry, are a total loser."

Kilgore struggled to say something, then he trembled and went limp, and beyond the hedge Remo could
swear he heard the chuckling of a little old man.

REMO FOUND CHIUN on a granite Roman bench in an untouched garden area amid the devastation of the Fortoul estate.

"I wondered if you would ever care to come rescue
me," Chiun complained. "I could easily have been
killed. This place is rife with madwomen." Chiun nod-

ded to Adoncia Fortoul, whose neatly severed head was resting on the second marble bench.

"You could never be easily killed," Remo said. He took the third bench, and they all shared a moment of beautiful silence.

"Peaceful here, when everybody stops blowing hot air," Remo said.

"Not as peaceful as Piney Point Beach Retreat, Site 14B."

"I guess the Fortoul dynasty won't rise again," Remo said.

"There will be some new clan of death dealers coming to take its place," Chiun said. "There is never a short supply."

Remo sighed. "Yeah."

The silence was shattered by more noise. The rustle of grass. The movement of branches. The huff and puff of barrel-chested breathing.

"Sounds like we're about to be apprehended by Gherhard's Grunts," Remo said. "Put your hands up, Little Father."

"You may play with your grunting friends. I prefer the company of Ms. Fortoul."

Remo found the Grunts hanging around the shadows of trees on the long, corpse-littered drive.

"Come on," Remo said. "Let's chat."

The Grunts froze in the shadows. They were highly trained Special Forces soldiers and they could make themselves practically invisible.

Remo shrugged—and vanished. The Grunts saw Subject Buck slip like a ghost into the trees.

Grunt Konk had a curious sensation of lightness, which alerted him to the absence of his submachine gun. He grabbed for his combat handgun. Missing. His ammo pack was gone. The knife sheath on his calf was empty leather. His garrote was gone from his belt, along with his radio, lipstick video pickup, headpiece microphone, signal flares and canteen. Somebody shoved him. He staggered out of his hiding place onto the drive—and fell on his face. The laces of his rubber-soled mission boots were tied together.

Lay flopped on the drive, then Shredder. Yeepod came last. He landed on the body of a Colombian and got blood all over him.

They tried to get up. They made it onto their feet and got smacked back down again by something that looked like Subject Buck but moved too fast to be a human being.

Then came their gear. Subject Buck piled it up in the middle of the road. The only items he held on to were the satellite phones. He lined them up in a row on top of his head and balanced them there while he dragged Gherhard's Grunts to Chiun's garden. He managed it all in one trip.

"Why did you bring them here?" Chiun asked.

"I like it here." Remo stretched the Grunts out under

the watchful gaze of Adoncia Fortoul, who was beginning to wither already.

"Let's make some phone calls, shall we?" Remo suggested.

30

Mark Howard worked whatever kind of magic Mark Howard knew how to do.

"Okay, Remo, have them make the call."

"Affirmative, Junior Leader." Remo handed another satellite phone to Yeepod.

"You phone your friend Shep now," he said. "Play it straight. Remember." He showed Yeepod his thumb and forefinger. "Pinchy pinchy."

Yeepod started tearing up again, and that set the rest of them into fits of sobbing.

"What's happening, Remo?" Mark asked.

"Give us a second," Remo said. "Boy, when you finally break a Special Forces guy, he breaks big."

Mark ignored that. Yeepod sniffed, ran his forearm under his nose and phoned his base.

"Grunt Three here, Base." His voice regained some of its old boldness.

"I expected to hear from you an hour ago. What's the problem? Where are you?"

"We're up to our asses in fucking alligators, Shep.

The Fortouls got wiped totally out by Subject Blow Hard."

"What about Subjects Buck and Mao?"

"Those fuckers got to Blow Hard ahead of us. They killed Blow Hard and they smashed his hardware. There's nothing left of him. This place is a slaughterhouse. We're getting the hell out before the Colombian military or some friends of the Fortouls show up to help themselves."

"What about Buck and Mao?"

"We're on their tail. They've got a safehouse in the jungle and they're leading us to it. It'll be the perfect place for us to introduce ourselves and get some of the answers you were wantin'."

"Good. Excellent."

Yeepod hung up and curled into a fetal ball.

"So?" Remo asked Mark Howard. "Did you get him?"

"We got him. He's in the Pentagon."

"And?"

"We must silence him immediately," Mark Howard said, with a peculiar lack of emotion.

It was the matter-of-fact cold-bloodedness of the consummate CURE director.

31

Throughout the long night, Thomas Shep received brief, regular reports from Colombia. Yeepod said they had taken up positions in a sealed-off storage room on the exterior wall of a safehouse in the Colombian wilds. Subjects Buck and Mao were waiting inside, and were expecting the arrival of their commanding officer any minute. Yeep could barely whisper because of his proximity to the subjects, which didn't stop him from using the F-word. In every sentence.

At five o'clock in the morning, Shep jerked awake. He was still behind his desk, deep inside the Pentagon. He had been dreaming he wasn't alone.

But it was just a dream. Nobody sneaked into other people's offices inside the Pentagon. *Nobody.*

"Hi Shep," said somebody.

Thomas Shep jumped to his feet. Two men were standing behind him. One was an elderly Chinaman in a singed robe. The other was a younger man with muscular wrists. There was no doubt as to their identities.

"Buck!" Shep gasped. "And Mao!"

"How'd you track us down, Shep?" Buck asked.

Shep stammered, "Del Carmon. The CIA has under-cover agents in the vicinity. I had them poke around. They came back with the your descriptions. Said you were in town the day after the fire."

"Okay. Good. Now how did you link the descriptions of those two people in Honduras to CURE?"

Thomas Shep stared at Subject Buck. His eyes got wider. His mouth opened, and out flowed the word "CURE."

"Yeah. CURE. That's who we work for. That's what it's called. How'd you make the connection?"

"Oh. Uh. Official orders in the mil-nets that traced back to transient personnel records."

"Just as I suspected," Subject Buck said, then took the receiver of Shep's telephone off the desk—it was off the hook. Had been the whole time. Somebody was listening in! "Did you get that?"

"We got," Mark Howard replied. "Continue the questioning."

Remo lowered the receiver and asked in a low, cruel voice, "What about back braces?"

"Back traces," Mark Howard said.

"Back *traces*," Remo corrected, although it made just as much sense either way as far as he was concerned.

"I tried finding where the orders and the fake records came from," Shep explained nervously. The man was getting an idea, finally, of just how much danger he was in. "I never got there. Swear to God I never did."

"Remo," Mark Howard said, "this is vitally important. We have to know if he is telling the truth."

"He lies by omission," Chiun announced.

Shep was startled by the songlike, piercing quality of the old Asian's voice. "I found nothing, I swear. Every trace came to a dead end. There was nothing more I could do. I had to get an enforcement arm in the field. So I recruited the Grunts. They think you two are in a safehouse in Colombia right now."

"The Grunts are on their way back to the training camp. You've been talking to a computer since yesterday afternoon."

"Really?"

"Pretty realistic, huh?" Remo said. "It even fools me sometimes. Well, Little Father? I think he came clean."

"I did come clean," Shep assured them.

"He has revealed all his petty secrets," Chiun said with a nod.

Shep asked, "What now?"

"Well, what do you think?" Remo asked.

"No. Please."

"You called me Mao," Chiun said, his words like acid. "I am not Chinese."

"You're not?"

"I am Korean. I am Sinanju."

"So?" Shep whined.

Chiun whisked his hand over Shep's face, placing his finger deep inside the brain of the most powerful bureaucrat of all time.

"So now you know," Remo explained.

Chiun's finger came out again so fast there was no blood on it. Shep's eyes rolled up. He was trying to look at the hole, but then his eyes stopped seeing anything.

Thomas Shep fell into his chair and slumped on his desk, just as though he was still napping.

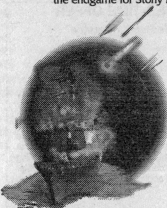

TAKE 'EM FREE

2 action-packed novels plus a mystery bonus

NO RISK
NO OBLIGATION TO BUY

... James Axler
Outlanders®

The war for control of Earth enters a new dimension...

REFUGE

UNANSWERABLE POWER

The war to free postapocalyptic Earth from the grasp of its oppressors slips into uncharted territory as the fully restored race of the former ruling barons are reborn to fearsome power. Facing a virulent phase of a dangerous conflict and galvanized by forces they have yet to fully understand, the Cerberus rebels prepare to battle an unfathomable enemy as the shifting sands of world domination continue to chart their uncertain destiny...

DEADLY SANCTUARY

As their stronghold becomes vulnerable to attack, an exploratory expedition to an alternate Earth puts Kane and his companions in a strange place of charming Victoriana and dark violence. Here the laws of physics have been transmuted and a global alliance against otherwordly invaders has collapsed. Kane, Brigid, Grant and Domi are separated and tossed into the alienated factions of a deceptively deadly world; one from which there may be no return.

Available at your favorite retailer.

GOUT36

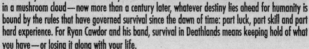